# Finding Home

Written By

## Laura Powell

Cover Design: Pixel Studios

ISBN: 978-1-7353597-3-1

FIRST EDITION

# Dedication

This book is dedicated to my sweet friend,
Jennifer Phelps, for being used by God to change
the course of my life, and for opening my eyes to
the joyful possibilities of new dreams.

What will you do on the day of reckoning, when disaster comes from afar?  To whom will you run for help?  Where will you leave your riches?''

-Isaiah 10:3

# Acknowledgements

I'm deeply grateful to Anne and Jerry Engelhardt, Rebecca England, Lynn Jackson, and Patricia Powell for taking the time to read, edit, and help shape this book. Your support means so much.

Thank you to Kara and Bryan Megginson for offering advice about farmland. Diana Moade, I appreciated the insights into type one diabetes. I've learned it's not an easy journey, and I'm glad you daily rest in God's care.

Just as in the first book of the trilogy, *Facing Love,* Springfield, Illinois area businesses and organizations are highlighted in this second addition of the Capitol Hearts series. The Apple Barn in Chatham, Downtown Springfield, Inc., Mariah's Steakhouse and Pasta, Ruby Electric, Inc., James Home Kitchen, the Springfield Municipal Opera, Blackhawk Roofing, and Charlie Parker's Diner are a few of the many quality businesses serving our community, and I am glad to spotlight them.

Finally, dear readers, I am very thankful that you would take a chance on a new author. I write with you in mind and pray that God would help you find daily contentment as you walk with Him.

# Table of Contents

**Chapter One**

**Chapter Two**

**Chapter Three**

**Chapter Four**

**Chapter Five**

**Chapter Six**

**Chapter Seven**

**Chapter Eight**

**Chapter Nine**

**Chapter Ten**

**Chapter Eleven**

**Chapter Twelve**

**Chapter Thirteen**

**Chapter Fourteen**

**Chapter Fifteen**

**Chapter Sixteen**

**Chapter Seventeen**

**Chapter Eighteen**

**Chapter Nineteen**

Chapter Twenty

Chapter Twenty-One

Chapter Twenty-Two

Chapter Twenty-Three

Chapter Twenty-Four

Chapter Twenty-Five

Chapter Twenty-Six

Chapter Twenty-Seven

Chapter Twenty-Eight

Chapter Twenty-Nine

Chapter Thirty

Chapter Thirty-One

Chapter Thirty-Two

Chapter Thirty-Three

Chapter Thirty-Four

Chapter Thirty-Five

Chapter Thirty-Six

Discussion Questions

Preview of Book Three

About the Author

# Chapter One

The same rain that nourished the seeds also watered the weeds, Ethan Adams mused, as he pounded in another ground stake for the hoop house he was building. He'd never personally seen the noxious weed kudzu, but he read that it could grow one foot per day. Ethan had seen pictures of it overtaking barns in the Appalachian Mountains and could understand why it was sometimes called "the vine that ate the South."

Ethan was thankful he didn't deal with kudzu in his Midwest town of Springfield, Illinois. However, he'd done enough yardwork to recognize the power of an aggressive plant. Building three hoop houses was his way of keeping the weeds out so the annuals, perennials and shrubs for his new landscaping business could thrive.

One hoop house was already completed, and he was halfway through hammering in ground anchors for the second structure on this fine fall morning. Besides keeping out weeds, the 120-foot long houses, made out of galvanized steel and wood and covered with polycarbonate plastic, also protected fledgling plants from high winds, cold weather and deadly ice. Shaped like the top of a covered wagon, hoop houses saved money because they didn't require extensive heating or cooling systems. And stretching his budget was a priority.

Ethan stood up and arched his back. Crouching down for hours was tough on his almost thirty-two-year-old body. For the past three weeks he had worked nonstop. The chilly October morning was warming up, and as he rolled his neck side to side, he took off his tan fedora to wipe his forehead.

While he was upright, he figured he'd stop for a drink. Gazing around the barren ground, he located his water bottle six feet away. As he walked to retrieve it, he looked at his land. *His* land. He loved saying those words. Twenty-three glorious acres.

He had purchased the long, narrow plot only three weeks earlier. Before taking ownership, the land had been farmed. Soybeans had been harvested the previous fall, before the acres went on the market, and sun-scorched chaff was all that remained.

Ethan's former home, a small bungalow on the east end of Springfield, had been purchased for the asking price, which gave him the funds needed to start this dream. Adams Landscaping didn't have a physical building...yet. Unless the Arctic Fox counted.

The twenty-five-foot long trailer was permanently parked on the plot. Although his new home didn't have much indoor living space, it had a full-sized bed, an eat-in kitchen, and a tiny shower. What he lacked inside, he made up for with spacious sunsets.

His old place was purchased by Illinois Congressman James Patton. The beautifully landscaped backyard caught the attention of fifteen bidders, but Patton won the yard, the home, and his first love and fellow neighbor, Danielle. Before Danielle, Ethan had been an angry hermit. Danielle was a social worker, and her kind spirit attracted Ethan. But James Patton held her heart, which crushed him, and made starting over seem like the right thing to do.

So many changes had taken place for Ethan over the past few months. Before he put his house on the market, he'd spent the summer living in his mom's apartment while he underwent pulsed dye laser treatments for extensive port wine stains on his face. He'd had them since birth, but the emotional wounds from the teasing and isolation were his deepest scars. Being raised by a single mom who worked minimum wage jobs her whole career meant there had never been money for extras like the surgeries.

Ethan had saved $100,000 by working from home as a medical transcriber. It had taken him ten years to build up enough equity to own land. He'd dipped into the fund to have the procedures done, and Danielle had been the motivation for his physical changes. Before he met her, he wanted to get away and live in the country so no one would stare at his hideous purple face. Now he had a flawless complexion, and he was alone. The irony was not lost on him.

He picked up the water bottle and drained the final sip of cool liquid. Then he walked to his yard hydrant.  This was his only water source on his property, at the moment.  Because the land was undeveloped, he had to have a water line put in.  He used the spigot to get drinking water and fill up the trailer's clean water tank once a week—as long as he didn't take more than five-minute showers or do many dishes.

What would Danielle think of his primitive living, he wondered as he pulled the handle on the steel spigot back and water gushed forth.  He put his hand under the cool flow before positioning his bottle to catch the stream.  Ethan shook his head as if to push away the memories of her.

No woman would want what he had to offer.  The Arctic Fox, a few hoop houses, and a man wearing thick sunscreen and a tan Fedora weren't really an appealing package, in his opinion.  Maybe in a few years he'd have enough income from the business to build a house but getting clients would be the biggest hurdle for Ethan.  All his life he'd been a loner.  He didn't know how to talk with people, and he certainly couldn't market himself.  No, he'd rather design, build, plant.  Ethan needed the skills he lacked the most.  Without them he'd remain a lonely man with a dream and a country sunset.

"I met the new neighbor today," Jedidiah said as he passed a bowl of corn to his wife,

Connie, in their farmhouse kitchen on a mid-October evening. "He's a quiet guy. Didn't say much."

"Where did you run into him?" Connie asked.

"I was harvesting in the field next to his property, so I just got off the tractor and walked over to say hello. He was working on those hoop houses."

"Oh, Dad," their daughter, Claire, interjected with a sigh.

"Your dad never knows a stranger," Connie smiled.

"His name is Ethan. Ethan Adams. Said he wants to start a landscaping business. Gonna plant rhododendron, boxwoods and barberries and such in those hoop houses," Jed continued.

"How old is he?" Connie asked, shaking salt on the vegetables.

"I don't know. Maybe late twenties?" Jed replied.

"Well, I'll have to bring him a pie or something," Connie said before turning her attention to their daughter, Claire. "How was your day at school?"

"Tiring," Claire Rogers replied, pushing the dainty white headband back farther onto her thick reddish-brown hair.

5

"Isn't it ironic that twenty-one little first graders can tire out our twenty-three-year old?" Jed chuckled.

"Was Greer acting up again?" Connie asked.

"Yes, but so was about a third of the class during the afternoon assembly," Claire replied after taking a sip of water. "We had a fundraising representative come to the school, and he really got the kids riled up. Of course, every first grader wants to win an iPad by selling the most magazines."

"You and Gretchen were the same way," Connie chuckled. "Every time Farmingdale Elementary had a fundraiser you wanted to sell the most of whatever it was you were to peddle."

"Speaking of Gretchen, has anyone heard from her today?" Jed asked.

"I got a text from her this afternoon," Connie replied. "She got an A on her Economics quiz."

"Any word if she's coming home for fall break?" Jed questioned.

"She didn't say anything to me. Claire, did she tell you what her plans were?"

"No, but she will probably be staying on campus," Claire sighed.

"I wish we saw more of her," Connie frowned. "She really loves college."

"Aren't you glad you went to school in town so you could eat your mom's delicious home cooking?" Jed asked, spearing another piece of baked chicken for his plate. Not waiting for her answer, Jed continued, "Will you go with your mom when she takes Ethan a pie? It would be good for him to meet you, too."

"Sure, Dad," Claire replied dutifully, with a feigned smile.

"Do you like pie, Jez?" a tender-faced young man seated at the bar asked the bartender.

"Sure, why?" Jezmeen Williams replied as she filled an ice-cold mug with beer.

"I had the best French silk pie this past weekend in St. Louis," the young man said. "Do you want to go with me sometime, to get a slice?"

"Absolutely, Collin," Jezmeen answered with a flirtatious smile, pushing the drink towards the young man.

It was a slow night at Finnegan's Taphouse. No matter the size of the crowd, the men were always drawn to the same thing, and it wasn't the flat screen televisions above the bar.

"Here, Jez," a man wearing a utility company uniform said as he pressed a twenty into the palm of Jezmeen's hand. "Thanks for the drinks. Keep the change, sweetheart."

"Thanks, love," Jezmeen replied with a wink.

With swift movements, the beautiful brown skinned bartender opened the cash register, deposited the twenty, made the appropriate change for the tip, and pocketed her earnings. Jezmeen had worked at Finnegan's for the past six years, and even on a quiet night she brought in a generous income.

The standard bartender uniform—-a white shirt and black v-neck vest—didn't leave much room for creativity but opening a few buttons and being artistic with her thick brown hair and makeup helped Jezmeen keep customers coming. And her striking hazel eyes were not to be forgotten. Like a chameleon, they changed with their environment. Sometimes yellow, sometimes brown, they sparkled like jewels.

When she was in high school, a modeling agency spotted her in the local shopping mall and asked her to sign with them. However, she couldn't get her mom to do anything with the paperwork, mostly because she was jealous.

"Hey, Jez," an overweight, balding man bellowed. "I'll have an Old-Fashioned."

"Comin' right up," Jez smiled.  She grabbed a chilled rocks glass and muddled a teaspoon of simple syrup and bitters.  "How was work, Ray?"

"Ahh, that young punk, A.J., tried to teach me how to do my job again.  These kids, like blondie down there," Ray said lowering his voice, "think they know everything once they get out of school.  A.J. forgets I've been a database administrator for twenty-one years."

"Well, I think maturity and intelligence are an attractive combination," Jez said.  She added two ounces of rye whiskey and three large ice cubes to the glass then stirred.  Topping the drink with an orange twist, she walked it over to Ray.

"A.J. doesn't have anything on you," she said, handing him his drink.

"Jez, I'm lonely down here," the young blonde Collin yelled, and Jezmeen shifted directions.

Until closing time, Jezmeen nursed the drinks and egos of lonely men who came to her to be filled.  They didn't even realize she had nothing of value to offer because she, too, was empty.

# Chapter Two

Jezmeen wore a towel around her head and a white bathrobe hugged her slender body. She searched the refrigerator for leftover pizza. Usually the head cook, Bernie, fixed her something to go, but she was tired of burgers and chicken sandwiches. The clock on the microwave read eleven. Monday through Wednesday, Finnegan's closed early, and Jezmeen was thankful her boyfriend Edward wouldn't be visiting until the weekend.

As she waited for the two slices of supreme pizza to warm, her mind drifted. She wondered what Edward might be doing on a Monday night at home with Amy...his wife. From what Edward had shared, not much. It seemed like a lonely and loveless relationship, or at least that's what he wanted her to believe.

For the past two years, Edward's Springfield apartment had been her home, and she had been his what? She couldn't bring herself to say the word mistress although she knew the role she played. Before Edward it had been Steve, before Steve it was Tyson. Jezmeen kept a list of all the men she had been with. The act of keeping a record made her relationships seem more legitimate. If she read the names, she could pull up a memory—at least for the ones that deserved an afterthought.

Edward was an architect from Chicago. She'd met him in the same place all her acquaintances formed the last six years- Finnegan's Taphouse. At thirty-five he was eight years older, but age didn't matter to Jezmeen. She'd learned many things by watching her mom's behavior before she moved out at seventeen. One lesson was that men were to be used for what they could provide in the moment, and then they could be discarded.

Sherry Williams was a hairdresser, and Jezmeen watched men trail through her mom's life like ants going to a picnic. Sherry was Caucasian. The dad she never met was Colombian and African American. Jezmeen was Sherry's only child, and Sherry was virtually non-existent in her life.

Jezmeen pulled the towel off her head and set it on the back of a kitchen chair, letting her wavy brown hair lay wet against her shoulders. She sat down at the table with the plate of pizza and turned on the television in the living room. Edward's apartment had an open concept, which made the space perfect for entertaining, but when you're the "mistress," that opportunity never arrives.

However, even though she dreamed of hosting parties, Jezmeen liked to be alone. No one needed anything from her in solitary moments, and she savored her space. Tomorrow's shift started at five, and she was confident that the bar stools would be filled with men who desired something from her.

Chewy meowed loudly at the end of Ethan's bed. When Ethan didn't respond, Chewy jumped onto his chest and began gently pawing his face. Ethan scratched Chewy's head, and he slowly sat up. He'd gotten used to the wooden cabinets that hung two feet above the mattress, so he no longer hit his head. The trailer had come with curtains for the three narrow windows in the bedroom, but Ethan could tell it was still dark out. Chewy, Ethan's bronze-colored cat named after the *Star Wars* character Chewbacca, had adjusted well to country life—especially the early to rise part.

Ethan had been getting up at six every morning, and Chewy liked the new routine. Before moving, Ethan had worked forty hours a week listening to physicians and other healthcare professionals and converting their recorded words into written reports.

He would have quit completely except he had no other income to rely on...yet. So, he continued to transcribe part-time. After trying out a few different schedules, he found that typing from five until nine at night suited his situation the best. Yet, there were times when he found himself falling asleep at his second job.

As he swung his legs out of bed, he thought about the day's work. There were many times he wished his dad was a part of his life, the current moment was one of them. Ethan had never met his father. He had left his mom before he was born, and Suzanne Adams rarely talked about him. She met his dad at a bar, which seemed ironic to Ethan since his mom wasn't a drinker.

Suzanne's friend had dragged her to a little dive one night, and there she hit it off with Wayne. Wayne Copeland. Ethan didn't forget many details about his dad. He knew little, so his mind stored each fact like it was a priceless treasure. Wayne and Suzanne dated for about three months. Long enough to conceive a child. A few years ago, his mom succumbed to Ethan's questions about his dad and shared that Wayne had been unfaithful, causing the split.

Ethan never learned why Suzanne hadn't contacted Wayne after he was born, but his extensive birthmarks may have been part of the reason. Suzanne was his most loving supporter, and she never made him feel bad about the way he looked, but he wouldn't have blamed her if becoming accustomed to his face took some time at first.

Only six weeks had passed since his last pulsed-dye laser treatment, and he still wasn't used to his new appearance. His mom told him he could be a model, but she said that before the surgery too. Suzanne claimed he had fine features and a chiseled jawline.

He certainly wouldn't ever be a swimsuit model, although his muscles were well-sculpted from the years of physical labor working on landscaping projects in his backyard and now at his business. No, his face would always have to be pasty white. His fedora, and liberal use of sunscreen, protected his face from the harmful rays that could undo the work of the procedures.

The forecast for the October day was full sun, and Ethan planned to bolt the channel pieces over the purlins and then cover the hoop house with plastic. When Ethan had finished installing the last purlin the night before, he stepped back and thought that the bare structure looked a little like the rib bones of a whale.

He'd done everything alone on the first structure, but he knew it would move faster, and be enormously easier, with an assistant. Too bad Chewy wasn't taller, Ethan thought as he headed to the kitchen to open a can of cat food.

"Mmm. Something smells good," Claire said as she dropped her large canvas tote on the floor in the mudroom.

Claire's mom, Connie, was busy wiping down the granite countertop in the kitchen but looked up with a smile when she saw her daughter enter.

"How was your class today?" Connie asked.

"Tiring," Claire sighed as she sank down onto the tan cushion of the bar stool across from her mom.

"Did you have to send any of the little angels to the principal?"

"Not today.  There was just a lot of tattle-telling.  'He pushed me.' 'She cut in line.' 'She splashed water in the water fountain.'"  That type of thing—all day long."

"I bet it gets on your nerves."

"That's an understatement," Claire said.  "But I have a new plan.  I borrowed a book from the library, *A Bad Case of Tattle Tongue*, and I'm going to make a problem-solving spinner over the weekend.  I'll be prepared by Monday."

"Sounds good."  Connie moved to the sink and began washing a large mixing bowl.  "I made our new neighbor a pumpkin pie.  It's cooling on the dining room table."

"I hope you made me one, too."

"I made you a crustless low-sugar specialty and a regular one for your dad.  He might not be in tonight until after eight, so I think you and I will be eating alone."

"I'm glad this week has been dry so he could continue harvesting the soybeans."

"Me too.  Even though it's long hours for him, he's less stressed when he gets to be out in the fields, not home worrying about the weather."

Connie set the large bowl on the drying rack next to the sink and toweled-off her hands.

"So, will you come with me to deliver Ethan's pie?"

"Sure. When I drove past on my way home, he was working on a hoop house, so it might be good to go now."

"Did you have a snack on the way home from school?" Connie asked with a hint of concern.

"Yes, I had a handful of almonds. I'm feeling fine."

"Okay, just checking," Connie replied. "I can't believe he's building those greenhouses all by himself."

"Maybe he's new in town and doesn't know anybody who can help him," Claire said, as she stood up.

"If that's the case, I'm glad we're going to go introduce ourselves. At least the Rogers family can be added to his list of acquaintances."

Ethan was frustrated. He'd spent the morning installing the channels, and then he tried to put the plastic covering over the structure. He knew, from constructing the first two, that even the slightest breeze could ruin his hard work, especially since he was working alone and had no one to hold the other side in place once he threw the plastic over the top.

He'd just started another attempt when he saw a maroon car pull up next to the Arctic Fox. A hardy breeze blew, sending the plastic right back into Ethan's body. Car doors slammed shut, and Ethan heard cries of alarm from female voices. He felt like a muffled mummy as he batted the plastic off his face.

"Do you need help?" came a cry from a lady in her fifties.

A young woman, dressed in black pants and a red and black striped sweater, followed. As she approached, Ethan noticed her gray-blue eyes were filled with concern. He felt his face and neck flush with red-hot embarrassment. Out of instinct he looked away, not wanting the visitors to see his birthmarks. Then he remembered they were no longer visible. Still, his legs were wrapped in polycarbonate plastic which seemed just as bad.

"Are you okay?" the young woman asked as she rushed to pull the plastic off his feet.

"I'm fine," he said gruffly. He kicked at plastic, trying to get himself free.

"Really, I can help you," she pressed, bending down to grab the material.

In a final effort to break out of the stronghold, he kicked hard one more time. His boot accidentally struck the young woman's outstretched arm and caused her to cry in pain.

"Are you okay, Claire?" The older lady addressed the younger.

The young woman grabbed her wrist, looked to the sky, and exhaled loudly, managing the sting.

"I'll be okay, mom," the young woman replied through little breaths.

Ethan felt horrible, but he didn't know how to respond. Growing up with birthmarks, he was always an outcast. After years of taunting, he was ignored, which was worse than the teasing. When he could take it no more, his mom allowed him to be homeschooled for his last two years of high school, and after he graduated, he worked for a short time at Walmart as an overnight stocker. After he quit, due to his lack of interpersonal skills, he became a recluse completely.

The only person he interacted with was his mom...until Danielle. But she was gone, and now he was alone with two females on his front lawn—one that seemed to be nursing a broken wrist thanks to him. He searched for the right words to say but felt awkward murmuring something comforting. So, he remained shamefully silent.

# Chapter Three

Edward would be at the apartment after her shift ended, Jezmeen thought, as she fixed Bob his third Jack and coke of the night.

"Here ya go, sweetheart," she smiled and handed Bob his drink.

"Do you want to go for a ride with me on the bike after you're done with work, Jez?" the man with the mustache and tattooed arms asked coolly.

"Aww, Bob, that's so nice of you to ask," Jezmeen said warmly. "Maybe another time. I've got plans tonight."

"Hot date?" he asked with a hint of jealousy.

"Not with someone as cute as you," she replied, knowing in truth Edward was much better looking than Bob.

Over the years, she had been known to accompany male customers out of the building after her shifts. The men that lined the stools were like hawks looking for an easy meal. Although Jezmeen threw out compliments with ease, she was selective with whom she allowed to escort her out. Men like Bob, who visited Finnegan's regularly, knew that she had those mesmerizing eyes set on two things—riches and power.

Jezmeen heard a holler for a beer, and she moved to get a mug. As she filled it with a golden brew, her mind drifted back to Edward. He no longer visited the bar when he was in town. Maybe he was jealous that she flirted with so many men. More likely it was because he didn't want word leaking back to his wife that he was involved.

This was the first time Jezmeen had been in a long-term relationship with a married man. At first, she felt conflicting emotions. Sometimes she felt badly for his wife and wanted to end the whole thing. But the tug of guilt vanished quickly. She'd long buried shame.

When Jezmeen was about five years old, she remembered her mom cutting a man's hair in their tiny kitchen apartment. Her mom's infectious laugh filled the space, and she recalled how she leaned over and kissed him on the neck. That man stayed with them for a few months. So many passed through over the course of her seventeen years of living with Sherry, she couldn't even recall their names.

Perhaps that was why it was important for Jezmeen to keep an account. When she was a teenager, she asked her mom why her love life was such a revolving door. Life's boring with one man. They pay the bills. Don't you feel safer when we have a man around? Sherry gave all sorts of reasons, and Jezmeen vowed to never be like her mom.

"Hey, babe," yelled a young man over the din of the Friday night crowd. "Can I get a whiskey on the rocks?"

"Sure thing, handsome," she said, throwing him a grin before swinging into action.

Edward would be waiting up for her. She'd be tired, but on Sunday he'd be back in Chicago. Then she'd have the place to herself, which was her favorite part of the arrangement.

"Do you have any ice?" the older lady asked Ethan.

"I don't think so," Ethan replied, knowing that the compact refrigerator's top two shelves held only microwave meals. Ice would be a luxury.

"I'm really okay," said the young lady.

Ethan's fedora had flown off his head when the plastic hit his face and a light gust rolled it towards the young lady. She stooped down to pick it up.

"I'm Claire Rogers," she said, handing him the hat with her good hand.

Ethan thought Claire looked like a college student. He'd seen plenty of shows on television that featured her demographic.

"And, I'm Connie Rogers. We're your next-door neighbors," the older lady replied, pointing to the white farmhouse to the left of his property.

When Ethan didn't introduce himself, Connie continued.

"We heard you met my husband, Jedidiah. Everyone calls him Jed."

Ethan remained silent.

"He said you're starting a business. Adams Landscaping, is that right?"

Ethan shook his head yes.

"We brought you a pie," Claire interjected, placing her arm behind her back so everyone would stop staring at it.

"It's in the car. I'll go get it," Connie said quickly.

"It looks like putting that plastic on is tough to do by yourself," Claire said nodding to the pile at his feet.

"The first two pieces went on okay," Ethan said bluntly. He felt embarrassed and awkward being alone with the young woman.

"Do you want my help?" Claire asked.

"There's no way you could help with one arm," he replied gruffly.

"If you just throw it over to the other side, I could hold it in place till you get it nailed down. That's what you're doing, right?"

"Yes."

"Claire, I forgot the whipped cream," Connie called as she stood by the car's back seat. "You can't have pumpkin pie without whipped cream. I'll just run home and get it from the fridge. It will only take two minutes."

Claire felt her heart sink. She'd have to make small talk with Ethan for longer than she expected. Talking with him was like chewing taffy—slow going and not very easy.

"Sure you don't want to try working together?" she asked with hopes they'd have something to do to pass the time.

"No. It's too windy."

They stood in silence for what felt like an eternity. Then Claire decided to try a tactic that worked with her fledgling students. If she could find a topic he was interested in, Ethan would probably be drawn out.

"Tell me about these," she said, gesturing to the greenhouses.

"The hoop houses?" Ethan asked hesitantly.

"Yeah. I don't know anything about them."

"Not much to tell. You grow plants in them."

This was going to be more difficult then she anticipated, and she hoped her mom would be back soon.

"What kind of plants are you going to grow?"

"Well, one will be for shrubs, another will be for perennials, and the last one will be for annuals. I made a planter box today for English laurel, but I'll also grow cherry laurel. Boxwood, barberry, hydrangea, rhododendron, spirea, forsythia, and firethorn will all be in this building for shrubs."

Ethan realized he had just rattled off a list of plants. His neighbor surely didn't care, did she?

"But that's enough about that," he said curtly. He didn't have visible purple marks on his face anymore, but that didn't make interacting with people any less uncomfortable.

"I like hearing about what's going inside," Claire said with a kind smile. "Don't forget my dad's a farmer. I've grown up my whole life hearing about planting, growing, and selling. Actually, you have quite a bit more variety than my dad. He just rotates between crops of soybeans and corn."

Feeling encouraged by her remarks and knowing that there was nothing else to do in the middle of the open field, he continued.

"In the perennial hoop house, I'll propagate daylilies, bleeding hearts, echinacea, delphiniums, and probably peonies. There are so many more I'd like to grow, but I'm limited on space...and money."

"What does propagate mean?" Claire asked with genuine interest.

"It's just a fancy way of saying I'll be taking cuttings from one parent plant to grow a bunch of new plants."

They heard a vehicle pulling onto the worn-down patch of grass in front of the trailer.

"I hope she found the whipped cream. Do you like pumpkin pie, Ethan? It's Ethan, right?"

He realized he had never introduced himself and felt flustered.

"Yes, Ethan Adams," he replied, sticking out his hand stiffly.

"Nice to meet you, Ethan," she said. His hand felt like sandpaper, just like her dad's.

Connie came hurrying over with a pie wrapped in a tea towel and a spray container of Redi-Whip.

"It was right where I left it on the counter," she sang. "How's your arm, Claire?"

Ethan wished he had been thoughtful enough to ask.

"Just a little tender," she said, touching it. "I'm sure icing it once we get home will help. Mom, Ethan was telling me about what he'll be growing."

"When will you be open for business?" Connie asked.

"The plan is to be ready by March."

"You won't be shoveling driveways this winter?" Connie asked, knowing that landscaping companies often offered different seasonal services.

"I don't have equipment for that yet. I work part-time as a medical transcriber. It's what I did full-time until I bought the land. Hopefully by spring, I can drop that job."

"Well, you're definitely a hard-worker," Connie said. "We've seen you building non-stop since you moved in."

Connie handed Ethan the dessert.

"We won't keep you, but we wanted to introduce ourselves. The only Rogers you haven't met is Gretchen, but she's away at college. If you ever need anything, please don't hesitate to call us. I wrote down our number."

Connie reached into her pocket and pulled out a notecard.

"Nice to meet you, Ethan," Claire said as she began to head towards the car.

"If you need help with the plastic covering, please call. I'm sure Jed would be happy to lend a hand," Connie said.

"Thanks," Ethan replied, wishing some thoughtful words of appreciation would leap out of his mouth. Whenever he interacted with new people, he felt a foggy haze come over him. And the new neighbors were so nice.

"Hope your arm's okay," he blurted, as Claire reached the car door.

Every third evening Claire changed the tubing on her insulin pump. When she was first diagnosed with type one diabetes at the age of four, her mom gave her daily injections. In 1999, at the age of ten, she watched Nicole Johnson win the Miss America title. Claire was fascinated and inspired by the dark-haired beauty contestant who wore an insulin pump during the competition.

Even though her parents said she could try one, she felt hesitant to be plugged into something all the time, and she worried her classmates would view her as sickly or odd. So, she continued to give herself daily insulin injections.

Having diabetes meant constantly managing math problems. She knew how many carbohydrates were in a sandwich or an apple off the top of her head, and she also knew how much insulin was needed to balance her blood glucose level.

But, by college, she was tired of having to wake up at the same time every morning to balance her blood sugar level, and she was tired of the multiple daily injections. So, she decided to switch to an insulin pump. It would keep her insulin level steady because it could be programmed to deliver different amounts throughout the day.

The small black device had become her constant companion since her freshman year. Now, standing by the bathroom sink, Claire took the pump out of her pocket. The process of loading the device with new insulin and inserting the cannula under her skin usually took her less than ten minutes because she had done it hundreds of times over the past four and a half years.

With swift movements, she loaded insulin into the machine, took off her old infusion set, unbagged the new tubing, and jabbed the tiny needle attached to the new set into her waistline. The right side of her stomach was tender from where she had pulled off the plastic from the last site, so she chose the left side this time.

Claire wore the infusion set high enough that it wouldn't hit the waistband of her clothing. Once finished, she stared at her reflection in the mirror. Her long-sleeve top was so loose, no one would even suspect she had life-saving liquid under her clothes.

Certainly, Ethan wouldn't have noticed. All of her outfits were carefully chosen because they could conceal what she was trying to hide. But her arm still hurt where he had kicked her, and she saw the purple coloring of a bruise forming.

Claire wondered why he hadn't reacted more compassionately when that happened, but she gathered he was pretty shy. It wasn't until she got him talking about his plants that he began to open up.

With his wavy brown hair, hazel eyes, and tall stature, he was very handsome, she mused. She liked men who were willing to work hard— probably because her dad modeled that quality so well. So many young men her age seemed unable to commit to anything. Claire found his desire to start his own business admirable.

Pumping a squirt of face wash into the palm of her hand, she applied it in a circular motion onto her skin. She wondered what he had thought of her. He seemed to be a good eight to ten years older than she was. He probably thought she was in high school. She didn't wear make-up and usually wore a headband because she didn't like loose hair in her face. Even though she looked young, she had always been mature for her age.

Maybe it was the early diagnosis of diabetes or it could have been that she was a responsible first-born child, but she had always been years ahead of her classmates in regard to good judgment.

During high school, she concentrated on her grades. In college it was hard to connect. She went to a local community college for two years and then finished at the University of Illinois' Springfield campus while living at home.

At the university, there weren't a lot of men in the elementary education program, and she didn't live in a dormitory. The church her family attended was tiny, and the few young gentlemen around her age were attracted to her gorgeous younger sister, Gretchen. Not that she blamed them—she was beautiful.

Claire toweled off her wet face. Maybe she would stop by Ethan's property in the morning to see if he needed help with the plastic covering. She wanted to get to know him better, and she had the perfect excuse to make it happen. She said a quick prayer that God would work out the details and turned off the bathroom light.

# Chapter Four

"Hey, babe, how did you sleep?" Edward asked, kissing Jezmeen on the curve of her neck.

Jezmeen felt Edward's hand stroke her thigh.

"Fine," she whispered, still waking up.

"What do you want to do today? It's almost eleven," Edward asked.

The bedroom was dark, thanks to heavy-duty blinds, and Jezmeen still felt tired from the late night with Edward after her work shift ended. She wanted to tell him that a few more hours of sleep would be nice, but she knew he wanted to spend time with her.

"What's the weather going to be like?" she asked.

Edward rolled out of bed and pushed up the blinds. Sun streamed onto the wooden floor.

"Looks nice out," Edward replied.

Jezmeen sat up and stretched. Even first thing in the morning she was a beautiful sight to behold. She rolled her neck from side to side knowing they would go through the same routine that took place every Saturday morning.

"Have you ever been to the Apple Barn?" she asked.

"No, never heard of it."

"It's in Chatham. About twenty minutes from here. It's cute. They make these amazing apple cider doughnuts. You can buy fresh fruit, gourds, pumpkins—that kind of thing. It's a fun place to go in the fall."

Edward's dark hair stuck up in funny angles, and he ran his hands through it a few times.

"I don't know, Jez," he said with a serious expression. "We might run into someone I know from the job. I bet it will be packed."

"Okay, how about we go to a movie?" Jezmeen replied even though she knew his answer.

"There's nothing good out. Plus, you never know who might see us."

"You want to go out to breakfast? Or brunch?"

"I think I'll order us something, Jez," Edward replied, walking to get his laptop off the desk. "And, you know what? We could rent a movie. I think that sounds like a good plan."

Jezmeen silently smirked. It was always the same.

"I'll jump in the shower then," she said.

"Would you wear that red sweater I got you? I love seeing you in it," Edward said.

Jezmeen walked to the closet, wishing they were going to the Apple Barn instead of hiding away at home. Home, Jezmeen thought. She had so many "homes" since she moved out at the age of seventeen. Whenever she left a place, she took her clothes and make-up. That was really all she had, along with a large savings account. Living off men made it easy to retain most of her earnings.

She always told herself she should spend some of her hard-earned cash once in a while, but in the back of her mind she knew why she was saving. One day her luck with the men might run out. It had for her mom a time or two and they'd end up crashing at a stranger's place or in her car. For the last ten years, Jezmeen always had a place to stay, but the nest-egg was there just in case.

Claire rolled over and winced. The tubing of her insulin pump was tightly wrapped around her arm. It didn't happen often, but it had occurred before, so she didn't panic like she had the first time. She carefully untangled the tube and checked the monitor. Everything looked fine, but the clock read six-thirty.

Normally on a Saturday morning, Claire liked to sleep in. But now that she was awake, she could see a clear blue sky out her bedroom window. She loved the horizon—day or night, and she never slept with the blinds drawn if she could help it.

Ever since she was sixteen, after a particularly moving week at church camp, she had read the Bible before her feet hit the floor. Reaching over to the bedside table, she followed the ribbon that held her place in the book of John. Her Bible was highlighted and marked with handwritten scribbles.

She read slowly, absorbing the words about Jesus being the vine and His children being the branches. Claire wrote in the margin, *"being connected to you brings life."* Once she was finished, Claire said a short prayer.

*Good morning, Father. Thanks for waking me up. You're in charge of my day. Help my words and actions please You. Amen.*

Then she swung her feet over the side of the bed and contemplated what she'd do after breakfast. Her thoughts went to Ethan and the tangle of plastic at his feet the day before. She decided to find out if he needed help with his project.

Ethan felt like cursing, but time with former neighbor, Danielle, had curbed his habit. He used to let foul words fly off his tongue, but now he had more self-control. And even though he was alone with the sunrise, he restrained himself.

The plastic would not stay in place. Every time he threw it over the middle, it would fall crooked or drift, so it wasn't centered. There wasn't much wind, but it seemed to blow at just the wrong times. How he had done the last two by himself, he couldn't fathom, but he had. And he wasn't about to call the farmer next-door. Ethan was much too shy—or stubborn. He considered asking his mom to help, but he knew she was working.

At least it was early, and no one was around to see him struggle. The day before had been a disaster. He still felt bad about kicking Claire and wished he had responded more appropriately. It was always easier to look back and see how he could have handled things differently.

It must have bothered him more than he initially realized because he couldn't get to sleep, and that hadn't happened since the first night in the Arctic Fox when he laid away worrying about the responsibilities that accompanied purchasing the land.  Many days he wished Danielle was at his side for the journey.

Before he met Danielle, he was an agnostic.  He had believed something, or someone, created the world, but everyone was left to their own devices.  Danielle shared a book with him, *Mere Christianity* by C.S. Lewis, and after talking through some of his major skepticisms, he came to believe that a man named Jesus really did walk the earth.  But when he left behind his house, he also walked away from the faith that had been stirring in him.

Ethan's hands were cold.  He hadn't been getting a good grip on the plastic with his work gloves, so he had taken them off.  With the morning temperature a brisk 45 degrees, he had decided to forgo his fedora for a black winter cap before he left the trailer.

Just as he was about to attempt another throw, he caught a glimpse of the young Claire headed his way.  With an exuberant wave, she bellowed hello.  Ethan noticed she was dressed for the weather with a puffy midnight blue winter jacket and coordinating pink and blue striped gloves and hat.

"Good morning!  How was the pie?" Claire called from fifty feet away.

"Half gone," he replied softly.

"What?"

"You can tell your mom I ate most of it for breakfast," Ethan said as she neared.

"I'm sure she'll be glad to hear you liked it."

Claire stopped in front of Ethan and took in the sight of his attractive face. Just the nearness to him made her heart skip. Then she looked at the half-covered structure.

"Well, it definitely looks like you can still use some help," she chuckled.

Ethan didn't think this was a laughing matter and took offense.

"I'll be fine without you. Look at the other two."

Claire felt the charge in his spirit and responded gently.

"Sorry. No offense was meant by that. I just happened to wake up early, and I figured I'd see if you were working on the project."

"Don't you have better things to do?" Ethan bristled, still hurt.

"I've got lesson plans to finish, a project to make for class, and some videos to watch," Claire replied with indignation, "so if you don't need me, I can go."

Ethan realized he had offended her.

"Here," he said, thrusting the plastic at her. "We're going to start in the middle."

For the next fifteen minutes, Ethan gave short orders to Claire, and she assisted him with ease. After the covering was over the top, Claire held it in place and Ethan fit the wiggle wire into the channel on the opposite side to bolt it down. When he finished, he walked around to where she was standing with her hands firmly holding the plastic against the frame.

"How did you do this by yourself?" Claire asked quizzically.

"Usually the covering is installed as one long piece, but since I didn't have any help, I cut it into sections."

Claire felt Ethan's body heat as they stood shoulder to shoulder. "Will that affect its durability?" Claire asked as Ethan maneuvered the wire into the channel's groove.

"I hope not."

"You're smart to position these east to west," Claire said.

Ethan was impressed that she would recognize such details. Her roots as a farm girl were showing.

"I'm trying to maximize the sun."

"You'll get plenty. There's nothing on your property blocking the light." Claire let go, as he finished the wiring.

"These things aren't heated. Saves money that way," Ethan said, stepping back to inspect their work.

He headed to the Arctic Fox to get the next piece of plastic that he had been storing on his couch. Claire followed.

"I noticed you don't have electricity out here yet. My dad says it's expensive to have it installed."

Ethan just kept walking, unsure of what to say. He was beyond broke. After paying for the land, trailer, generator, and a water line, he had run out of money. His mom had loaned him the ten-thousand dollars so he could buy three greenhouse kits. With his transcribing salary cut in half, he used his income to pay for groceries, the water bill, plants for the business, and the gas he needed to run the generator.

"Your generator is quiet," she said as they approached the Arctic Fox.

Ethan gave her an incredulous look. How did she know what a generator was?

"We have one for our house. Sometimes the power goes out," Claire smiled. "I didn't think those things were supposed to run all the time though?"

"I only use it when I really need to."

"How do you keep your food cold?  You do have a refrigerator, don't you?"

"Yes, I have a refrigerator," Ethan said haughtily.  He felt ashamed, living like a vagabond.  "Look, the arrangement is only temporary.  In a couple of months, I'll have enough saved up to get electricity out here."

"That's good," Claire replied, backing off.

"Wait here," he grunted, as he headed inside.

For the next two hours, Ethan and Claire worked side by side.  Claire would ask an occasional question about his business when they were near, and Ethan replied with minimal words.  By nine-thirty, the sun was inching up the horizon, and Claire noticed she was feeling shaky and light-headed.  She knew that meant her blood sugar was low.

Ethan was fitting the last of the wiring on his side, and Claire felt obligated to hold her side a little longer.  The next few minutes dragged by, and Claire waffled about what to do.  When she began to feel slightly sick to her stomach, she knew she needed a snack.

"Hey, Ethan," she called out.  "I've gotta go." She didn't wait for him to reply.  Her solitary thought was on making it home.

# Chapter Five

"Can't you just skip whatever it is you do on Sunday mornings?" Edward asked Jezmeen as he set the alarm on his phone.

"Sorry," Jezmeen replied, rolling over so her back was now towards Edward.

"But you're going to be tired," Edward retorted. "It's already three a.m."

Edward was right about that, she thought. Although her shift at Finnegan's ended at one, she had to count the money in the register, wipe the counter and bottles of alcohol, clean the blender, and sweep behind the bar—among other responsibilities.

Back at the apartment, Edward had been waiting for her to arrive. She was drained after entertaining Edward all morning and working an eight-hour shift at the bar. But her Sunday appointment wasn't something she cancelled.

"You're right," she sighed, fighting the urge to say something sarcastic. She was overtired and just wanted to go to sleep. "I don't want to get up that early."

"Then don't."

When she didn't say anything, Edward continued with a frustrated sigh.

"What time will you be back?"

"The same time as always."

"Ten-thirty?"

"Yes."

"Well, I guess I'll just leave to go home after I wake up. You know Amy expects me by mid-afternoon."

"Okay."

Then he kissed her on the cheek and turned off the bedside lamp.

Every Sunday afternoon Ethan did the same thing. He took his laundry to his mom's apartment. She was a cashier at Walmart, so sometimes she was working, and he had the place to himself. This week she was off and anxious to talk with her only child.

Suzanne, a petite, dark-haired lady who tended to go too heavy on the black eyeliner, was in her early fifties. She had worked retail jobs her whole life, and when she wasn't making a paycheck, she enjoyed doing puzzles in front of the television.

Growing up with a single mom who worked night and weekend shifts meant that Ethan learned independence earlier than most kids his age. After high school, he lived with his mom for a year and then moved into his own apartment until he raised enough money to buy his first home.

While he felt a strong connection to Suzanne, since she was the only family he had ever known, he wasn't one to share heart-felt, emotional conversations. He really didn't let anyone in that far. But he always updated her on his projects and goals, and that seemed to satisfy her. He had already put in a load of darks, and he was relaxing on her couch when she brought him a cold can of root beer.

"It sounds like I'll have to drive out to your property later today to see the greenhouses," Suzanne said as she sat down beside him and set her can of soda on the side table. "How long did it take you yesterday to finish covering the last one?"

"A couple of hours," Ethan replied, shuffling through her puzzle pieces, looking for the rest of a marbled white cloud.

"How come it went so fast?" Suzanne asked, bending over the coffee table to help sort through the pieces.

"I had help from a neighbor."

"Who? That farmer, Jedidiah, you told me about?"

"No, his daughter."

Suzanne raised her eyebrow.

"The farmer has a daughter?" She asked with a smile.

"Two."

"Are either of them cute and single?"

"Mom," Ethan groaned.

"What? You have this beautiful face." She touched his cheek with her hand.

"Only since the laser surgeries."

"No, Ethan, you've always been handsome. You're just now catching on to what I have always known."

Suzanne located a white puzzle piece and tried it in the open space in the top right corner with no success.

"Claire Rogers helped me. I haven't met the other daughter yet."

"So, what's Claire like?"

"Young."

"Like in high school?"

"I don't think so. I actually never asked."

"Ethan, how are you going to get to know anybody if you don't ask questions?"

"I have no desire to get to know anybody— let alone Claire."

"How will you run a business with those skills?"

"I don't have to be friends with all the customers, Mom. I perform a service. Get in. Get out. Get paid. That's all there is to it."

"Oh, Ethan," Suzanne sighed and shook her head.

They worked quietly on the puzzle while the television show droned in the background.

"Are you staying warm enough out there in the trailer?" Suzanne asked.

"Yes, Mom."

"And Chewy looks like he's doing okay."

Ethan had brought the cat, and he was curled up on the top of the cat tree Suzanne had at her apartment just for him.

"The little stinker has tried to escape a few times."

"Are you sure you don't want me to keep him here?"

"Nah."

Ethan knew that even though he liked his bachelor lifestyle, he'd be lonely without the furball.

"So, what's next now that the hoop houses are finished?"

"I need to get the cuttings started and then build some more of those boxes with fiber glass lids to keep the starter plants warm."

"When are you going to get business cards made, so I can hand them to my co-workers?"

"Not any time soon. I need to get the greenhouses up and going first."

"But Ethan you need to get the word out about your services."

"Why?

"Don't you want jobs to start rolling in?"

"I want to have the plants started first."

"Couldn't you buy what you need from other local nurseries once you get landscaping work?"

"Sure, but I'll make more if I can sell my own."

"It's your business," Suzanne sighed. "I just hope you can stay afloat. I don't like to see you working two jobs."

"It's only for a short season."

Suzanne located another white cloud piece and pushed it into place.

"I hope that's the case."

When Claire graduated from high school, her parents remodeled the loft area of their old farmhouse to make a large suite with a bedroom and bathroom. Jed and Connie convinced Claire that living at home and going to college would be the safest option, given her medical condition.

She would have protested. Claire's friends were all going away to universities to experience life on their own. It seemed as if she was missing a milestone by staying home. But having relied on them in the past, she felt safer with them around. And she had always been compliant. Her sister, Gretchen, was the more likely one to be independent or make rash choices—like last Thanksgiving when she came home with a tattoo on her wrist or spring break when she went to Cancun and posted some questionable pictures of her fun on Facebook.

Claire's role in the family was set. She was dependable. Honest. And she tried to please her parents. The smile she wore wasn't always an accurate reflection of how she felt, but she displayed it all the same.

As she sat at the long worktable her dad had made, she cut out the words she printed for the problem-solving spinner for her class. Claire went into education because she loved children. Now, having her first classroom, she found great joy in her job.

The day before, when she ran away from Ethan, she had felt no joy—only embarrassment. Once at home, she ate a granola bar and felt better. But secretly she had hoped Ethan would come and check on her.

She had been with him all morning, and she had bolted on him with no warning. Didn't he think that was odd? Claire didn't know what she had expected, but the time they had spent together fell flat. She knew nothing more about him, and he never asked anything about her.

She wasn't one to chase relationships, but she liked qualities she saw in him. Even if the outcome of the previous day wasn't satisfactory, she was thankful she had helped him finish his project.

Looking out one of the large windows that faced the road, she wondered if she would live at home forever with her parents. Claire loved Connie and Jed, but at the age of twenty-three, she felt a longing to spread her wings. But where would she go? And how would she survive without their help if her diabetes flared up? For now, the twenty-one little ones she'd spent her days with would have to be enough.

When Jezmeen arrived back at the apartment late Sunday morning, Edward was gone, and she was thankful. She breathed a sigh of relief. Using the elastic hair tie on her wrist, she pulled her brown locks into a messy bun, and headed into the kitchen to get a bite to eat—the first of the day.

She never missed her Sunday morning appointment—at least she hadn't in almost ten years. She couldn't. As she passed by the granite-topped kitchen island, her eyes fell on an envelope. Sometimes Edward left her extra spending money or wrote her a love letter.

She'd heard lines before from many men. *Your eyes are beautiful. Your body is fine. I love your lips.* But she'd never had anyone compliment her character. At the moment that didn't matter. Jezmeen opened the envelope hoping for some Benjamin Franklins to appear, but instead she found a solitary note.

*Dear Jez,*

*I'm sorry to tell you like this, but I couldn't bring myself to do it any other way. We've had a lot of good times together, but the building I was working on is done. It has been for a month, but I couldn't bring myself to let you go. Now I have no other choice.*

*When Susan and I were shopping for groceries, we ran into a co-worker of mine, and he spilled the beans that things in Springfield were complete. He asked what I was doing with all my spare time.*

*Then I had to lie to Susan and tell her I still had loose ends to finish up. I gave the landlord my two-week notice. I hope that's enough time for you to gather up your things. I left some money on the bed in case you need it to get started at a new place.*

*You'll always be in my heart and in my dreams.*

Jezmeen let out a deep sigh. Her memory drifted to a moment with her mother. One night, after not seeing her mom's latest boyfriend for a week, she asked where he had gone. Sherry said he wasn't coming back, but it was fine with her because she didn't really like him anyways.

Never once had Jezmeen felt any longing for Edward. It was a relationship of convenience, for both of them, and now she would move on. But where would she go? Her flirtatious ways made her popular with the opposite gender and an outsider with women. She had no female friends, and Sherry had moved to Texas—for a man. Jez had the nest egg, if she needed it, but she wasn't worried. She already had her eye on some fresh prey.

# Chapter Six

**4 MONTHS LATER...FEBRUARY 2012...**

"Are you going to stop by?" Jezmeen hollered to Nick from the bathroom where she was curling her hair.

The tall man with dark-blonde hair appeared at the door frame and leaned against it.

"Nah. I don't want to risk running into Clarissa."

"I don't think she's working tonight," Jez replied, not really knowing if that was the truth. She secretly liked making Clarissa jealous.

"That's what you said last time." He grabbed her side flirtatiously.

"Hey, this thing is hot," she whined, almost dropping the curling iron.

"I think you want me to run into her," Nick said. He grabbed a dirty t-shirt from the bathroom floor and picked it up.

"Well, what are you doing to do tonight then?"

"Probably go to Dan's to hang out."

"You mean drink beer and play video games."

"Don't wait up," Nick said. "If it gets too late, I'll crash at his place."

"Translation— if you get too drunk."

Nick whipped the t-shirt at her in a playful manner. "Hope work goes well," he said before walking away.

Jezmeen set the curling iron down and studied her appearance in the mirror. She'd lost a little weight due to the stress of the move, but she was pleased with her tinier waist. She certainly looked better than Clarissa.

Clarissa was Nick's girlfriend, before Jez broke them up. She and Clarissa worked together at Finnegan's for the last three years, and Clarissa had always been kind to her. She was the only female staff member who tried.

Jezmeen knew that stealing Nick would jeopardize any relationship they had, but she needed a place to stay, and Nick had always been friendly. Since Clarissa was a waitress, Nick often came in before Clarissa finished her shift and sat at the bar. Jez used her moments with him wisely, especially after her break-up with Edward.

All she had to do was share the sob story about her heartbreak and potential homelessness, and Nick let her move in—even though he said it was strictly platonic. He was still dating Clarissa, after all. Jez knew that wasn't enough. She had to have his full investment, otherwise she could be kicked to the curb. So, within a month of living with him, she had stolen him away.

Clarissa no longer talked with Jez, which wasn't a surprise. However, she did rally the rest of the female staff, and some of the males too, to heckle her. Sometimes she'd find a nasty note in her purse, one time the side of her car was scratched with a key, but the scariest moment was when a group of servers waited for her by her car one night, when the bar closed. Words were spoken, punches attempted, and Jez barely escaped without a black eye or broken arm.

After that she talked with her manager, who had vacillated over the years between liking and tolerating her. Begrudgingly, the boss called a staff meeting and outlined proper behavior at work and off the clock, which silenced the crowd for the time being.

Jez chose "devil's food cake" lipstick and applied a thin layer before puckering and dabbing the excess. She heard the din of the television in the living room and thought about how much she genuinely liked Nick. He didn't fit the rich and powerful profile of men she usually dated.

Nick worked at a local hardware store and was a few years younger than her. He was playful, likeable, and cute. The more time she spent with him, the stronger her feelings grew, although she never let herself explore the depth of her emotion.

A little immature, Nick liked to spend nights when she worked with his buddies, but she never worried about him straying. He was loyal. Even when she moved in, he was completely transparent with Clarissa, and when he found himself "falling in love," he broke things off with Clarissa before anything happened between them. Maybe that's why she liked him so much.

Edward had contacted her only once since his departure in October. He was on a business trip in St. Louis, and he wanted her to meet him at his hotel. Now that she had Nick, there was no need to pander to his demands, and she politely declined.

Jezmeen spritzed hairspray onto her locks before turning off the light. Work awaited. Maybe one day she'd hit the jackpot and meet someone *really rich* so she could quit her job.

Winter had been brutal for Ethan. When the temperature dropped into the teens outside, Ethan had to put extra layers of plastic on his plants inside the hoop houses. But he was still worried about them freezing, so he warmed buckets of coals and put them in each structure for extra warmth.

Besides trying to keep his plants from dying, the outdoor water faucet froze. Fixing it set him back hundreds, and he wished the man who installed it would have told him it needed insulation. Next, in a careless move, he placed a bucket of coals too close to a side wall covered in plastic.  Within twenty-four hours, a hole had been burned through, and he had to repair it in the negative ten-degree weather.

Finally, one morning Ethan woke up to find one of the plastic tarps on a greenhouse had collapsed, due to a pile of snow resting on top. The perennials in the "The Eternal Forest" were almost crushed.  On a particularly quiet winter day, he'd named the three greenhouses and used a wood burning tool to create wooden signs that he hung in each one.  "The Eternal Forest" held plants that would live for years, "The Once Again Woodland" housed annuals, and "The Green Jungle" held shrubs.

Only once did he leave Springfield during the course of the season, and that was when he had his six-month appointment for a laser treatment to keep his birthmarks at bay.  Even though he knew what to expect, having gone through three treatments over the summer at his doctor's office in St. Louis, he was still stunned by all the blueberry-sized purple dots that the laser inflicted.  Ethan was thankful that he didn't have to worry about visitors during the two-week recovery period.

When he lived in town, he had become friends with Danielle through her persistent acts of kindness as his neighbor.  Now in the country, the Rogers hadn't visited since Christmas when Connie brought a plate of homemade cookies to his door.  The neighbors on the right were an older couple who lived in a ranch-style home.  He only saw the man of the house occasionally when he used his snow blower to clear the long drive.

Ethan rarely got lonely, but that didn't surprise him. From his earliest recollections, he could entertain himself for hours on end. Before he became interested in plants, he liked building, drawing, reading, and studying animal behavior. And if he had more time, he would take up caring for animals again.

Since his outdoor work had slowed down, he returned to full-time hours transcribing, which was necessary considering he had yet to run an electric line to his property. His goal was to have it in by the end of March, and if he didn't have any further financial setbacks it could happen.

But he didn't want to transcribe forever, so he needed customers. Every time his mom nagged him for not advertising, he came up with excuses. He didn't have a printer. Why market himself when it was so cold? Who would he tell?

Truthfully, Ethan knew he was scared stiff to interact with people, so he put it off. Maybe he didn't need buyers, he mused. He could grow plants for himself and make his own blooming barrier to keep people out.

He always believed that if his birthmarks were gone, he'd be a different person. No longer would he be uncomfortable around others, and he'd become the outgoing man he dreamed he could be.

Back when he read the Bible, he recalled a passage about how he could become a new person. It involved believing in Jesus. Through study, he'd determined a human named Jesus had lived over 2,000 years ago, but Ethan's conclusion was that He was just a good man, maybe even a prophet, but certainly not the Son of God. It seemed far-fetched that one man could save all mankind by dying and rising again. If faith in Jesus was what it took to be a "new man," he decided to stick with the old.

Ethan let a curse word fly out of frustration. His breath blew billowy white clouds, as it hit the cold air. One of the beauties of winter was waking up whenever his body decided it was alert. This morning, the temperature was his alarm. Even under the comforter he didn't feel warm. Ethan had already outfitted the bedroom windows with special curtains to block the chilliness, so instinctively he knew something was wrong with the battery-powered generator outside.

Heating his trailer must have strained it beyond repair. He dreaded pulling his legs out from under the covers, but he needed to confirm his suspicions. When he went to the bathroom, the toilet seat was freezing, and the small window was framed in ice crystals. Ethan went back to the bedroom and tugged on thermal underwear, sweatpants, and a heavy winter jacket.

It was dark out when he stepped onto the trailer's slick steps. Reaching the generator, he unplugged and reconnected the power cord. And then just for good measure he kicked it. If he wasn't worried about waking the neighbors, he would have let out an inexhaustible groan.

He was broke and now he'd have to hand over eight-hundred dollars for a new generator. For the past few months, he'd managed to save a majority of his earnings. But all the money set aside was earmarked for an electric line, and he was still a few thousand dollars short.

His mom's latest suggestion, to make a Facebook page to advertise Adams Landscaping floated to his mind. She even said she'd do it for him. With the month of March only days away, and warmer weather forecasted, he knew he should start lining up jobs, but he was nervous. Did he really know enough?

Sure, he'd read books for years, plotted hundreds of designs, and understood plants and trees inside and out. But did that translate into practical know-how? Could he make a client happy?

It was too early to find an open hardware store, so headed to the "Green Jungle." After he pulled up the many layers of plastic covering on his plants, he saw twenty-five happy hydrangeas. They would take a few more years to mature into pot-sized plants to sell, but for now they were healthy and on-track.

A few of his other shrubs were slow growers, too. The boxwoods wouldn't be ready for the market this spring or summer. Actually, Ethan thought, as he looked around, most of the plants in this hoop house wouldn't be big enough to be attractive to buyers. This only depressed him more, so he left and went to the "Eternal Forest."

Lifting off the tarping, Ethan saw white dust on the green foliage, covering ninety percent of the plants in the one area. He instantly knew what that meant—powdery mildew had attacked his perennials. He yelled at the top of his lungs in anguish, and quickly went down the rows of flowers, checking to see if all of them had succumbed to the fungus that grew because humidity was trapped within the tarp.

All of the plants on the east wall were affected, which meant he had been keeping them too warm, and now he'd have to buy a fungicide to treat the lot. He was bleeding money, and he wondered why he'd even taken on this challenge.

# Chapter Seven

## MARCH 2012

Claire had finished her lesson planning for the weekend, so she decided to channel surf. An episode she'd already seen was being replayed on the *Food Network*, so she tried the *Home and Garden Television* station as she relaxed in a blue recliner up in her loft.

A special feature called *Unbelievable Backyards* had just started, so Claire set the remote control on the side table and settled in. Halfway through the episode, Claire sat up in surprise. A Springfield, Illinois backyard was being featured.

The host of the show and a handsome politician were touring the gardens behind his house in the Southern View neighborhood. Claire thought the backyard was breathtaking with a waterfall boasting color-changing lights, whimsically patterned pathways, and finely manicured flower beds and tall grasses. But the main focal point was the stamped concrete patio with a pergola that had a lattice top that could open and close with a hand crank.

The politician explained that he had bought the property, and he could take no credit for its beauty. He gave merit to Ethan Adams, who previously owned the home and landscaped the backyard. Then the host elaborated that the property caught the eye of a fan of the show who sent in pictures from the internet when the house went on the market.

For the next few minutes, Claire was enthralled as the host pointed out why certain plants worked so well in each space and how the design was ingenious.  When the show transitioned to commercials, Claire ran down to tell her parents.  Their neighbor would be famous, she exclaimed, and she hoped he could keep up with all the business that would soon come his way.

"Adams Landscaping," Ethan said as he answered his cell phone.  He was repotting plants in "The Once-Again Woodland," while he cradled the phone to his ear.

"You'd like a landscape design for your back patio?  Can I get your address?  Then I can schedule a time to come out and look at the space."

Ethan searched the greenhouse for a piece of paper or a pen, knowing he wouldn't find what he needed.  This was the third call of the morning, and every time he went outdoors to start a new task, he forgot to bring writing utensils and paper.

"Hold on a second," he grunted, and he bolted back to his trailer.

"Okay, go ahead," he said as Chewy jumped onto the kitchen table and rubbed his arm.

"3112 Brick Mill Road." He was about to hang up when the customer reminded him they hadn't scheduled a day and time for him to come.

"Oh right," he sighed. "Let me pull up my calendar," he said, trying to open the online program.

"How's Saturday at nine?" He offered. Without offering a goodbye or thank-you, he hung up, flustered.

He couldn't stand talking on the phone, and that's all he seemed to be doing the last two weeks. Ever since the HGTV episode aired, featuring his backyard, people from all over the city and surrounding towns were calling to ask for his help with their landscaping needs.

Ethan had known that an HGTV crew filmed his old backyard. The producer of the show had called to get his permission and ask if he wanted to be interviewed. The thought of being on camera terrified him, but he allowed the crew to use whatever footage of the yard that they wanted. The producer hadn't promised the segment featuring his designs would make the cut. So, he was surprised, along with the rest of Springfield, when it was highlighted.

Since he didn't have a television, he hadn't seen the show, but the local paper sniffed out a story and called him. Their write-up caused a second wave of interest in his services, even bigger than the first, since they gave out his contact information and highlighted pictures of the plants in his hoop houses.

Ethan had hoped to start propagating trees, now that the ground was warm enough, but he had stacks of phone messages to follow up with, designs to plan, quotes to print, and jobs to schedule. He felt like a pack-mule carrying a large load up a mountain.

His mom offered to help, but Ethan knew she didn't have the organizational skills that it would take to aid him. Ethan scratched Chewy nonchalantly on the neck as he looked around the kitchen. He had post-it notes on every cabinet and little scraps of paper on the table. He saw that the nightstand behind his bed held more notes, too.

A few of his design plans had floated to the floor, and Chewy had placed some dusty paw prints on top, hopefully as a stamp of approval. Ethan exhaled and looked down at the paper under the heel of his hand. Saturday nine a.m. 501 Bellerive Rd. He had forgotten to put that appointment on his calendar, and now he was double booked. Ethan yelled out in frustration, startling Chewy who jumped down and ran to the cat tree in the bedroom.

Then the phone rang—again.

Jezmeen quietly opened the pantry and grabbed a protein bar out of a box. She didn't want to wake Nick. It was early Sunday morning, and she was on her way to "exercise class." At least that's where Nick thought she was going.

After shoving the bar into her purse, she opened the silverware drawer and picked up the stash of cash Nick left under the utensil holder. She flipped through the wad and took a twenty. Nick hadn't exactly shared where he kept his spare bills, but she saw him linger too long by the drawer once and figured it out. Jez never took the big bills. She figured that would be too noticeable.

She had started with fives and tens. Once she realized he didn't seem to keep track of the exact amount he kept in the drawer, she worked up to twenties. When she first started taking cash from the men she was with, she rationalized it, saying she'd spent it on dinner or groceries. When that wasn't always the case, she reasoned that everything was to be shared in a relationship.

She checked her watch and saw that it was eight-thirty. If she wanted to be on time, she needed to go. Grabbing her cell phone, she saw the date flash, as she powered it up. March 28. It was her mom's birthday.

Where was her mom these days, she wondered. Seven years ago, she had moved to San Angelo, Texas with her boyfriend, Tom, who was a wind turbine technician. He relocated for a better paying job, and her mom followed. Sherry would be forty-eight today. She had Jezmeen when she was twenty-one.

A few years ago, Sherry called saying Tom had proposed. She wanted to know if Jezmeen would go to their wedding, if they had one. Jezmeen said it probably wouldn't fit with her work schedule. Then, a few months later, her mom phoned again to let Jez know the wedding was called off, but Tom was still around.

Sherry had been married twice. Once when Jez was three and the other when she was fourteen. Jez didn't recall too much about the first marriage, but she vividly remembered how depressed her mom became after the second betrothal. Sherry cried to her repeatedly during the months following the nuptials, saying Richard didn't pay enough attention to her and there was no real love between them. Jezmeen had never been married, and with those memories, she didn't plan to.

She considered calling her mom to wish her a happy birthday when she got back, but then she decided against it. When was the last time her mom had done anything on her birthday? It had been years since she'd gotten a card or a call. No, Jez determined, she would give Sherry the same treatment. Like mother, like daughter, she smirked.

"Adams Landscaping," Ethan groused.

"Hello, is this Ethan Adams?" a deeper, older voice asked.

"Yes."

"This is Lawrence Conwell. I own Tryton Building Products. We're located in Indianapolis, Indiana. Been around for thirty-two years."

Ethan wondered how far he'd be willing to travel for work. Indianapolis was quite a few hours away.

"I have a friend at the *Home and Garden Network*. She happened to be one of the producers of the episode that aired a few weeks ago featuring the backyard you designed. She sent me pictures of your pergola, and I was fascinated by the hand-cranking element for the lattice top. I'd like to talk to you about buying your concept and manufacturing it for sale in the big-box stores. It hasn't been patented yet has it?"

"No."

"That's fine.  We'd do that for you.  We'd also deal with the manufacturing, marketing, and distributing.  Those are our specialties."

Ethan was dumbfounded, and Chewy was distracting.  He'd come down from the cat tree, and was meowing loudly, reminding Ethan he had forgotten to feed him breakfast.

"Sorry," Ethan muttered.  "Cat.  Umm.  Let's see.  You want to buy my idea?"

"That's right, Mr. Adams.  I think you've got a real winner."

Ethan had two orders for his pergola sitting on his table, but he never considered his design to be that special.

"Umm.  What's your name again?"

"Lawrence Conwell," he chuckled.  "But you can call me Larry."

"Okay, Larry, how would this all work... if I *did* decide I want to do this deal?"

"Well, I'd draw up some paperwork.  Send it to you.  Do you have a fax machine?"

"No."

"I could email you then.  It would state what the terms would be, but I'd like to own the product and pay you a royalty."

"I'd get a percentage of each sale?" Ethan asked, clarifying.

Chewy jumped onto the kitchen counter and demanded, with a louder howl, that he was through waiting.

"Yes, that's right, Mr. Adams."

Ethan headed towards the pantry in a daze. Chewy appreciated the movement in the right direction and stopped his commotion.

"I guess I'd like some time to think about it."

"That's fine. When would you like me to call you again?"

"I don't know," Ethan replied, retrieving a can of cat food. "Maybe in a couple of days?"

"That's fair. In the meantime, feel free to check out our website and what we do. Just type in Tryton Building Products, and you'll find us. Thanks for your time, Mr. Adams. I look forward to speaking with you again soon."

"Okay," Ethan replied, and he hung up.

He robotically opened the can and scooped it into Chewy's food dish, then filled up the water bowl. The happy cat pounced over to the food and began eating. Ethan walked back to the kitchen table, in such a stupor he stepped on a design plan laying on the floor, and it stuck to his shoe.

Just weeks ago, he was hopeless, staring into a bleak future that needed momentum he couldn't muster. Now, he had plenty of customers and the potential of a money-making invention. It seemed like an easy decision—look at the contract and if all was equitable, take the deal. But if he had such a winning idea on his hands, maybe he should manufacture it himself and make a larger percentage of the income while maintaining the rights to his invention?

If Danielle was there, she would have told him to pray, he thought. But he didn't know much about that, so he did what he knew to do. He called his mom.

# Chapter Eight

Ethan walked up two flights of stairs with a hamper full of dirty clothes, thankful his mom's apartment wasn't on the third floor.  He was fumbling for his key when his mom opened the front door.

"Let me help you with that," Suzanne said, taking the handles of the mesh container from him.  "I was walking to the kitchen, and I heard you out there."

"Thanks, Mom.  I really appreciate you doing my laundry today."

"Don't you want to come in, even for a minute?" she asked.

"I wish I could, but I'm swamped.  I have to finish the brick work for a path at one of the jobs sites, then swing by a house in the same neighborhood to take pictures of their space so I can write up a design for their front yard."

"But Ethan, it's Sunday, and you haven't had a day off in weeks."  Suzanne leaned against the door frame.  "Have you put in your two weeks' notice with the transcribing service?"

"Not yet," he answered, feeling impatient to get going.  "I don't want to stop until I see money coming in.  The down payments on these first couple of jobs are only covering the cost of materials at this point."

"When do you sign the papers with Tryton Building Products?"

"Mr. Conwell is coming next week."

"I still can't believe he's going to pay you a million dollars for a hand crank."

"That million isn't coming in all at once. You know it's spread out over two years."

"But you're getting five percent royalties on every kit sold, too," Suzanne replied.

"Those kits won't be on the market for months."

"Oh, Ethan, stop grumbling," Suzanne smiled. "I'm so proud of you." She pulled the laundry hamper into the hallway. "But I'm worried about you, too." Are you even sleeping?"

Ethan didn't answer.

"Why don't you hire someone to help you?"

"I want the work to be up to my standards. Who knows what I'd get?"

"Well then, find someone to do your secretarial work. How behind are you with your scheduling?"

"I don't know, at this point. My answering machine is full."

Suzanne stepped into the hallway and reached up to put her arms on her son's shoulders. "It's okay to accept help. If you don't find some, I will."

"Okay, Mom," Ethan grunted. He pulled his mom into a hug. "Thanks again for helping me with my laundry. I really appreciate it."

"You're welcome, sweetheart. Don't work too hard."

Suzanne loaded her vehicle with Ethan's clean laundry, went to a drive-through to get him something to eat, and then headed to his trailer. When she had texted him an hour earlier, he said he wasn't close to being done with the brickwork.

The sun didn't set until after seven, and Suzanne was sure Ethan would work until dark. She pulled up next to the trailer, popped the trunk, and grabbed the basket of neatly folded clothes. After she inserted the key to open the trailer, she used the hamper to press against the front door, causing it to swing wide open, and out streaked a copper-colored fur ball.

"No, Chewy," Suzanne screamed, dropping the hamper on the floor. She knew Ethan had perfected some move with his leg that kept Chewy inside, but she had forgotten all about the escape artist.

The cat dashed for the road, and Suzanne's heart dropped. She took off in the fastest sprint her fifty-four-year-old body could manage. Chewy ran past her car and was almost to Farmingdale Road when Suzanne saw the next-door neighbor pushing his blue garbage container to the edge of the curb.

"Hey," she cried. "Grab that cat!"

Jedidiah Rogers looked up and saw Chewy headed his way. Jed quickly opened the lid, rummaged for a second, pulled out an empty brown box, and set it on the ground in front of the trash can.

Chewy slowed and sat down on his haunches about ten feet from the box. It was then Suzanne caught up to the duo. She began to make a move to grab Chewy when Jed held up his hand in opposition.

"Wait. Cats can't resist boxes," Jed whispered.

They watched Chewy lick his front paw casually, as if ignoring them altogether.

"I think I need to try to catch him," Suzanne said in an equally hushed voice. "If I don't, he might try to run across the road."

"I've never had this trick fail. We used to have indoor cats who would escape."

After a few agonizing minutes, Chewy nonchalantly padded towards the box, and after walking around it a few times, he hopped inside.

"Thank you," Suzanne said, as she picked up the box and cradled it against her body. "I'm Suzanne, Ethan's mom. I was dropping off some things for Ethan, and Chewy got out."

"Nice to meet you. I'm Jed," he replied. "It's a good thing my wife just happened to get an online order of clothes today, and the recycling bin was already full."

"I had no idea that would work. You really saved the day."

"Happy to help. I just happened to be in the right place at the right time. How's Ethan doing these days?" Jed asked as he watched Chewy clean his face.

"Busier than ever."

"We saw his design on *HGTV*. Well actually our daughter did, and she let us know. That was really exciting. We haven't seen a lot of him outside, so we figured business was going well."

"A little too well," Suzanne sighed. "He has so many calls coming in, he's having trouble staying on top of things. I keep telling him he needs to hire someone."

Jedidiah's eyes lit up. "That's funny. Our daughter, Claire, was just talking tonight at dinner about wanting a summer job. She's a teacher but was a part-time administrative assistant for a dentist during college."

"She sounds like a perfect fit," Suzanne exclaimed, noticing Chewy's squirmy movements, hoping to get out.

"Do you think she could start now? I mean for a few hours in the afternoon? My son will probably balk, so *I'll* hire her. I can't offer more than minimum wage to start, but in the future that could change."

"I'll ask her, but she's the type of young lady who likes to help out, so I imagine she will say yes."

"You really are a life-saver," Suzanne smiled. "Thank you *so* much for saving the cat— and Ethan."

Jezmeen knew she couldn't be stuck in Nick's apartment all day. Every April eighth she relived all the memories that took place ten years ago. There had been so much happiness, uncertainty, and pain mixed in a twenty-four-hour period. Since Nick didn't have to work, she decided it would be a perfect time to take him shopping.

A few weeks earlier, one of the waitresses at Finnegan's had come in wearing a new diamond necklace. It sparkled brightly, and ever since she had wanted something similar. She dressed with intention that morning, putting on tight-fitting jeans, a snug, white v-neck top that left nothing to the imagination, and tall wedge sandals. Nick had been out with his buddies the night before, so while he was still sleeping, she curled her hair, did her make-up and put on large hoop earrings. Her appearance was certain to make men do a double-take.

Then she went into the kitchen and fixed bacon and eggs for Nick. The smell of the sizzling pork brought him out of the bedroom and into her arms. After several minutes of enjoying her lips, Nick asked if it was his birthday and he didn't know it.

"No, silly," Jezmeen lilted. "I just wanted to show you that I appreciate you. Sit down, hon. Do you want orange juice?"

He sat down at the small island, and she brought him a plate of food.

"Since we both have the day off," she said casually, "I thought we could go to the mall."

"Oh, do you need something?" he asked as he took a bite of the crisp bacon.

"No, but we haven't done that before, and I just want to spend time with you."

"We could spend time here," he replied with a mischievous grin, "getting to know the bedroom." He grabbed her by the waist and kissed her again.

She laughed and took a sip of his orange juice.

"You're so funny, Nick," she flirted.

"If it's really what you want to do, fine," he said. "Just give me fifteen to take a shower."

Two hours later they had window-shopped at a few clothing stores, a candle outlet, and a home-goods retailer. They had just finished eating puffy pretzel sticks from *Auntie Anne's* when Jezmeen spotted her target—*Kay Jewelers.*

"Nick," she exclaimed, "can we go in there?"

"Why?" he grimaced.

"Just to look."

"I guess."

At first, she light-heartedly pointed out pieces that were gaudy or expensive. Then, she carefully approached the necklaces. She had already spent time online selecting the piece she wanted, and when she got to the second case, she saw it.

"Isn't that beautiful?" she whispered.

"What?" he asked, distracted.

"That necklace," Jez replied pointing to the half carat pear-cut diamond on a cable chain.

"Sure."

A male employee, dressed in a suit and tie, approached the couple.

"Can I help you?" he asked.

Jezmeen threw her eyes his way and smiled.

"I'd love to see that one. London Nights, I think it's called," she said.

"Perfect choice," he replied, opening the case and extracting the necklace. "You can try it on."

As she centered it on her neck, she pulled up her hair and asked Nick to do the clasp. The employee positioned the standing mirror to face her.

"That looks lovely with your eyes," he said.

Nick didn't like the man encroaching and said, "Yeah, Jez, that looks really great on you."

"You think?" she asked innocently, looking at both men.

"Oh yes," the employee commented. "I think you could model that for us," he said, pointing to a picture of a woman on the wall.

Nick's agitation was increasing at the attention Jez was getting, and she couldn't have been more pleased with how the scene was playing out.

"Nick, honey, do you think..." She stopped, knowing exactly what she was doing. "No, it's too much to ask," she continued. "Never mind," she said, beginning to unhook the necklace.

"There's a sale today," the employee said. "This just happens to be twenty-five percent off."

"How much is it?" Nick asked.

"$638, but it's usually $850. That's a great deal. This piece doesn't go on sale often."

Nick's face went white. "Sorry, Jez, that's a week's paycheck."

"Oh," she naively. "It's just that nobody's ever bought me a diamond before," she lied. "I've never owned a piece of nice jewelry."

"But you'd never be able to wear it to work," Nick objected.

"Why not?"

"Don't you think it's too flashy? Too extravagant?"

"I don't think so. I would think of you all the time I was wearing it," she said. Then she flashed a grin again at both men, trying to remind Nick of all the hungry piranhas that she served.

80

"Well," Nick began, thinking deeply. "Maybe another time. I can start saving for it."

Jezmeen didn't expect Nick to be such a tough nut to crack, but she really wanted that necklace.

"It's okay. I couldn't expect you to know it's my birthday today," she lied again. "No big deal. Let's go,"

"We'll take it," Nick said.

# Chapter Nine

## APRIL 2012

"Mom, it's not going to work. Where would Claire have office space? It's not like she wants to take calls out of the Arctic Fox? Plus, I only have one business number. And, really, is there that much for her to do?" Ethan ranted.

Suzanne and Ethan sat across from one another at his tiny kitchen table. A few days after Suzanne's conversation with Jedidiah, she received a call from Claire saying she would be interested in learning more details about the job. Not wanting to move forward without Ethan's permission, Suzanne scheduled an evening to talk with him about hiring Claire.

"Ethan," Suzanne sighed. "Look at this place."

It was covered with papers, post-it notes, landscape designs, leftover plates of food, tuna cans licked clean, and dirty laundry in the bedroom.

"She's not going to be my housekeeper."

"I know. But you're disorganized. You have too much going on. Claire has had a few years of administrative experience. She can handle your schedule, return calls. You'll keep more jobs than you're losing now. You can't do it all, honey."

"Where's her salary going to come from?" Ethan sighed.

"I'll pay it for the first two months. After that, you should have your first check from Tryton Building Products. I think you'll be able to cover the cost after that."

Suzanne took a drink of her diet soda.

"I don't know, Mom," Ethan sighed.

Ethan knew he needed the help. He'd gone the last four weeks averaging four hours of sleep a night. Larry Conwell was coming in two days to look at Ethan's pergola design and sign the papers finalizing the deal.

He was salivating over the potential of having more money in his possession than he ever had before, even if it came in increments, but he was running on fumes and stressed to the max. He already knew he needed to quit his transcribing job, but he couldn't let go of that income until Tryton's check came through.

Since the television show, over one hundred phone calls for work had come in. Some were simple requests for lawn mowing or yard clean-up. Others were for landscape design. He scheduled as many as he could. But he knew he'd lost a fair share of business because he couldn't return calls fast enough, and he wondered what that had done for public opinion of Adams Landscaping.

Ethan had a new appreciation for workers who had to acquire their own customers. Quoting new jobs took up about fifty percent of his time. First, he'd go to the client's home, talk with them about their desires, take pictures of the space, then go home and draw up a plan, estimate a cost, print out an invoice, and mail it.

Because his designs were so innovative, most potential clients wanted to hire him. This thrilled and terrified Ethan. But after he began the first few jobs, he found the work so satisfying he almost dreaded ending the day to go to his transcribing job.

After inhaling a microwave meal or take-out for dinner, he typed medical records from nine until two a.m. During the day, while he dug holes, planted flowers, spread mulch and created fire pits...and took incoming calls. The idea of hiring an administrative assistant was tempting.

Suzanne pressed her hand against his, calling his attention back to her.

"When I talked with Claire on the phone earlier today, she said she'd be willing to help in the greenhouses. Remember, she grew up on a farm. She seems like the type of girl who will really work hard."

Ethan's ears perked up when he heard she could help with the plants. He desperately needed to give his stock attention, and maybe she could even help sell them.

"Where would she work?" he asked, stifling a yawn, while looking at his watch. It was almost nine, and he needed to start his second job soon.

"Why not make her a space in one of the hoop houses? Just create her a simple wooden counter."

"And what about phone calls?"

"I'll add a second phone line to your plan. Then, she can take your phone and handle incoming calls."

"It sounds like you have this all figured out," he grunted, only for show.

"So, is it a yes? Can I hire Claire?"

"I guess," Ethan replied, hoping his contact with her would be minimal.

Claire sat at the desk Ethan constructed for her in "The Once-Again Woodland." The plants that needed the most attention and were the likeliest to sell in the approaching months lived there. Her backdrop was a myriad of annuals—marigolds, geraniums, petunias, begonias, and impatiens. Most had already begun to bloom, sharing their bright pink, fiery red, and dazzling yellow hues.

She had been working for Ethan nearly two weeks, and after the first day, when he met with her for about twenty-minutes to give her some basic instructions and a tour of the greenhouses, she had not seen him at all.

Besides not seeing Ethan, the job had been a perfect fit so far. Thankfully, she was a self-starter. Working just two hours each weekday afternoon suited her fine. When school concluded at the end of May, she'd start full-time hours.

After her schedule had been set, her first matter of business was to organize the paperwork chaos. She had been given permission to scour the Arctic Fox, which she did with expediency. Claire learned that Ethan had a friendly cat, who's diet consisted of a variety of fast food- based on the empty sacks lining the counter. And Ethan wasn't much of a decorator.

She located all the loose scraps of paper and set to work creating a calendar for Ethan. Claire decided to make a large wall size paper calendar. She'd keep it at her workspace, and Ethan could check it as he'd like. She also linked his personal calendar on his new cell phone with the one on his business phone line, so he could also have an accurate copy electronically.

It took her a few days of driven focus to get his appointments straight. Once that task was complete, she called all of his clients to confirm the schedule and thank them for their interest in

Adams Landscaping. Then she made him a binder of the designs he'd made, using tabs to create sections for full sun, mostly shade, back yard, and front yard plans.

She also made copies of all the plans he was currently using with customers and created a separate binder with tabs by clients' last name, so he could take it with him to jobs. All the while she was taking care of these backlogged tasks, she fielded new phone calls and tended the plants. Claire liked the work and found that it stretched a different part of her brain than the ways she used it in her classroom.

As she was taking a phone call on the first Friday afternoon in May, Ethan walked in. She looked up, gave him a small wave, and a smile.

"So, I have Ethan down to stop by your house in two-weeks, on Saturday, May 15th, at 4:00 p.m. Thank you for your interest in Adams Landscaping. We look forward to helping you in the weeks to come, and if you have any questions please don't hesitate to call. Have a great day."

This was the first time he heard her interact with a customer, and he was impressed. Ethan walked a few feet away, while he waited for her to be done, and he was pleased to see that the plants at the beginning of the row looked healthy.

"Hey," he grunted as she finished the call.

"Hi Mr. Adams," she replied, not knowing what she should call him since he was now her boss.

"It's Ethan," he said, answering her silent question, taking off the fedora, and running a hand through his wavy hair.

"I was just finishing up for the day," she said, straightening the papers on her desk, hoping he wouldn't see how nervous she was to be around him. "You'll see I scheduled four new client visits for the second week of May. I think now we'll have to start booking three weeks out."

Ethan nodded in understanding. "I noticed you organized the plants by the amount of sunlight they need," he said. "And I see you added signage to explain what's in each section, name stakes in the plants, and price tags on the black pots."

"I hope that's okay."

Ethan was thrilled with the changes she had made to all three greenhouses in a very short time span. The spaces were inviting and orderly.

"It's fine," he muttered, not knowing how to give a proper compliment.

Ethan dead-headed a pink petunia and looked around for the garbage can he kept inside.

"I moved it to the back, so it would be out of the customer's way," Claire commented, noticing what Ethan was looking for.

He headed to the left corner, and Claire trailed like a puppy.

"Has my mom paid you?" Ethan asked.

"Not yet, but I believe she's stopping by tomorrow to give me a check. Then your first payment from Tryton goes through."

"She told you about that?" Ethan looked up in surprise, as he discarded the petals.

"I'm so happy for you," Claire exclaimed. "I love the pergola you have out front. I think that's a great marketing tactic. People can see it, try it, and they'll want to place an order."

"The one out front was just for Mr. Conwell to see. It's getting disassembled and going to a client," he said as they headed back to the front.

"I still can't believe it," Claire continued. "All this attention for your business, and now a product of yours will be sold in stores. It's so amazing."

Many of his customers wanted to talk about his instant notoriety, and since he didn't like to talk period, he gave the same answer to everyone. He heard Danielle say it a time or two, back when they were friends.

"It's been a blessing," he replied.

Claire's eyebrows rose in surprise. She must not have taken him for the religious type, he rationalized, and he wasn't in the mood to correct her. The phrase just seemed to stop the conversation, which was his goal.

As they approached the front door Claire asked, "I guess you'll lock up?"

Ethan nodded in agreement.

"Well, I'll see you tomorrow morning at eight. I've been making a few signs at home for Farmingdale Road, so I'll get those up before I start."

Ethan became apprehensive. "I can't pay you for hours outside of the ones you work here," he complained.

"I know," Claire replied, sounding hurt. "I just like coming up with ways to help your business, and I enjoy doing projects like that."

"Oh, okay," Ethan replied, relaxing a little. "Tomorrow then."

# Chapter Ten

## MAY 2012

The Rogers were enjoying Sunday dinner around the kitchen table. With Jedediah's long hours in the field, Sundays were family favorites since Jed took time off to eat dinner with his girls.

"How is everything going at Adam's Landscaping?" Jed asked Claire. "Your Mom tells me you're enjoying it."

"Helping Ethan get organized has been so much fun," Claire gushed. "And he even asked me to hire three people to help him."

"He asked you to do the hiring?" Jed asked, raising an eyebrow.

"He's shy. I don't think he really likes talking to people all that much, and I really didn't mind. It was actually pretty enjoyable. Ethan's calling me his office manager and letting me make the new guys' schedules, so I don't think it seemed too odd."

"Has he been selling many plants?" Jed questioned.

"On the weekends we've been busy. I was surprised at how many customers came that first weekend without advertising."

"The signs you made must have helped," Connie said.

"It was nice to see the extra effort pay off," Claire replied.

"How are you able to manage all the work on Saturdays? It sounds like too much for one person," Jed asked.

"I asked Ethan if one of the new hires could help out, and he agreed. He's sold so much during the month of May, he'll probably run out of spring plants by the end of June. Most of the shrubs are too small to sell this year. But he had me start cuttings for mums back in April, so we will have those in the fall."

"We?" Connie asked with a smirk.

Claire became flustered, and Jed saved her by changing the subject.

"So, he has you propagating plants," Jed chuckled.

"Yes, why are you laughing?" Claire replied indignantly.

"Well, you've always told me you never wanted to take over the farm, but here you are growing things."

"It's a satisfying feeling to see something bloom that you planted," she smiled. "But I'm still not planning on taking over the Rogers farm."

"I'm just glad you're done teaching," Connie added. "I know you made it through, but it was hard to see you working so many hours."

"You'd never believe the schedule Ethan was keeping," Claire replied. "He finally quit his medical transcribing job about a week and a half ago. Before that, his mom told me he was barely sleeping."

"Is his mom still the one paying you?" Jed asked.

"Yes, but this will be her last weekend to drop off a check." Claire sat back in her chair. "I'm so glad he has *someone* watching out for him. He's such a loner."

"We're thankful he has you." Connie said. "Didn't you tell me that a few customers have called to complain about his stand-offish behavior?"

"Yes, but I've watched him interact with people in the hoop houses, and that's just his style," she replied, trying to defend him.

"You might need to teach him a thing or two about customer service," Jed interjected.

"Maybe, if it ever came up," Claire said.

"If it doesn't, he's bound to lose customers. There are a lot of landscaping companies in town competing for the same jobs," Jed said.

"I'll just have to do my best to represent his business well," Claire replied.

"Well, if anyone can do that, it's you," Jed said. "Alright ladies," Jed said, grabbing their plates, It's my turn to do the dishes."

"Ethan!" Claire said, startled. She stepped inside the green house with her umbrella. "I was wondering why the door was unlocked. I hoped I hadn't forgotten to close-up yesterday."

"The rain's going to push the Anderson job back a day," he said as he looked over the color-coordinated schedule on Claire's desk.

"I thought about that on the walk here. I'll call them to let them know."

The phone rang, and Claire scuttled around Ethan to reach the call. As she curved her arm around his body to grab the cell phone, he turned to move out of her way and ran into her slender frame. She felt his muscular chest and her heart palpitated faster.

"Ethan's Landscaping," she said, flustered. Quickly correcting herself she continued, "Adam's Landscaping. This is Claire, how can I help you?... Yes, his pergola design is amazing. Yes, that's right. It will be out in big-box stores in the next year. Correct, he is still building them. I agree, the write-up in the paper about his invention was nice. No, Tryton Building Products still lets him build them for his customers." She paused listening. "Well, we're running almost two months out with construction. Great, I'll put you down. Can I have your name?"

Ethan strode off to the chrysanthemums, half listening to the conversation.

"You got an order for a pergola," she said after hanging up. She found him pouring some potting mix into a black, plastic container. "Do you think V.J. and Mark could work on building it, if you showed them your design?"

"I don't think so," he huffed.

"Well, you're booked until the end of July."

"Is the customer willing to wait?"

"Seemed like it. Maybe, if you're able to get the Sutton's job started at the end of July, you could let V.J. and Mark finish it up, so you could get going on it sooner," she suggested, not wanting to overstep her bounds, although she noticed he tried to do everything himself.

"Andrew's still doing all the mowing jobs, right?" Ethan asked, moistening the soil with a spray bottle.

"Yes, and if he doesn't have much work that week, he could always help on the Sutton project."

"Okay," he relented. "You can schedule me to start the pergola at the end of July, and V.J. and Mark can finish up the Sutton job."

Claire silently rejoiced. It was the first time he had agreed to letting V.J. and Mark work on their own. Maybe he was trusting them more. Or maybe he was trusting her? She had liked the way Ethan's body had felt against hers, but she shook off the thought as soon as it crossed her mind. He was her much-older boss who never showed any interest in her.

Since she began working for him, it was hard for her to deny she hoped to run into him each day. Not that she ever thought that would happen literally—until today.

Even though he had never been particularly kind, she couldn't help but like him. She used up a few pages in her journal trying to figure out what it was about Ethan that captured her. He didn't seem to be a Christian. He wasn't tender or warm. She'd come to realize that it was his work-ethic. He was so like her own father. And he needed someone. Claire knew he was lonely, even if he never would admit it, and she longed to bring him the happiness he seemed to lack. She was lonesome, too. Now that they were together, for the first time in weeks, what would they talk about?

# Chapter Eleven

"I forgot to tell you that the Twilight Series lights you asked me to order are going to be shipped on Monday," Claire said breaking the momentary silence. She was glad she thought up something to say, but she wished it was a topic other than work.

Ethan pushed an empty black container towards her.

"Mind helping?" he huffed.

"Not at all," she replied, used to his curt attitude. "I'll fill them with the potting mix. You're better at the transplanting."

"You did fine with the ones you had to do," he replied, offering her a rare compliment.

"Since it's raining today, I guess that pushes back the completion day for the Johnson project, too?" Claire asked, trying to make small talk while they worked.

"Unfortunately," Ethan sighed.

"Has it been hard getting used to the uncertainty of this job?"

"It's not like transcribing. There, I put in my hours and was done."

"Which job do you like better?" Claire asked, enjoying the soothing patter of rain on the plastic tarp overhead.

"Without a doubt this one. I love seeing a blank canvas come to life, or a corner untouched in a yard become full of color. It's really rewarding. Better than anything I've ever done." Ethan was surprised at how the words came tumbling out, and his cheeks colored. He turned away to grab a small mum so she wouldn't notice.

"That's wonderful," Claire exclaimed. "My dad is always saying that God gives all His children gifts and talents. How we use them is important to Him."

Ethan was quiet.

"It seems like you're really good at what you do," Claire said.

"Thanks. To be honest, I feel pretty overwhelmed most days. You know how I'm pouring the concrete patio this week for the Johnsons?"

Claire shook her head in agreement.

"I've only done one stamped concrete patio before, and that was in my backyard. There I could take my time, go slowly, watch YouTube videos. I don't think the Johnsons would trust me as much if I was stopping to watch 'how-to' tutorials," he smiled.

Claire had never seen Ethan smile before and her heart pounded faster. As he opened up, she felt her connection to him grow. "You could always watch the videos the night before."

"That's what I did last night.," he laughed. "I just hope I remember what I've learned."

"What's the hardest part?"

"Probably leveling the ground. I have the equipment I used when I did mine, but I just want it to be precise."

"Well, if worst comes to worst you could have Mark or V.J. run to your truck and do the watching, then come back and tell you how it's done," she teased.

"Mark and V.J. were good choices," he said, complimenting her decision to hire them.

"I'm glad to hear that. They seem to be hard-workers."

"They are, but I think they like to have fun on the weekends. They keep inviting me to go to this bar."

"Is that your kind of scene?"

"Never has been before."

"Me either," Claire replied. "What would you think about—"

Claire was about to offer him an alternate plan for weekend fun with her, so he'd have an excuse not to go to the bar the next time he was asked, and she would have a reason to spend more time with him. But she was interrupted when the phone rang.

"I better go get that," she said, putting down the potting mix, taking off her pink floral work gloves, and reluctantly going to take the call.

Nick rolled over and kissed Jezmeen, as she was waking. He had been waiting for a half-hour for her eyes to open.

"Good morning, Jez. Did work go okay last night?" he asked, running his hand over her cheek.

"Yeah," she mumbled, still not quite alert.

"I see you're still wearing your necklace," he smiled. Nick ran his hands over it, as it rested on her neck. "It really does sparkle like your eyes."

"I tell all the customers you gave it to me," Jezmeen lied, hoping Nick would believe he'd marked his territory.

"You don't have to go to Finnegan's until six, right?"

"Right," she replied, rolling over to face him.

"How would you like to meet my parents? It's my dad's birthday, and the family's having a little party for him at my parent's house at noon."

"What time is it now?" she asked, warily.

"Eleven."

"I wouldn't have time to get ready," she replied. "How close do they live?"

"About ten minutes, but we don't have to be on time. I just really want you to meet them. After all, you moved in during the month of November, we started dating in December, and now it's April. I have this beautiful girlfriend, and only my buddies have met you." He kissed her neck.

Jezmeen didn't want to go. She hadn't met any of her boyfriend's parents in years. It was better for them both. She learned from past experience, it only made break-ups a hundred times harder. Playing it cool, she pulled out her phone.

"Well, let me check to see if anything's on my calendar."

She grabbed her phone from the bedside table and put in the password.

"Oh, Nick," she sighed. "I'm so sorry. I forgot I have a mandatory staff meeting today at two," she lied.

"Why do you have a staff meeting?"

"Finnegan's is rolling out a new menu, everyone's required to attend and try all the new dishes. We talk about prices and specials."

"But you just make drinks."

"Sometimes bartenders take food orders."

"Couldn't you come for an hour?"

Jez gave him a look.

"By the time I got dressed and ready, we'd be late, and then I'd have to leave early. I don't want my first time meeting your family to go that way."

"Okay," he exhaled. "I guess I'll go hop in the shower."

Jezmeen felt a rare sense of remorse as Nick headed to the bathroom. She knew she couldn't keep saying no to his requests to meet his parents. As much as she liked Nick, she had no desire to settle down—especially not with him. He was too apathetic. He didn't seem to have any goals. For all she knew, he'd be working at the

hardware store his whole life.  There was no future
with him.  It was time to start scouting again.

# Chapter Twelve

## AUGUST 2012

Ethan counted the empty chairs lining the bar. There were eight. The three television screens in view were playing various sporting events. Having never followed any teams, competitive athletics held no interest for him. V.J and Mark were bantering over a trade made for a baseball player earlier in the day.

He didn't know what to expect when he agreed to go to Finnegan's Taphouse with his two employees on a Wednesday night after work. The forecast for Thursday called for rain, and the August day had been hot and long. V.J. and Mark said a beer would hit the spot, so they had driven right from a job after convincing Ethan to follow in his work truck.

Before they left the job site, V.J. gave Ethan a container of deodorizing body wipes and told him that was all he needed to clean up. When they got to the bar, Ethan wanted to wear his hat inside, but Mark told him to take it off. So, he held the fedora in his lap and felt just as uncomfortable as he thought he would.

They'd sat down a few minutes earlier, and the bartender had been busy with the other portion of the L- shaped counter since they arrived. But as the woman with the silky brown hair and gorgeous figure turned their direction, Ethan could see why his buddies liked the place.

"Hey, Jez," V.J. said, as the woman neared. "How's work treatin' you?"

"It's been slow tonight, V.J.," she replied. "But you and Mark are bringing some sunshine in from the outside. You are so tan."

"Yeah, but look at him," V.J. teased, pointing to Ethan, "he's as white as the paste I used to eat in preschool."

"You ate paste in preschool?" Mark asked quizzically.

"Didn't everybody?" V.J. responded.

"Evenin', friend," Jez greeted Ethan.

"This is the boss man, Ethan," V.J. said introducing him.

"Ah, so you're the young millionaire landscaper," she replied with an alluring smile.

Ethan could barely catch his breath. He had never seen eyes so arresting.

"He's kind of quiet," Mark jumped in.

"'Till you get to know him," V.J. said.

"Well, I hope to get to know you better," Jezmeen said.

"Don't be flattered," V.J. interjected. "She says that to all the guys."

"And I always mean it," Jez replied warmly, keeping her gaze on Ethan. "What can I get for you gentlemen?"

After they had placed their drink orders, V.J. and Mark returned to their conversation about who the Cardinals organization needed to get for their pitching line-up, while Ethan sat in silence. He knew he was staring, but he couldn't help it. She was the prettiest woman he'd ever seen. V.J. noticed Ethan's stare.

"She's taken, man. Believe me, I've asked," V.J. said.

"Plus, she's a little too mature for you," Mark joked. "Why don't you send a drink to that blonde over there?" he continued, more serious.

"Hey, she's cute, and so's the one next to her. I'll do it," V.J. cut in.

When Jezmeen brought their draft beers, she stopped to visit—first with V.J. and Mark about baseball, and then she moved her attention to Ethan.

"So, the boys tell me you're the only millionaire they know who lives in a trailer," she said, putting a hand on her curvy hip.

"I'll be building a house late fall," he replied gruffly, for that seemed to be the only way he knew to continue a conversation. And he didn't feel the need to tell her he wasn't a millionaire...yet.

"V.J. told me you invented something-" Jezmeen was interrupted by a holler from a man at the other end of the bar needing a refill. "Excuse me, handsome," she said. "I'll be back."

An hour later, Ethan was on his third beer, and seated by V.J. and Mark were the ladies they had their eyes on earlier. With his employees caught up in their own conversations, Ethan only stayed with the hope that Jezmeen would return to talk, like she said she would. The bar had gotten busier, but Ethan didn't mind watching her move. She was graceful, confident, and charming. Everything he was not.

Ethan rarely drank. He didn't like to spend the money, and he generally liked the taste of soda more than beer or wine. Maybe he would prefer mixed drinks, but he'd never tried any. Not used to the effects of alcohol, Ethan had begun to feel warm and relaxed by the second drink. V.J. had ordered two plates of wings, but he'd only gotten two before they were devoured.

"Hey boss man," V.J. hollered over the din of the music. "I think Mark and I are going to show Samantha and Tori the capitol at night. It's only a few blocks from here. You okay to drive home?"

"Sure," Ethan smiled, feeling relaxed. "Go for it. They'll love the view," he blabbered.

"Thanks for getting the tab," V.J. shouted, throwing his arm around one of the girls.

Ethan watched them go, and he looked at his watch. It was a little after eight. With four chairs empty next to Ethan, he would have felt awkward and lonely, but his drink was good company.

"Hey Jez," he yelled, "V.J. said I need to get the tab."

Jezmeen was in the middle of pouring a beer. She was surprised at how busy it had been, but with Ethan's friends gone, and two patrons about to leave, it would soon quiet down.

Ethan originally intrigued her, but now that he was on his way to the land of inebriation, he seemed like all the others. Still, she knew Nick was becoming too attached, and she was going to need a move-out plan...soon.

"Be right there, Ethan," she smiled.

She dropped off the beer and brought over the receipt.

"Why don't you stay awhile. After that couple leaves, I won't have much to do, and I still haven't heard what you created."

"Sure thing, Jez," Ethan drawled. He felt confident and fearless. Beer was helpful, he reckoned.

After printing out a bill for the two bar dwellers at the corner, Jezmeen headed back to Ethan.

"You're good looking," Ethan said boldly with an impish smile.

"Thank you. You're quite handsome yourself. You probably have a dozen girlfriends," she flirted.

"Nope, not even one, but there is someone I like," he said childishly.

"Aw, that's too bad. I was hoping you were single."

Ethan gestured with his hand for Jezmeen to come closer. She leaned across the bar toward his mouth.

"The person I like is you," he whispered into her ear, and then he laughed.

She let her hair glide across his cheek as she pulled away.

"I don't think you'd be telling me that if you hadn't had three beers," she whispered into his ear.

"Probably not," he grinned. "It's this stuff," he said, pointing to his nearly empty mug. "Uh oh, I'm almost out. Should I get another one?"

"I don't think so, big guy," she replied. "You're going to need a ride home as it is."

"I can drive," Ethan huffed.

"Not tonight, but if you're still here when the bar closes, I can give you a lift."

"That is *so* nice of you," he gushed. "You are really, really nice."

Two hours later, he drained his fourth beer and ate the burger she requested he get to counteract the alcohol. All the while, he told her the story of his life— complete with his love of plants, port-wine stains, and being raised by a poor, single mom.

Ethan found out they had the latter in common and she was a good listener. Occasionally she had to attend to other customers, but she remained attentive as the night progressed. When the crowd diminished, and the noise lessened, he grew sleepy. He watched Jezmeen clean up the bar and count out her tips. She worked hard and made good money he noted.

She told her boss she was giving someone a ride home, and by that time he was practically falling asleep.

"Okay, Ethan, let's get you home," Jezmeen said, as she grabbed her purse. "Night, Stan," she called to her boss.

"Where'd you get that pretty necklace?" Ethan asked as they walked out.

"My great grandma," she lied. "Family inheritance."

Jezmeen hadn't driven a customer home in a long time. But she felt completely safe with this guy. He was a typical introvert—quiet unless intoxicated. And he was immature. She didn't have to fear any aggressiveness from him. Ethan was cute and harmless. Their relationship could be symbiotic until it no longer served its purpose, just like all the others.

# Chapter Thirteen

Ethan woke to his feline alarm. He had no idea how long Chewy had been pawing at his face. As he sat up, his head felt like the fifty-pound decorative boulder he moved to the Smith's front yard the week before.

Chewy mewed incessantly, obviously hungry, and Ethan checked his watch. Six a.m. Looking out the window, the morning was gray, but there was no sign of rain.

He grabbed his phone and pulled up the weather. He silently cursed. The storm that was forecast to hit Springfield was moving slower than predicted, and the impending showers wouldn't be coming until late afternoon.

Swinging his legs over the side of the bed, he tried to stand up. His movements were weak and wobbly. What had come over him the night before? He knew it was the four draft beers and the smile of a beautiful woman.

Ethan groaned as he remembered the ride home and how he had asked Jezmeen to pull over on Jefferson Road so he could lean out and vomit. Under the influence, he had felt so free and confident. In the dim light of morning all he felt was embarrassment.

As he opened a can of food for Chewy and filled his water bowl, Ethan knew he needed aspirin— and his truck. What had he hoped to gain by getting a ride from Jezmeen? Sure, he avoided a D.U.I., and if he hadn't been so sleepy and nauseated, he could have held a conversation with the beautiful bartender.

Now he'd have to get a lift back to Finnegan's, and he felt miserable. Today was to be the start of an outdoor kitchen project. He'd only done one other build of its type since Adams Landscaping opened, and Ethan knew he didn't have the fortitude to tackle it with the fatigue he was fighting.

He poured himself a glass of water and then headed to the bathroom to search the cabinet for pain medicine. After swallowing two pills, he sat on the toilet lid and tried to think.

He'd have to switch to constructing the firepit. That would be easier to oversee. They'd need the concrete mixer, stored in "The Green Jungle," bags of cement, and bricks.

He could send V.J. and Mark for the cement and bricks, but he'd have to load the mixer. And he still needed his truck. Hopefully Claire would be willing to take him to Finnegan's when she started her shift at nine. Until then, all he wanted to do was go back to bed. After he texted V.J. and Mark what they needed to get and when to meet him at the job site, he set his phone alarm for eight forty-five and went back to sleep.

Claire had hoped that it would rain. It hadn't in weeks, and her dad's crops needed the water. Plus, rain meant more time with Ethan. Since she'd be returning to the classroom in two weeks, her job with Adams Landscaping was resuming part-time hours. She'd work one hour a day, returning calls and scheduling jobs. Then on Saturdays, she'd be working a half day, taking care of payroll, invoices, the books, and answering the phone.

Moving to reduced hours meant less contact with Ethan, and they had been spending a lot of time together. Most days, Ethan came back to the hoop houses at lunch to check-in. He liked to go over his schedule, check on the progress of supplies he'd ordered, and talk about his future ideas.

Lately he'd wanted feedback about buying bigger equipment. When Andrew was hired, Ethan purchased a riding mower and a flatbed truck attachment for him. But his personal push mower, wheelbarrow, blower, and edger were all stored in the back of "The Green Jungle," when not in use, and Andrew could use some upgrades.

He also wanted a small Bobcat. Renting them got expensive. And he needed to buy two work trucks. One of the requirements for being hired was owning a truck, but Ethan knew that arrangement had only been temporary, and he was paying his workers extra for gas and the wear and tear on their vehicles.

He'd asked Claire to investigate deals on used trucks and Bobcats. In her organized fashion, she'd created a spreadsheet with prices, mileage, and other details. She didn't mind helping him, in fact she liked that he valued her opinion.

Only on the rainy days did Ethan seem relaxed, and occasionally that led to conversations about themselves. He'd asked what she thought about farm life and teaching, and she'd found out about his long love of plants.

As he told it, when Ethan was seven, he and his mom moved into an apartment complex at the end of the school year. The owner of the apartment, Mr. Jones, was an avid gardener, and his mom gave him permission to work alongside him any time he was outside working on the flower beds.

Mr. Jones had given Ethan a book about flowers which he still owned. He also taught him how to draw up simple landscaping plans, based on color, height, texture, and flowering time of the plants.

At the age of eighteen, Ethan moved out of his mom's place and turned his first apartment into a greenhouse of sorts. Within a few years, he'd gotten his own house and had begun to put dreams into reality.

Claire savored every new piece of information she found out about Ethan, but he never seemed to notice her interest. He seemed clueless about women. At least he hadn't picked up on the signals she was trying to give out. She laughed at his jokes, touched his arm or hand whenever it fit the moment, and would stay late just to talk. She even invited him multiple times to church with her family and brunch afterwards—even if he always turned her down.

In their teen years, Claire had watched her sister Gretchen flirt with guys all the time. Interacting with young men was easy for her. But Claire had always been more reserved, so even those small gestures meant a lot—even though Ethan didn't know it.

As she walked over to the greenhouses, she wondered how she'd be able to juggle two jobs. Sure, she'd done it in the spring, but it was only for a few weeks. Now he wanted her to continue to manage his schedule year-round. He'd been flexible to say she could work from home once the mums were sold in September, and he assured her that once cold weather came, calls would taper almost completely.

Ethan had decided to let other companies take care of the snow in the winter, so he could cultivate more plants. Ethan was always thinking ahead, and she liked that. If only he had that same foresight in his love life, she sighed, as she neared the "Once Again Woodland."

The cellphone's alarm sounded, and Ethan covered his face with his pillow. He envisioned waking up refreshed after two more hours of sleep, but he only felt groggier. Falling back asleep for fifteen minutes, Ethan became alert again when he heard a car driving on the gravel outside his trailer.

Moving as if he had mud on his feet, he threw on a clean work shirt and jeans, before washing his face and brushing his teeth. The cool water was refreshing until it ran out. One of the drawbacks of living in a trailer was that the clean water tank only held so many gallons, and it needed to be refilled.

Chewy's litter box was emitting a noxious odor, and when he opened his pantry for a granola bar, he found the box empty. So far, the day was not going at all as planned. He grabbed the cash box for Claire's register and hurried out the door.

When he arrived at the "Once Again Woodland," Claire was nowhere to be seen. A blue car was parked on the gravel, so he busied himself deadheading mums until Claire and the customer entered.

"We only take cash, credit cards, or checks," Claire said as she held open the door for a middle-aged woman.

"Oh, Ethan," Claire exclaimed, catching him out of the corner of her eye. "I didn't know you'd be here this morning. Mrs. Ferrell, this is Ethan Adams, the owner of Adams Landscaping."

"Nice to meet you," Mrs. Ferrell said. "Your plants are beautiful. I just wish you had more to choose from."

"We're pretty picked over right now," Ethan replied. "But these mums will be ready in September, and by next spring I plan to double the inventory."

"Your signage is wonderful," Mrs. Ferrell said. "My neighbor told me about you, and these greenhouses are delightful."

"Claire here gets credit for that," Ethan said.

Claire warmed at the compliment as she printed a receipt for Mrs. Ferrell's selections.

"Thank you for your business. Please come back for our mum sale in September," Claire said, handing her a flyer she had made for the upcoming event. As soon as the door closed, Ethan asked his question.

"I need to get my truck. It's in a restaurant parking lot. Would you take me?"

"Oh no! Did you have car trouble?"

"No," Ethan replied curtly, indicating he was offering no other information.

"Okay," Claire drew out the word. "Well, my car is parked at home, so why don't you walk with me to get it."

Claire locked the greenhouse on the way out.

"Thank you for bringing the cash box when you came. I was surprised it wasn't there when I got in this morning. Hope you are feeling okay," Claire said.

When Ethan didn't respond she continued. "Do you need to lock up your trailer?"

"No, I already did that."

"I thought it was going to rain today," Claire said, making small talk as they headed towards her house.

"Me too," Ethan sighed.

"It's really humid. I can't imagine it will be fun to be outside today."

"Or in the greenhouses," Ethan replied. "Actually, would you have time to look into how to get electricity to the property? I haven't had time, and I know it's way overdue."

"Definitely. I bet you'll be glad to have your trailer relying on something other than the generator."

Ethan nodded. "And you really need fans."

They arrived at the front door of the Rogers's white farmhouse.

"You can come inside. I just need to get my keys," Claire said.

Ethan followed her into the hallway and then into the kitchen.

"We keep our keys in a basket on the counter," Claire said as she reached the empty wicker container. "That's odd. I thought I had—oh wait I left them in my purse, and it's up in my room. I'll be right back."

Claire hurried away. With nothing to do but wait, Ethan found himself extremely thirsty. Probably the body's way of washing out the alcohol, he reasoned. He wondered if it would be rude to get a glass of water. Eyeing a relatively clean glass in the sink, he grabbed it and went to the refrigerator's water dispenser. As he poured himself some cool liquid, he looked at the pictures in front of him. There was a "save the date" card for a wedding, a magnet with a medical number, and a photo of a middle-aged Asian couple.

Taking two long gulps, Ethan began to feel better, but with his mind off of his physical woes for a moment, he went right back to thinking about what a fool he was in front of Jezmeen. He'd heard of love at first sight but didn't believe in it. Yet, he felt something. Even when he lived next-door to the beautiful Danielle, there wasn't an instant spark.

He had to apologize to Jezmeen. Thank her properly for the ride home. And he wanted to see her again. What should he do to show his remorse— and affection? Flowers? Chocolates? A handwritten note? He should ask Claire, he thought, she'd have wisdom. Just then she ran into the kitchen, purse over her shoulder. She looked so fresh and youthful, with her hair pulled back into a ponytail and her tan work shirt hugging her petite frame. Over the summer, she'd convinced Ethan to get employees matching shirts.

"Sorry, I was parched," Ethan said, setting the glass back in the sink.

"You could have gotten a clean glass," she laughed. "They're in the cabinet next to the refrigerator, if you need one again."

"What's with the Asian family?" Ethan said, pointing to the picture he'd seen.

"Oh, they are missionaries we support."

Ethan gave her a quizzical look.

"We send them money each month so they can tell others about Jesus in Tianjin, China."

"Brainwashing," Ethan said under his breath.

"The message of the cross is foolishness to the one who is perishing," Claire said, quoting a Bible passage.

Ethan shrugged, neither having the energy nor the desire to get into a religious discussion.

"Different question," he said, hastily changing the topic.

Claire began walking towards the front door, and Ethan followed.

"What's a good way to show a girl you like her without being too assertive?"

Claire locked the door behind them, and she pushed the key fob to unlock her car.

"Hmmm. I'd say be a good listener. Try to remember something that she brings up in conversation— especially something that she likes and get it for her. If she says she loves Mel-O-Cream doughnuts, find out her favorite kind and deliver it to her. By the way, I'm more of a steel-cut oatmeal girl, if you were wondering," she smiled.

Claire hopped into the driver's seat. "Where am I taking you?"

"Finnegan's Taphouse."

Claire's eyebrows rose in surprise. Now she understood why he looked more pale than usual.

"V.J. and Mark finally convinced you to go out?"

Ethan nodded.

"Well, I'm glad one of them gave you a ride home."

"They didn't," Ethan said, leaning his seat back slightly. He began to feel motion sick, as they backed out of the driveway.

When he didn't offer any more information, Claire switched back to the original topic.

"Let's see, besides being a good listener, flowers definitely say you're interested. And since you know a lot about flowers, you probably could pick out something unique."

They rode in silence for a short while. When Claire pulled up to the stop sign, she took a right to head into town.

"What are you working on today?" Ethan asked.

"Invoices. Returning phone calls. Ordering the lighting for the Kendall job. Watering the shrubs in "The Green Jungle." Oh, and looking into Bobcats and electricity. Why? Is there something you want me to add to the list?"

"I know you have a lot on your plate, but if you have a chance in the next few days, I'd really like to start building a house now that the second check from Tryton has come in. Since you have the printer hooked up to your laptop, would you find me some floor plans for small ranches?"

"Isn't that kind of a personal decision? I mean I'm happy to help, but how would I know what you'd like?  There are so many different choices."

"Claire, if you haven't figured it out yet, I trust you."

"Thanks," she replied softly.

"I'm thinking three bedrooms, two baths, at least a two-car garage, and a basement.  The layouts will vary, of course, but I'll look through them and pick one I'd like.  Just don't pick out anything too grand.  I want simple and inexpensive— if that's possible."

# Chapter Fourteen

As Jezmeen drove down Illinois Highway 97, towards the big mum sale at Adams Landscaping, she thought about the tangled web she'd weaved. Since she'd met Ethan at the end of July, he'd visited her at Finnegan's at least once a week.

Thankfully, Nick no longer came to the bar. His break-up with Clarissa made it too awkward. She was also grateful Ethan had not gotten as drunk as he had on their initial meeting. However, he'd become partial to Old Fashioneds, and after two drinks he became talkative and relaxed.

His work buddies sometimes accompanied him, but most often he came alone, and she knew he was giving up precious sleep to spend time with her when he closed down the bar some nights.

Two days after she'd met him, he'd showed up at the bar with a bouquet of New-Day rose-striped gazanias. At least that's what he called them. Supposedly he contacted four florists in St. Louis before one referred him to a larger business in California who overnighted the striking flowers to Springfield. He said they reminded him of her eyes. Unfortunately, she had to throw them away. She certainly couldn't bring them home to

Nick's apartment, and there was no other place to put them.

Ethan wasn't her type. He was far too insecure, but over the course of the past six weeks he revealed that the money he was receiving from Tryton Building Corporation was going into a savings account to build a house and expand the business. He had more jobs than he could manage, and royalties would soon start coming in from his invention.

So, Nick was being phased out. She'd done it before. This time it wouldn't be as easy because she genuinely liked him, but that didn't matter. Her own feelings hadn't mattered for ten years.

The complex part was the Arctic Fox. She certainly wasn't going to move into that tiny thing, and he'd only just begun to let her help with new house details. As Ethan had become more serious about her, he'd let her help pick the final floorplan, and she convinced him to up his budget.

A half-a-million-dollar home would certainly be more impressive than a small ranch, she explained. In addition, she reasoned, he had a newly branded reputation to uphold now that Springfield had become familiar with the up and coming young professional. Plus, he worked so hard— shouldn't he get to have something nice to show for it? Her smooth words persuaded him to build a luxurious two-story—complete with a circular drive, fountain, decorative hedges, and a grand front porch to greet visitors.

Ethan hadn't asked her to live with him once it was built, but she felt confident their relationship was headed in that direction. Now she only had to get the builders to hurry up so she wouldn't have to live in the small trailer.

He picked a local company to do the job, and they'd already poured the foundation for the basement, but there was much to be done. If she could get Claire out of the picture things would move even more quickly. She was too useful to Ethan, and Jez could tell Claire had feelings for him.

Jezmeen first met Claire on a rainy Saturday morning when Ethan showed her around the greenhouses. His "little secretary" was diligently working the whole time they were in "The Once Again Woodland," and she'd introduced herself as Jez entered.

Ethan seemed to trust Claire more than he trusted her. Every transaction he made had been researched by the young assistant and increasing the budget for the new house didn't sit well with Claire. So Jezmeen changed that.

She kissed Ethan on a steamy August night after the bar closed. He wasn't drunk, but she could taste bourbon on his lips. They had stood outside by their cars, talking about his house plans.

Most men would have made a move after three weeks of friendship, but Ethan admitted he'd never had a girlfriend before. It seemed odd to her, that a man of his age would have remained single so long. But when she remembered his former port-wine stains, she realized it made more sense. Yet, he was so timid. He had never touched her, hugged her, or even kissed her on the cheek.

That night, when he leaned his back against his truck, she let her body draw into his. She rubbed her hand across his cheek, then she brought her lips to his. After she'd awakened the desire, Ethan found time to make that happen at every private encounter, and as he felt more comfortable with her, he gave her more ownership of the project.

As Jezmeen pulled into the gravel parking lot, she noticed it was fairly busy for eleven o'clock. She put her car into park and turned off the engine. Flipping down the visor to get to the mirror, she checked her lipstick, hair, and eye make-up before getting out to fight the crowd for some mums.

Claire watched Ethan put his arm around Jezmeen's waist. So much had changed about her employer since he'd met the enchantress. He'd lost focus. At least on Adams Landscaping. His house plans were another story.

And he was always tired. He'd go to the bar and then ask her to push back the start time on his jobs so he could sleep in. Then, when he did manage to squeeze in time to talk about the business, he was grumpy.

He said he didn't have the finances to do the extras, like purchase the work trucks, because he needed the money for the new home. Ethan declared that once the next check from Tryton came in, he'd have more leverage. But Claire found the man she'd come to admire for his hard work ethic and for his frugal ways was changing.

She was changing, too. Claire had been back with students for four weeks and managing two jobs was starting to wreak havoc on her body. The stress was beginning to affect her diabetes as well. Her blood sugar was continually high. In turn she was dealing with headaches, constant dehydration, and unwelcomed irritability.

Claire was often complimented by parents for her sweet, patient demeanor, but in the last week she'd snapped at them multiple times, and even her students knew she just wasn't herself.

Of course, planning the chrysanthemum sale hadn't helped. With Ethan struggling to get jobs done on schedule and trying to build a pergola to be a display model in time for the sale, he'd left everything else up to her.

She'd ordered four dozen apple cider doughnuts from the Apple Barn, picked up cider to go along with them, lined up V.J. to give out samples of the treats and Mark to help write

129

receipts for mums, mailed the press release, put a post on the Facebook page that she'd created for his business over the summer, and ordered and picked up signage.

Somehow, she fit that in on top of lesson planning, grading, calling parents, and teaching twenty-one first graders how to walk through the halls quietly. Her mom and dad weren't happy to hear she was out in the dark, the night before, putting out signs while Ethan was at the bar spending time with Jezmeen. When she dwelt on it, she wasn't thrilled either.

She could see why he liked Jezmeen, she thought, as she wrote out a receipt for a customer. She turned heads. Claire instantly recognized the physical attraction between the two, but what else did Ethan see in Jezmeen?

"Thanks for stopping," Claire said with a smile. "And here's a coupon for ten percent off all greenhouse purchases in the spring."

"Could I talk to someone about that pergola?" a man asked Claire, as he stepped to the register.

"Oh sure, let me get the owner," she said cheerfully. "I'm sure he'd be happy to answer whatever questions you may have."

"Ethan," she called.

He was a few feet from the cash register, walking through a row of mums with Jezmeen. Hearing Claire's voice, Ethan walked over to the customer and led him outdoors. Jezmeen picked up a mum and carried it to the cash register.

"Good to see you, Claire," Jezmeen said, voice dripping with artificial honey.

"You picked out a nice one," Claire replied.

"The mum or Ethan?" she smiled.

"Both, I guess," Claire said and then regretted it. She didn't want Jezmeen to think she liked him.

"We just have to get Ethan to do a little better being comfortable talking with people, and then he'll really get this business going," Jezmeen said, as she put her hand in the back pocket of her jeans.

Claire started to write out a receipt, ignoring the statement.

"Ethan said I don't have to pay for this one," she said. "I was just coming to get one of those coupons you're handing out."

"Oh, sure," Claire said, taken aback.

*Can you break a fifty?* Claire heard the phone vibrate against the wooden counter. Mark texted that he needed change. She opened the cash drawer and counted out the change for a fifty.

"Excuse me for a moment," Claire said, handing Jezmeen a coupon, as she left Jezmeen standing at the counter.

Jezmeen quickly looked around. Claire had left the register unlocked. What better way to make Ethan dislike the little servant, she mused. The only customers in the area were back at Mark's cash register, where Claire was dispensing change. Acting with swift speed, she pocketed a handful of bills. Then she went to find Ethan, realizing there was no need to be near the scene of the crime.

It had been a long time since Ethan had sat in his recliner. With a glass of bourbon at his side and Chewy on his lap, the night was quiet. Ethan couldn't remember the last time he'd just relaxed. Since the *HGTV* episode aired over six months ago, Ethan had been squeezing out every inch of energy his body held.

Now the first annual fall mum sale was complete, and they'd sold about seventy-five percent of the stock. He'd known that greenhouse space would be limited, and months earlier he'd done the mathematical calculations that told him exactly how many three-quart containers he could fit into his 120-foot building.

One-hundred had lined the walls in the "Once Again Woodland," and he moved out the other 100 he'd grown in the "Eternal Forest" onto the lawn. Claire had brought in bales of straw to display the outdoor pots. Varying them in height, she said, would look more attractive. And she was right, as usual.

Ethan scratched Chewy on the head and thought about how Claire had left the sale crying. It ended at five, and after she had counted out her cash drawer, she found she was over $700 short. She thought maybe she had given some extra money to Mark when she made change for him, but his drawer came out with the correct balance.

Claire couldn't recall any time she had been away from her post and left it unlocked, but she promised Ethan she hadn't taken anything. She never had before, and she'd handled all the transactions for the past five months.

Ethan had given Claire a key to his trailer, and every night she made a "drop off" of her cash drawer. She'd even done bank runs for him when he couldn't. It just didn't make sense, Ethan thought. Where could that much money have gone? That was almost half the net profit for the entire sale.

It had been months of work to cultivate and nurture the plants, and he realized it seemed like a lot of time had been wasted, but his heart ached for Claire. Ethan was grateful that Claire had been honest with him, when she realized what was missing. Her loyalty meant more than the money.

After he paid for the food samples, signs, employee checks, and containers, he'd barely make a profit, he mused unhappily. He hadn't mentioned that to Claire, but since she kept the books, she'd be aware of the margins.

He took a drink of the amber colored liquid and thought about something happier. Ethan still couldn't believe a girl as gorgeous as Jezmeen would be seen with him, but he was taking it one day at a time and enjoying the ride.

It had been so nice of her to come to the sale, Ethan thought, as he leaned the chair back into a reclining position. V.J. and Mark gave him high-fives after she left. Her skin-tight jeans fit her like a glove, and the barely buttoned white shirt cinched around her waist, showing off her tight abs when she raised her arms.

V.J. and Mark said that Jezmeen was into him because he was "the millionaire boss man." Ethan wondered how much that played into her decision, but he didn't want to ask, and she didn't offer information about what she saw in him.

In a couple of conversations, Jezmeen casually asked what it would be like if they lived together. Ethan had never seen himself as the kind of guy to "play house" with a woman. He liked his own space too much. And if he was so into the girl, he'd put a ring on her finger. But he wondered if that was her way of hinting at something.

It had only been six weeks since he'd met her, but he'd already questioned, half a dozen times, if she was "the one." How would he know? He couldn't ask V.J. or Mark. They just played the field.  His mom had never been married.  Maybe he'd ask Claire.  Her parents seemed content.

Poor Claire, he thought, as his mind drifted back to her.  Even though he reassured her he wasn't mad or worried that she had stolen from him, she wouldn't be consoled.  And she'd worked so hard to pull off such a successful sale.  All the marketing was her idea, and he really hadn't been much help over the last few weeks.  Maybe he'd bring her a few of the leftover doughnuts on Sunday.  She always had Sundays off, and he knew he could find her at home.

# Chapter Fifteen

**DECEMBER 2012....**

Claire looked at herself in the mirror. Make-up was in order since she was going to a Christmas party— even if it was just downstairs. Over the past three months, she'd gotten to know Jezmeen better, and while she didn't think most of her suggestions were helpful, she could've used advice on eyeshadow. Claire opened the lid of the case with eight colors and decided on a dark gray shade.

Gretchen was home for winter break, and her boyfriend, Tim, had arrived earlier in the day so he could be a part of the weekend festivities at the Rogers' house. Her mom had also given Ethan and Jezmeen an invitation to the intimate family party. When Claire protested, Connie insisted that they were neighbors, and Ethan was her employer.

Jezmeen had moved into the Arctic Fox in October. The story she heard from V.J. was that Jezmeen had a boyfriend when she met Ethan. Someone who knew her boyfriend caught sight of Jezmeen and Ethan kissing in Finnegan's parking lot and shared the news.

That gossip got her kicked out of the shared apartment, and she'd gone crying to Ethan who took her in. Since Jezmeen entered the picture, work had not been the same. Ethan had set up Saturday afternoon meetings with her to discuss the business, and Jezmeen attended whenever she wasn't scheduled to work.

When she was present, Ethan became quiet— letting Jezmeen take over, and her vision included a winery, grape vines, and a storefront. Ethan had never mentioned wanting to expand in those directions, but he didn't protest loudly. Instead he let Claire close down her ideas. Jezmeen gradually acquired all the house planning, and Claire gladly gave that project to her.

Claire shut one eyelid and gently swept on the smokey hue, while it fluttered to stay shut. She'd been feeling okay the past couple of days, but it had been a long and harrowing fall. She knew her lightened mood was attributed to the Christmas break ahead.

During the past three months, Claire gradually realized the joy she'd found at Adams Landscaping had vanished. Then she started re-evaluating everything. She'd recently turned twenty-four, was living at home, working with kids she loved, but feeling very lonely. She wanted a change. Independence. New friends. Fresh purpose. For weeks she'd prayed for direction, and in the last few weeks it became clear where God was sending her.

She ran a finger over the shadow, brushing off the excess. Claire was going to announce her plan at the party. She figured there would be less of a chance that her parents would explode, since they had guests.  Claire added blush to her cheeks and finished with a warm plum lipstick. Taking a final glance, she wagered she looked almost as good as Gretchen and Jezmeen tonight.

"Claire tells me things have slowed down considerably," Connie said to Ethan.

Connie was seated on the loveseat, next to Jedidiah.  Each dressed in red sweaters, they were a cute pair, Ethan thought. The fireplace was going, and the big meal he ate brought sleepiness and relaxation.  Originally nervous about going to a social gathering, Jezmeen insisted they attend once they opened the invitation.

Since she'd moved into the trailer, things between them were different.  Some changes he welcomed— like sharing a bed.  Others he loathed.  Storing her clothes at the back of "The Eternal Forest" was one of them.

Had she not come crying to him about having no place to turn, he probably would have recommended she find an apartment.  But there hadn't been a lot of time to think, and their opposing work schedules meant they didn't see each other too often— until late November when leaf-raking eased.

"Yes, things have really quieted down," Ethan responded.  "We had one order come in for a pergola. It's a Christmas gift, but the customer doesn't want it delivered until winter has passed, so I've got time to build it."

Ethan saw Jezmeen across the room laughing with Gretchen and her boyfriend. She looked stunning with her hair pulled back, but tonight he was most taken with Claire. Dressed in black pants and a black lace top, adorned with a stunning necklace and eyes done up with charcoal shadow, she had a captivating beauty he'd not noted before.

"When does your invention hit stores?" Jedidiah asked, pulling him back into conversation.

"At the beginning of March," Ethan said.

"That's so exciting," Connie replied. "And your house looks like it's coming along."

Jezmeen sat down on the arm of the overstuffed chair where Ethan was sitting and immediately joined the conversation.

"We're thankful the frame and roof are up, so they can work inside," Jezmeen said. "Ethan and I were surprised they were going to work during the holidays, but Ken, our builder, said he'd have the wiring guys in this week. Can you believe we'll actually have a house with electricity?" she laughed.

"The greenhouses have electricity now, don't they?" Jedediah asked, as Claire, Gretchen, and Tim sat down on the brown couch facing the fire.

"Yes.  I'm very happy to say I won't have to heat them in creative ways, like I did last winter," Ethan said.

"And you managed to get two more greenhouses up before the cold weather hit," Jed continued.

"I would've liked to get some rows of trees planted, too, but I guess that will have to wait 'till spring now.  The ground's frozen," Ethan said.

"When will you be in your house?" Jedidiah asked.

"If all goes according to schedule, it could be March.  But the realist in me says it will probably be May."

"Not if I'm out there with doughnuts every morning," Jezmeen replied.

"Well, I guess since we're all here now, we'll do our white elephant gift exchange," Connie said.

After numbers had been drawn, presents chosen, swiped, and reselected, the laughter and chaos of the game died down.  Then Connie said she'd like to sing a few Christmas hymns, and Ethan groaned silently.  He'd never been much of a vocalist, and he probably wouldn't know the words.  As if she heard his concern, she began passing out lyric sheets.

When Connie sat back down, Claire stood up, and Ethan wondered if she was going to do a solo. Instead, she surprised them all.

"Before we start singing," Claire began, clutching her lyric sheets nervously. "I have an announcement to make."

"You found the criminal who took the money from the mum sale?" Jezmeen blurted, and Ethan felt his heart drop. Why would she say such a thing?

Claire's v-neck lace top showed her white skin reddening. "No, I wish I had an answer to that mystery, but sadly that is not what this news is about," she continued, regaining her composure. "I've decided I'm moving to China."

Claire lay in bed, unable to sleep. The excitement of the night overwhelmed her senses. When she had told everyone that she was moving to China there had been an uproar, as she expected. She explained that she was planning on working as an English as a second language teacher on the weekdays at a training school and helping the missionary family her church supported. Everyone understood her goals, but they didn't all agree that she should go.

Actually, no one but Gretchen supported her. Well, Gretchen and Jezmeen. She knew Ethan's girlfriend would be happy to see her off. Thankfully, her parents didn't bring up their concerns about how she would manage her healthcare until after everyone left.

Claire fielded the group's questions with ease. She already knew her plan. Tianjin, China was the third largest city in China, and missionaries, Li Wei Wang and his wife, Bingquin, had been in communication with Claire for weeks. They helped her locate a school to teach at and secured an apartment to rent in their building.

Her new employer would pay for transportation to the country, and Claire planned to go as soon as the school year was done in May. She tried to laugh when she said this was her formal way of giving Adams Landscaping her notice. Even though this was what she wanted, she felt badly leaving her mom and dad— and Ethan.

When Gretchen asked her why she wanted to move, she answered as honestly as she could, without saying it all. She'd always been drawn to the Wangs ministry. Every time they visited her church, she felt her spirit stir. God had set every piece in place, and she felt ready for a change. She was young, unattached, and traveling now made perfect sense.

Not according to Ethan or her parents, though. Each found time, before the night was over, to challenge her decision. When she got up, during the hymn singing, to go get a drink, Ethan followed. Alone in the kitchen, Claire felt her heart pound. He gazed at her, as if they'd never met.

Claire wanted to hold onto the way it felt for him to look at her like that. It meant something, even if she didn't know exactly what. Ethan asked her to reconsider. He didn't know how he would run Adams Landscaping without her. He'd double her salary. Get air-conditioning for the "Once Again Woodland." Hire an additional administrative assistant until school was out, so she didn't have the stress of working a full-time job in the spring.

Claire suggested Jezmeen take over her position. She liked to have a say in all the details of the business, anyhow, she mentioned. Ethan said it would never work. Jezmeen wanted to keep bartending, and she didn't have Claire's organizational skills.

When he questioned if she'd officially signed a contract with any school, he seemed relieved to hear she hadn't. He said he would hold out hope that she'd change her mind.

An hour later, after Jezmeen and Ethan had left, and Gretchen and Tim retired to their rooms for the night, Claire was helping her mom and dad clean up in the kitchen when they began their barrage.

Had she thought about how she'd manage her diabetes in a foreign country? What if the strain of moving brought about trouble with her blood glucose, like working two jobs had in the fall? What would the school where she was working currently think of her leaving after only two years?  If she ever wanted to return to Springfield to work again would that be held against her?

Claire knew her mom and dad's concerns came from a place of love.  She also recognized they had helped her handle everything about her healthcare since her diagnosis.  Letting go was frightening.  Part of her wondered if she could captain her own ship but moving to China was one way to find out.  Sure, it was drastic.  But it meant she'd get away from the huge house going up next door, a business she had grown to cherish, the loneliness she felt living at home with her parents, and the man that had looked at her with searching eyes—for the first time ever.

# Chapter Sixteen

## JANUARY 2013...

Ethan hadn't slept well in over three weeks. He'd welcomed in the new year with Chewy and a shot or two of bourbon, since Jezmeen had to work. That had been fine with him. Sharing three-hundred square feet with a woman whom he was just getting to know felt awkward— especially when they were both home together at night.

He would've liked to blame his lack of rest on Jezmeen coming in late, but he knew the real reason— Claire was leaving. When his mom hired Claire last spring, he'd been drowning. She was the best thing that happened to Adams Landscaping, and he was seriously concerned.

In his sleepless hours, Ethan contemplated new ways to convince her to stay. He'd already given her his initial ideas at the Christmas party, and those didn't sway her. In a vain attempt to change her mind, he'd asked her to meet him at the "Once Again Woodland" to write a job description and show him the program she used to make the work schedule each week.

She'd kindly agreed, and Ethan knew it might be his last chance to state the case of why he needed her more than China did. He'd chosen an afternoon when Jezmeen would be at work, so she wouldn't interfere in their conversation. Ethan needed something more than money to entice Claire, and he hoped the words that often failed him would come through when he needed them the most.

"Wow, it's warmer in here than I thought it would be," Claire said, pulling the swinging door shut behind her to keep out the cold air.

"There's a space heater up here by the counter," Ethan replied, pointing to a brown box by his feet.

"I bet it's nice to have electricity this winter." Claire unzipped her coat but left it on.

"The Arctic Fox is happy not to have to run on a generator this year," Ethan said.

They exchanged pleasantries about their Christmases, and Ethan asked how her return to school had gone. With the small talk out of the way, Ethan knew what he needed to ask next.

"So, how'd your parents take the news about China?"

Claire began fumbling with the zipper on her jacket.

"About as well as I expected them to. They're having a hard time with the idea, but I think they'll come around. We talked with the Wangs together over Facetime a few nights ago, and that seemed to help."

"Oh," Ethan replied, not even trying to hide the disappointment in this voice.

"Well, Claire, you know I asked you here to help me write the job description for your position, but I want to let you know I've had a hard time sleeping the last few weeks."

"I'm so sorry to hear that," Claire said, eyes filled with concern.

"It's because I'm worried about losing you...as an employee," he added hurriedly. "Back in August, I was standing in line to get some bags of mulch at the store, and I overheard two people talking about my business. One said that we did the best work in town and had the most outstanding customer service. You single-handedly created a positive image for me in our community. Do you realize how huge that is?"

"That is so sweet, Ethan. Thank you, but you're the one that did the physical work."

"And you're the one that offered the customer service. I haven't told anyone this, but before my mom hired you, I was unable to eat, and I was barely sleeping. I was a nervous wreck. I couldn't keep up with everything, and I thought about calling it quits before I even got started. If you hadn't come along, I don't think that Adams Landscaping sign would be in the front lawn."

"Well, I may have helped you with some things, but I also cost you $800." Claire looked down at her boots.

Ethan saw the hurt etched on her face, and he felt caught up in compassion for her. He reached out and laid his hand on hers, as it rested on the counter. She looked up at him, and their gaze locked intently for a long moment.

"Claire, whoever stole that money should be prosecuted. It wasn't your fault. Is that why you're leaving?"

Claire withdrew her hand from under his and went back to running the zipper up and down.

"Do you realize I've lived at home my whole life? A majority of my coworkers are married with children. Most of the people at church are my parents' age, and the last time someone told me he loved me it was on the playground while I tied his shoe." Claire laughed at her life. "I need a change."

"So, it's settled?" Ethan sighed.

Claire nodded, and the zipper quieted.

"I guess we should start working on the job description," Ethan said with resignation.

"Sure you don't want to offer the position to Jezmeen?"

Ethan pushed the power button on the laptop.

"I'm afraid Jez only cares about the things she finds appealing." Ethan silently recalled how Jezmeen had spent a half-hour showing him pictures of ceiling fans for the new family room the night before. "She has her heart set on turning the land into a vineyard, and you and I both know that's not what a landscaping business does."

Ethan entered the password into the login box. "Why don't we switch places? You type faster than I do."

Ethan got up from the stool, and Claire moved to sit down. As she pulled up a blank file in Microsoft Word, Ethan leaned over her shoulder to watch her work, and she felt his breath against her cheek. She longed to reach up and touch the stubble on his face. Comfort him. Take away his worries. Yes, Claire thought, it was time to leave.

When did the shine wear off? Ethan wondered as he inspected the progress of his newest plants. He'd been propagating roses, and they looked like they were doing well.

He walked down the rows of plants in the "Eternal Forest." The temperature gauge that hung on the support pole read forty-five degrees. He was thankful the space heater was keeping the structure warm, so he didn't have to put hot coals in the hoop house and worry about burning the plastic, like he did the winter before.

Rays of January sunshine streamed through the thin tarping, and Ethan was glad to be able to work outside. Jezmeen had the day off, and she tried to convince him to go browsing for furniture for the new home, or the "grand mansion," as she had begun to call it.

He insisted the plants needed his attention, so she'd gone alone hours earlier and could be back any minute. The trailer felt so crowded with two. More likely it was that he was uncomfortable being around her when he wasn't slightly, or more than slightly, buzzed.

Afterall, he had a supermodel walking around his place— as much as you could walk around three hundred square feet. When she moved in, things changed between them. Maybe it was because all she wanted to do was talk about the "grand mansion." Or it could have been because he saw past her physical beauty. Jezmeen had morning breath, she left dirty dishes in the sink, rarely cooked, and liked to spend his money. And their relationship felt fake—like it all was an act to her.

His mom met Jezmeen once. They'd gone to Suzanne's apartment on Christmas Day. Jezmeen claimed she had no family to visit, which made it easy to share the day with his mom.

When Jezmeen was in the bathroom Suzanne whispered, "She's a dangerous beauty, Ethan. Be careful. I'm not sure I trust her." Perhaps it was this warning that removed her façade. Whatever the reason, Ethan felt the tug of dissatisfaction grow.

"I'll take one order of fried rice with orange chicken and one order of mixed vegetables with teriyaki beef," Jezmeen bellowed into the drive-through intercom.

She'd spent a long day browsing bedroom sets, comforters, and curtains. When she was in junior high school, one of her teachers assigned a research project on future careers. Jezmeen waffled between learning about doctors, because they made lots of money, or interior decorators, because she loved making things look pleasing to the eye.

In the end, she chose to write about becoming a doctor because she thought it would impress the teacher more, but she still loved watching television shows on design when she had time.

Jezmeen inched forward, after the young girl on the other end of the microphone gave her the total. She'd asked Ethan for money to pick up dinner, and he obliged reluctantly. With the mounting costs of the new home and furnishing the entire place on his salary, he'd asked her, if she was going to live there, to chip in.

All she could think to do was lie. Attending an expensive private college for a year caused her to incur serious debt, she told him. He'd questioned when she'd be done paying off her "loan" so she could help with expenses, but she told him it would take years.

Jezmeen was having so much fun working on the designs for the "grand mansion," she almost would have been willing to part with a small chunk of her nest egg to help furnish the place. She remembered decorating a room for *him* back when she was only seventeen. Jezmeen had been so excited to spend some of her hard-earned waitressing money on the room. She scoured magazines and websites to come up with the perfect look. And the day she came home to the beautiful room and *he* wasn't there to share it with her was the worst experience of her life. That was the moment she became her mom.

# Chapter Seventeen

The wheels of Claire's large black suitcase clicked against the gleaming cream tile at the Tianjin airport. With her backpack secured against her shoulders, she felt like a true international traveler. Now that she had arrived at her final destination and grabbed her checked piece of luggage off the conveyor belt, some of the exhaustion from the last twenty-seven hours dissipated. The layovers in Chicago, Tokyo, and Hangzhou weren't long enough to do any sightseeing.

Claire had been too excited to sleep on the planes, so a good portion of her time had been spent watching movies, looking at magazines, and trying not to worry too much about her insulin levels. Since stress usually raised her blood sugar levels, she'd tried not to be overly anxious.

She'd left Lambert-St. Louis International Airport at three in the afternoon the day before, and it was now five in the evening in the eastern hemisphere. Claire headed to the lobby, following the English subtitles on the signs, where she was meeting her missionary friends.

Claire hadn't seen Li Wei Wang and his wife, Bingquin, for over a year. They visited her Springfield church every two years, when they were itinerant stateside, raising money for their work. Since returning to China, the Wangs had a baby girl, and Claire was anxious to meet their newest family member.

Her flights had surprisingly run on schedule, so when she rolled into the lobby, she scanned the crowd for the Wangs. Not seeing them, she set down her backpack and unzipped the pocket containing her cellphone. A message from Li Wei awaited.

*So sorry. We won't be able to meet you at the airport. Tyler Stephens will be picking you up. He'll explain. You can trust him. He's attended our home church for the last two years. Looking forward to seeing you soon.*

Claire sighed and readjusted her headband. How was she going to find Tyler Stephens?

"Claire?"

She glanced up from her phone. A tall, slender man with dark brown hair, brown eyes, and a fair complexion, shared a wide smile beneath a thick brown beard. He held a small sign that said "Claire Rogers" in his hands.

"Are you Tyler?" she asked.

"The one and only," he said, with a deep voice that exuded confidence. "I was watching the board and saw your flight had arrived. The Wangs gave me a description of a pretty young lady, so you were easy to spot. But the crowd that just came through blocked my path."

Claire noted his kind words as she put her phone back into the pocket and zipped it.

"Let me help you with those," Tyler said, grabbing the heavy tote and rolling suitcase.

"Thanks," Claire replied. "Are the Wangs okay?" she asked worriedly.

"Yes, but little Li Na is not."

"Oh no, what's wrong with the baby?" Claire said, instinctively following his self-assured stride towards the exit.

"She has a fever, and Li Wei got an unexpected call from one of the members of our church. Someone's grandma passed away after a long bout with cancer. So, Li Wei went to comfort the family while Bingquin stayed at the apartment with the baby."

"I'm sorry to hear about all of that," Claire said. "Thank you for filling in as taxi-driver."

"My pleasure," he said, giving her another warm smile, as the automatic doors slid open and they stepped outside. "Welcome to Tianjin."

"That looks perfect," Jezmeen said to the two men who were positioning the new sofa in the living room.

"Where do you want the chairs?" one of the sweaty men asked.

"On each side of this window," she replied.

Jezmeen watched them walk on the freshly laid wood floor out to their truck. Even though she barely slept the night before because of excitement, she felt no tiredness. Jezmeen had never been so happy.

Her stomach rumbled, and she reached into her shorts pocket to check the time on her cell phone. Out tumbled a white envelope. Claire had stopped by on her way to the airport. She came to the new house, as the movers were carrying in the master bedroom set. Jezmeen offered to give her a tour. She would have loved to show off the place. But Claire said she didn't have time. Instead she handed Jezmeen the envelope and asked her to give it to Ethan.

While the men carried the heavy bed upstairs, Jezmeen quickly scanned the letter and counted the bills. Eight hundred dollars of Claire's teaching salary had been saved to pay back Ethan for the money that had never been recovered from the fall mum sale. As Jezmeen bent down to pick up the envelope, Ethan walked in.

"Hey, Jez," he said, looking as hot and sweaty as the movers. "What's that?" he asked, as she stuffed it in her pocket.

"Just receipts for all the furniture," she lied.

"You stayed on budget, didn't you?"

"Of course," she smiled. "I'd hug you, but you're grimy. Actually, can you take your shoes off? I don't want the new floors messed up."

"Aren't those guys already doing their share?" Ethan asked.

The two movers came in carrying an oversized white chair.

"They're wearing booties," she said, pointing to their shoes. "What do you think?" Jezmeen asked, excitedly, waving her hand around the room.

"It's formal."

"Don't you like it?"

"Looks trendy," he said, taking in the light gray walls against the white furniture.

"They'll be some pops of navy blue and lime green with throw pillows and knick-knacks. I'm sure you'll love it once it's all put together," Jezmeen replied, trying to mask the sadness she felt over his lack of enthusiasm with her design.

"We're going to go to lunch after we move in the other chair," one of the men said.

"That's fine," Jezmeen replied. "We just have the family room, dining room, and kitchen furniture to do once you come back."

"Sounds good," the man said, heading towards the front door.

"Do you want some lunch?  Or would you rather see the upstairs first?" Jezmeen asked, still bubbling.

"I ate a sandwich on the way here from the job.  Oh, and I got you one.  I figured you'd be too busy to think about what to eat."  He handed her the brown sack he'd been holding.  "It's got you a roast beef and cheddar from Panera.  That's what you ordered the last time we went there."

Jezmeen kissed him on the cheek.  "You're so thoughtful," she said sincerely.

"Do you want to eat?" he asked.

"I'd rather show you the bedroom furniture," she said, grabbing his hand.

After Jezmeen gave Ethan a tour of the three bedrooms and the office, they headed back downstairs.

"So that's what thirty-thousand gets you," Ethan said as he followed her slender figure down the steps.

"You do like it, don't you?" Jezmeen asked, honestly desiring his approval.  She'd worked for months putting together floor plans with design ideas, scouring home decorating magazines, and looking at stores all over town.  She'd consulted him in the beginning of the process, but as business picked up in March, he gave her complete reign of the project.

"I do," Ethan replied, noting the neediness in her eyes.  It was the first time she'd wanted something intangible from him, and even though her taste was more fashion-forward than his, he didn't want to crush her spirit.

"You're not mad that I couldn't chip in, are you?"

Ethan followed her to the kitchen where she stopped at the marbled gray and white granite counter and set down the bag.

"No.  You told me you'll start contributing to our household needs once you're done paying off your student loan."

Jezmeen felt a tinge of guilt as she opened the sack containing her sandwich.

"Do you know if Claire left?" Ethan asked, as he watched Jezmeen take a bite of her roast beef.

With her mouth full, all she could do was shake her head 'no.'

"So, she didn't stop by or anything?"

Jezmeen swallowed.  "No, why, did you think she would?"

"Well, she's leaving for China today.  I just thought—"

"I'm sure she was too busy," Jez said hurriedly. "Plus, I don't know why she would. It's not like you two were really close or anything."

"What's Chewy going to think of all this space?" Ethan smiled, changing the subject.

"We'll never find him," Jez laughed.

"You look happy," Ethan said, taking in Jezmeen's beautiful face.

"I am."

"I'm glad," Ethan replied. He wrapped his arm around her waist and felt her let out a contented sigh.

Tyler lifted Claire's heavy suitcase into the trunk of the Wangs' car while she set her backpack in the backseat. Feeling weary and hungry, Claire realized she'd forgotten to do her third insulin check of the day.

While Tyler was loading the suitcase, she'd quickly looked at her pump. Noticing her blood sugar was low, she pulled a peppermint out of her pocket and began sucking on it. Claire noticed Tyler was wearing khaki shorts and a light blue polo shirt as he sat down in the driver's seat. She'd worn jeans for traveling, thinking the air-conditioning on the flights might make her chilly

The weather in Tianjin was milder than Springfield, but it was still a warm eighty degrees.

"We're going to hit rush hour," Tyler said, as he put the key into the ignition. "So, I was thinking instead of sitting in bumper to bumper traffic, would you be open to stopping for dinner? There's a nice buffet a few miles from here. They have American and Chinese food."

"Sure," Claire replied. She was thankful to have the opportunity to get something to eat. For the next few minutes, Tyler concentrated on exiting the airport and finding the restaurant. Claire wasn't much help, being new to the city.

When Tyler pulled into the parking lot, he said, "Sorry we haven't been able to visit yet, I'm anxious to get to know a fellow American English teacher. That was my first time driving anyone out of the airport. I've always taken a taxi."

Claire was about to open her door when Tyler beckoned her to stop.

"Hold on. I'll get it for you," he said, dashing around to the passenger side.

The buffet restaurant was on the first floor of a fancy hotel. Once inside, Claire took in the sight of all the food stations. Sushi rolls, kabobs, seafood, fruit, and trays of beautifully decorated desserts caused her mouth to water. As they stepped to the register to pay, Tyler declared it was his treat. Claire politely accepted. Once Claire had filled her plate with a variety of choices, she made her way to the table where Tyler was seated.

"I hope I didn't make you wait too long," Claire said. "There were too many options."

"I always go for sushi. It made my decision easy," he said, pointing to the pile of neatly wrapped green and white rolls on his plate. "Would you mind if I prayed?"

"Not at all."

After Tyler whispered words of thanks for Claire's safe arrival and their food, Claire opened her eyes to see him taking in her face. She felt like she had the weary traveler look, and she smiled awkwardly. Tyler picked up his chopsticks, embarrassed that she caught him looking at her.

"So, how long have you known the Wangs?" Claire asked, trying to get the conversation rolling. She fingered the chopsticks but decided to go with the fork.

"Almost two years. I came here to teach English at Nankai University, and one of my students invited me to a game night the Wangs were hosting a few weeks after I moved here."

Tyler ate a circle of raw salmon wrapped in rice in one gulp. "Ah. That is good stuff. You don't have any on your plate. You don't like sushi?"

"Never had it," Claire replied.

"Here. Taste this." Tyler said, picking up a piece wrapped in seaweed and extending it towards Claire.

She gently took it from him and popped it in her mouth. "Not bad," she said.

"When's your first day with students?" Tyler asked.

"In about two weeks. Next week I report for training and prep work. How about you? Do you have the summer off?"

"No, I'm teaching two classes. Developmental Reading and Writing and Introduction to Written Argument and Research."

"Wow, your classes are much different than mine. I'll be playing games and singing songs with my little ones."

"That would tire me out."

"I imagine it will do the same to me," Claire laughed. "Where are you from, Tyler? How did you end up in Tianjin?"

"What, I don't look like a native?" he teased.

"No," Claire giggled.

"I'm from Bloomfield, Iowa. Population 2,640. Actually 2,639, since I'm not there. After I graduated from the University of Iowa, I taught English for three years at a high school in central Iowa and got my master's degree online. By the time I was done, I was ready for a change.  One of my friends from college had taught English as a Second Language in China, much like what you will be doing at the training school, and he loved it.  So, I decided to apply for a job, and here I am."

Tyler took a drink of water and continued.  "How about you?  The Wangs told me you taught at an elementary school stateside, and that you met them through your local church, but that's about all I know."

"That's about it," Claire smiled.

"I guess I can write your autobiography now," Tyler joked.  "Seriously, are you running from something or chasing adventure?  It seems like most Americans living in China are doing one or the other."

"Maybe a bit of both."

"Me too," Tyler replied.  "And for that reason, I declare you my new best friend."

# Chapter Eighteen

Claire excused herself to go to the bathroom before she headed to the car. Tyler had talked her into another bite of sushi and an almond cookie, and she needed to deliver a shot of insulin to balance out her carbohydrate intake. He said he'd pull the car up to the door and wait for her.

She was grateful the Wangs had warned her that public restrooms were quite different than what she was used to. She had a pack of tissue in her purse, since the Wangs told her it wasn't often supplied.

The toilet itself was flush with the floor. A garbage bin was in the corner, as she learned no paper could be put down the drain. Thankfully, her stall had a door. Tucked away from sight, she programmed her pump to deliver the appropriate dose of insulin.

After finishing up, she washed her hands and stared at her reflection. Her hair hung haphazardly around her shoulder blades, so she took the hair tie that on her wrist and drew her thick mane back into a low ponytail. Then she wiped her forehead with a paper towel before heading into the lobby.

As she walked past the counter where three Asian attendants checked in hotel guests, she thought about her new friend, Tyler. He was outgoing and chivalrous. She wondered if he was like that with all women, or if she was an exception. He certainly wasn't shy with his kindness. Once outside, Tyler was waiting at the side of the car to open her door.

"My lady," he said, his words rich and smooth.

"I'm not sure how to take all this gallantry," she smiled. "Does your dad open doors for your mom?"

"No, it's just my thing," he replied, walking around to the driver's side, as she slid into her seat. He checked the mirror, looked at the printed directions, and pulled forward.

"Tell me about your parents, Claire," he said.

"My dad's a farmer, and my mom was a home-economics teacher before my sister and I were born. They've been married twenty-seven years. How about you?" Claire replied.

"I haven't been married— ever," he teased. "Actually, I'm completely unattached. You?"

Claire laughed. "Me? I'm single, too, but I *meant* what are your parents like?"

"My mom's a nurse, and my dad's an Over-The-Road truck driver."

Claire watched Tyler ease onto the highway, and they were able to pick up a little speed before slowing down for a pocket of traffic.

"Any siblings?" she asked.

"I have an older sister who's married and has two children.  And you said you have a sister, too?"

"Yes, one, Gretchen.  She's a junior in college, studying business.  You'd like her.  Everyone likes Gretchen."

"Well then I'll have to meet her one day," Tyler said confidently.

There was a lull in the conversation, so Claire switched topics.  "How do you like the Wangs?"

"I love them.  I'd grown up going to church on holidays— Christmas and Easter.  I didn't attend at all once I got to college.  When I went to the game night, I didn't know they'd be praying for everyone before we left.  It felt a little awkward, but I kept going back.  The Wangs invited me to Tuesday night Bible study and church on Sundays.  I always made excuses why I couldn't go.  To be honest, I just wasn't comfortable with either."

Tyler signaled to change lanes and moved over into faster moving traffic.

"But I had a lot of questions about the Bible, sin, suffering.  That kind of thing.  One evening, after we finished playing cards, I began to ask Li Wei a bunch of questions.  He was able to answer them all in ways that made me think and said a few things that stung me to the core.  He invited me to Bible study again, and the next Tuesday I went. Within a few months, I made the decision to become a believer."

Tyler pointed to a large Ferris wheel that stood atop a bridge.

"Have you heard of the Eye of Tianjin? I'll have to take you there one day— if you're not afraid of heights."

"I saw pictures of it when I was learning about the city. It looks scary."

"So, you wouldn't do it?"

"I don't know. Maybe. I'd have to feel really brave that day."

"Well if you go, you'll have to see Ancient Culture Street, too. They're not very far apart."

"Have you seen all the major attractions in your two years here?"

"Most of them. The life of a university teacher here leaves you with plenty of free time. I only teach four classes each semester during the school year, and just two in the summer."

"I hope I can find time to explore the city. The training center said I'd be working forty hours a week, and I promised the Wangs I'd help them get a children's Bible study up and running."

Claire watched Tyler maneuver the traffic with ease. "How'd you learn to drive like this, being from Iowa?"

"I've driven in Chicago a few times. Traffic here actually feels easier to handle."

"How do you get around the city?"

"Bus, mostly. But a lot of the places I go are in walking distance."

They passed through a residential district.

"We're getting close to your apartment. I bet you're exhausted."

"For the past twenty-seven hours, I've been too excited to notice, but now that we're near, and all that delicious food is settling, you're right. I'm tired. Thanks again for picking me up and taking me to dinner. I really appreciate it."

"Don't talk like this is the last time you'll see me. Tomorrow is game night, and if you're up for it, I could use a partner for Euchre."

Ethan walked into "The Once Again Woodland," a little before five. The place was empty, and his new assistant, Hannah, was on her phone. She looked up, startled.

"Oh, hey Ethan," she said, pushing the phone into her pocket. "I didn't expect to see you."

"Jezmeen has the night off, so we're having dinner with some friends," Ethan said, striding over to the worktable. "Did we have many customers today?"

"Maybe twenty or so," she replied.

"Any word on when the lights will be in for the Edwards job?"

"Sorry, I forgot to check. I'll write it down to call the store tomorrow."

"Were you able to water everything in "The Green Jungle?" Ethan said, beginning to walk down the row of annuals, deadheading plants as he went.

"Shoot, I started but forgot to get to the last row. I got interrupted by a customer, and then I didn't get back to it. I'll write that down, too."

Hannah pulled a blank piece of paper out of the printer and jotted items down. Then she drummed the pen against the counter.

"Well, boss, it's five. Do you mind if I go?"

"Did you count the money drawer?"

"I was just getting to it when you came in. Do you want me to stay late?"

"I'll do it," Ethan grunted, waving his hand toward the door.

"See you tomorrow," Hannah called, grabbing her purse.

Ethan sighed as soon as Hannah left the building. She was nothing like Claire. Claire would have had all the plants watered, his Facebook page updated, calls to customers made to check on their satisfaction, and the drawer counted by five.

At least Hannah kept his schedule straight, Ethan thought. When Claire left, Ethan took back over everything except watering the plants, dealing with calls, and making his schedule. He didn't trust Hannah with the bookkeeping, payroll, Facebook page, and other marketing ventures. When he hired Claire, he had been too overwhelmed to refuse the extra help.

Ethan moved behind the counter and began counting the money. After tallying the daily register, he locked the box, tucked it under his arm, and headed for home. The Arctic Fox had been sold the day after they moved into the new house," so his stride took him down the freshly asphalted drive.

With the greenhouses flanking the front, the half-mile driveway led him to the two-story brick house. The yard was still in disarray. The front boasted leveled dirt showing signs of weeds, and the back still had the faint traces of row crops as far as the eye could see. Jezmeen had been on him to get the landscaping done, but Ethan had no spare time—especially when she kept scheduling special dinners. This was their third one in three weeks.

Since they moved in, she found prominent people in the community to invite over. Last Monday, it had been a city alderman and his wife. Then it was the executive director of Downtown Springfield, Inc. Tonight, it would be Lenny, from the Chamber of Commerce, and his girlfriend. Over the years, she'd met all these acquaintances at Finnegan's.

Entertaining people wasn't his style, but Jezmeen insisted he needed these social functions to help the livelihood of his business. She said networking was the key to sustainability. Ethan reasoned if that was the answer, he'd be burned out before he had a chance to find out the truth.

The blacktop reflected the heat of the day. The high had been ninety-five, but it felt like over one-hundred degrees midday. V.J and Mark had finished pouring a concrete patio around three, while Ethan left to check out a potential job. His hands felt cramped from planting shrubs all day, and his back and legs were tired.

Why did he agree to having people over he wondered as he neared the front door. Truly, he hadn't. Jezmeen asked if it was okay and he gave a reasonable list of excuses, but she had gone ahead with the plans anyways.

Maybe she was getting bored with his company, or maybe she really wanted to help his business, he didn't know.  Since they moved into the new house, they'd only had two nights together where she wasn't at work, or they didn't have guests, and those evenings had been purely carnal for Ethan.  There was momentary pleasure, but somehow it all left him empty.  How could he have "it all" and still feel so lonely?

He sat down at one of the four white rocking chairs that lined the long porch and took off his work boots.  Ethan speculated what the rockers cost him.  He'd given Jezmeen a $30,000 checking account in March, to furnish the home.  The last time he'd checked the balance, back in May, it was nearly depleted.

"Hey" Jezmeen said, sticking her head out the front door.  "You better hurry up and take a shower.  Lenny and Shawna will be here by six."

"Do you want to come sit by me for a minute and tell me about your day?" Ethan asked, patting the rocking chair next to him.

"It's too humid out here," Jezmeen groaned.  "I just did my hair, and it will fall."

"Which restaurant made dinner?" Ethan questioned, knowing Jezmeen had yet to cook a meal since they'd moved in.  Take-out or Finnegan's Taphouse frequently graced the table.  On nights when she worked, Ethan ate the frozen meals he'd come to love in his bachelor days.

"Mariah's," she said, looking fantastic in white capris, a form-fitting silky red top, and wedge sandals.

"Why are we doing this again?' he asked, peeling off his socks, enjoying the feeling of freedom from the constriction of the cotton against his skin.

"Lenny's with the Chamber, remember? He can tell you what the perks are for members. You might want to join."

"I was doing fine before all this 'networking.'"

"All the cold air is getting out," Jezmeen said disgruntled. "Come inside if you want to have a serious discussion."

"Never mind," Ethan replied, resigned. "I'll go take a shower."

# Chapter Nineteen

Jezmeen eased onto the highway. She'd prepared a thermos of coffee before she left, and after she was safely in the flow of traffic, she took a sip. Getting up on Sunday mornings, after working Saturday nights, proved to be difficult, but Jezmeen was determined.

Almost nine years had passed since she learned where she could find *him*. Before she'd become a bartender, she had been a food server. One evening, she overheard a private conversation between two women as she waited for drinks to be prepared for her customers.

The woman shared so many details in two minutes, Jezmeen knew where to look for him. When the woman pulled out her phone and showed a picture of him to her friend, exclaiming how handsome he was, it took all Jezmeen's self-control not to catapult over the bar and pull the phone out of her hands.

Jezmeen thought she'd lost him when they last parted. At first, that was what she wanted, but as time went on, she wondered if she'd made the right choice. Only days after she'd eavesdropped, she tracked him down. The Sunday morning she made it to the parking lot, she thought she might hyperventilate with worry that she'd be seen, or throw up—she felt so sick to her stomach. But she'd pulled into a spot far from the door, and no

175

one seemed to notice her. Yet, she spotted him immediately.

Overcome with mixed emotions- joy, sadness, anger, love- she knew that she wanted to see him every week. Sometimes she showed up and he wasn't there, then she worried about his health and where he could be, but then he'd be back the next week and all was right with her world again.

A few times a year she'd wish her life was different. She'd think about how she could change the past, but every time she went down that path it ended with the same conclusion—what had transpired could not be undone.

Jezmeen put on the turn signal for her exit and thought about Ethan. He was working, just like he did every Sunday. She wondered if he needed to take time off, but she knew it was "busy season" and winter would come again.

This winter would be easier to weather, she reasoned. The grand mansion was all that she had ever hoped to have in a house. She assumed that the beautiful place would make Ethan happier than he had been at the trailer— less reserved and distant. But he continued to seem dissatisfied, and it troubled her that she couldn't figure out why. Even if she didn't have strong feelings for him, she wanted him to be attached to her.

Jezmeen prided herself on being able to figure out most men, but Ethan remained a puzzle. She recognized that the dinners with company were wearing on his nerves, so she cancelled the one for the week ahead. But when she suggested they watch a movie at home instead, Ethan claimed he needed to catch up on landscaping plans for new clients.

She was grateful that he had so much work coming in because she had visions for the future of his business that required capital. But she didn't like how he was pulling away. When they first met, he was bewitched. Now it was like she almost had no power over him—and that thought made her heart palpitate with fear.

The stoplight changed color, and she turned left onto the frontage road. Jezmeen had been carrying a trump card in her pocket for months, knowing that she may need to use it with Ethan. And now was the time.

Two weeks of living in Tianjin felt like two months. On the bus to work, most everyone spoke in Mandarin, and there were times Claire just wanted to silence the unfamiliar hum of noise. Even though her apartment was clean and cozy, it didn't feel like home. Everything around her smelled, looked, and felt different.

The first week, she Facetimed with her mom almost every day. With thirteen-hours between them, 10 p.m. calls meant Connie could chat over a mug of coffee at 9 a.m., back in Springfield. They both fought back tears, and succumbed to a few, as they adjusted to life apart.

Claire never realized how much value there was in knowing more than one language. She couldn't understand her students when they wanted to converse with her, and the students' parents didn't always speak fluent English either. It was a humbling experience to live in a country as a minority. The Chinese people were friendly, but it was hard to make connections—especially when she didn't speak Mandarin.

Claire's saving grace had been Tyler. The second night in Tianjin, when she joined him at the Wangs for game night, he introduced her to everyone and kept her laughing for almost two hours. The Wangs spoke highly of him and claimed he'd become an avid student of the Bible.

She also learned he had been quite lonely when he first arrived. He'd never been a big fan of the bar scene, and he didn't know anyone in Tianjin. It wasn't until he connected with the Wangs, and started making friends with the people in the game night group, that he became attached to Tianjin.

Without Tyler, Claire would have been more homesick. The Wangs had their new baby to attend to, and she didn't want to intrude on their private life, so when Tyler asked her to dinner a few nights a week she went.

She'd shared with her mom much of what she'd learned about him in the short time they'd known each other. He was twenty-seven. He loved acting and had been in many plays in high school and college. If he wasn't a teacher, he might have been a pilot because he loved to travel. One Chinese New Year, he spent his break in Russia and the next year in Beijing.

Claire didn't let her mom know how many times he'd casually found a way to wrap his arm around her shoulder when they sat next to each other on the Wangs' couch, or how he seriously looked like he wanted to kiss her two days earlier when they said goodnight outside the entrance to her apartment building.

Today Tyler was going to take her to Walmart after church so she could get a blender. She'd known her apartment wouldn't have an oven—most Chinese homes didn't—and the microwave was sufficient. But she found that she missed her morning smoothies.

As Claire picked out an outfit for the June morning, her thoughts shifted to something her new co-worker, Trina, had said. Trina was only a year older than Claire, but she looked much more mature. She said Claire needed a style overhaul.

Claire had mentioned to Trina that her two classes of kindergarteners had gotten a little wild. Trina offered some sage advice about speaking more slowly and moving at a less frantic pace. She also suggested that making a visual schedule and offering more learning games, as rewards, would help.

While they were talking, Trina noticed Claire's stress level was high, and she suggested a pampering lady's day was in order. There was a huge mall close to Claire's apartment. Trina knew which stores held the best sales, and she said Claire would feel better if she invested a few hours in self-care.

As Claire put on a lilac sundress and slipped on a pair of sandals, she studied herself in the bathroom mirror and felt she was lacking something. She dug around the top drawer of the bathroom cabinet and found a large claw clip. Taking off her brown headband, she drew her thick locks back and twisted her hair up before securing the clip.

Then she turned to the side and studied the French twist. Claire pulled out a few strands of hair around her face and decided she liked the new style. She wondered what Tyler would think, and then for a quick second she thought about Jezmeen. Jezmeen had worn her hair in a similar fashion a few times and always looked lovely. Claire made a mental note to ask her mom how Ethan and Jezmeen were doing the next time she talked to her.

"Jez, I don't know why you invited so many people this time. I've told you before, I don't like big crowds," Ethan said as he buttoned the white dress shirt she'd laid on the bed for him.

"You never had a one year anniversary party for Adams Landscaping, and now that you got your first royalty check from Tryton for the first run of your pergola kits, it's the perfect time to celebrate," Jezmeen called from the adjoining master bathroom where she was applying eye shadow.

"This better be the last one for a long time," Ethan grumbled.

"I promise, after this one, no more for at least a month," she said, coming out of the bathroom.

Ethan thought she looked stunning in her strapless white dress, and he felt badly that he'd been ignoring her for weeks. It wasn't that he didn't care for her. He still found her madly attractive, and she was a fantastic hostess. But ever since they moved into the new house, he felt suffocated, and he didn't even know why.

Afterall, V.J. and Mark told him daily they'd be happy to change places with him. And when he'd gotten the first royalty check from Tryton for $50,000, he should've been more pleased. He had plans to build a proper storefront next to the hoop houses, get the stump grinder that would make work easier, and pave a parking lot for customers. But Jezmeen had other plans for his money. Plans he'd listen to and not act on, but even new work goals didn't thrill him the way they had the year before.

"Will I know anyone who's coming tonight, besides V.J. and Mark?" Ethan asked, as Jezmeen came and sat beside him on the bed. She rubbed his neck lightly with her fingers.

"I think you'll be pleasantly surprised at the guest list," she said.

"Did you invite my mom? If you didn't, and she gets wind of this, I'll never live it down."

"Oh shoot," Jezmeen said innocently. "I totally forgot. But we'll have her out to the house another time. Plus, it's not like she'll hear about it from anybody at *Walmart*."

Ethan caught the jab but didn't want to start an argument right before the party. "Let's just try to make this a short night," Ethan grunted. "I've still got to get up and work tomorrow."

# Chapter Twenty

"Abide in me, and I in you. For a branch can't produce fruit if it's severed from the vine," Li Wei preached.

Li Wei was seated on a wooden chair in the living room. His Bible was resting on his lap, and Bingquin was in a chair at his side. Claire was holding Li Na in her arms, and Tyler had his arm resting behind her head on the back of the couch.

"Think about it, friends—Jesus says we have to be connected to Him for anything good to come from our lives. We have to know Him, drink from Him, eat from Him, draw living energy from Him, for if we don't, we can't produce a bountiful harvest."

Li Wei scanned the room. "You might say, Pastor Li Wei, what does that look like? And I would tell you, it's reading the Bible, talking to Him through prayer...listening too, and resting in Him.

Li Wei closed the Bible as he wrapped up his message. "Let us strive to stay connected to the source of all goodness. Let us reflect His light to the world...And now let us pray."

The room was full. The sea of Asian faces made Tyler and Claire stand out, but there was beauty in collective nationalities worshipping together. After the prayer ended, Bingquin started the group in song.

Claire didn't want to wake the baby, so she hummed softly, but she heard Tyler's lovely, deep voice add harmony to the chorus. She'd listened to him sing, sometimes in English and sometimes in Mandarin, for the past four Sundays, and never tired of the sound.

When the song ended, Bingquin gave announcements for the upcoming week—Tuesday night Bible study, Thursday night games, and the new children's Bible study led by Claire and Tyler—starting on Friday in two weeks.

Claire had been prepared to lead it alone, but Tyler said he would help. Bingquin told her she was surprised. Tyler had always said he wasn't into kids. Regardless of what changed his mind, she was thankful for his assistance.

Bingquin approached Claire and gently scooped the still sleeping Li Na into her arms.

"Thank you, sweet Claire, for giving my arms a short break," Binquin said.

"It was my pleasure," Claire replied.

Li Wei had been talking with another parishioner but moved to his wife's side as the conversation ended.

"How do you like teaching at the training school?" Li Wei asked.

"It's great. I love the students. They're eager to learn, *usually* well-behaved, and they give great hugs- just like my first-graders did back home," Claire replied.

"I couldn't do it," Tyler chimed in, joining the conversation. "You have to tap dance, do cartwheels, and sing songs for those kids to stay focused. That would wear me out."

"You were in plays and musicals," Claire retorted. "It's certainly in you."

"Sure, doing one show at a time, not all day long."

"Maybe you'll add a theater component to the children's Bible study," Bingquin suggested, as she rocked Li Na side to side.

Claire looked at Tyler, "What do you think? Could you do a little skit each week about our Bible verse?"

"Only if you'll play a part, too," he replied.

"Absolutely," Claire said.

"Thank you for letting us borrow your car today," Tyler said to the Wangs. "I think we'll be back in a few hours."

"No rush," Li Wei said, taking the keys out of his pocket. "We'll be here all afternoon."

"Hey, Claire, here's what we need to fix this week for dinner," Tyler joked, pointing to a dead crocodile laying on a bed of ice holding a large orange in its mouth.

"I can't believe this is Walmart," Claire said. She stared at the scaly reptile, thankful it wasn't alive. "You've showed me a tank of frogs, a bunch of pig faces, cases of "diet" water—whatever that is, and a whole section of chopsticks. Now you lead me to a frozen crocodile."

"It tastes like chicken," Tyler teased.

"You've had it?"

"Sure. A couple of times. Many Chinese people love it."

"No thank you," Claire retorted, laughing lightly.

"So, you've got everything you need?"

Claire looked in the cart.

"Seems like it."

"Let's go checkout. There I'll get to show you how they package Snickers bars with batteries here in China. Don't ask me why."

"I told my mom that I felt comforted knowing there was a Walmart within a few miles of my apartment. Sometimes I feel like I'm halfway around the world."

"You are," Tyler laughed.

Claire blushed at her blunder.

"Are you hungry?" Tyler asked as he pushed the cart into a check-out line.

"Definitely," she said. She had hoped he would want to do lunch. There wasn't much lesson planning to do, since the training school built ten hours a week for that into her schedule. And she didn't have a television at her apartment because she would only be able to get Chinese stations.

"In keeping with the theme of the morning, I think McDonalds is in order," Tyler said, giving her a wry grin.

"Oh no," Claire moaned. "Do they sell crocodile nuggets?"

"You'll just have to wait and see."

"I can't believe you bought all of this food," Claire laughed as she set down the bag onto a clean table.

"When you come to a Chinese McDonald's you have to try all the foreign delicacies," Tyler said, grabbing a seat across from Claire. "Fried chicken, crisscut fries, mashed potato burger, and taro pie," Tyler said, pulling each item from the bag.

"I hope the taro pie is edible," Claire said skeptically.

"It's good," Tyler said. "I've had it before. A taro is a purple tuber, similar to a potato. It's slightly sweet, and the fried breading is amazing." He looked up at her. "Do you want to pray tonight?"

After Claire said a prayer of thanks for the provision, she excused herself to go to the bathroom. She needed to bolus before all the carbohydrates hit her system. When she returned, Tyler was still waiting to begin.

"I'm so sorry," she sighed. "I should have told you to go ahead. You're such a gentleman."

"You bring out the best in me," Tyler said. He watched Claire sit down, lay out a paper napkin onto the table, and reach for a piece of chicken.

"I have to say that works both ways, because listening to you ask questions at Bible study really has me thinking deeper than I ever have before."

Tyler cut the burger topped with mashed potatoes and placed half on the napkin Claire laid out at her place.

"Christianity is still new to me," Tyler said. "The more I read the Bible, the more questions I have. Was it like that for you when you became a Christian?"

Claire put her hand to her mouth, as she finished chewing a fry.

"I kind of wish that was the case. Whenever I share the story of my faith, I feel like it's vanilla ice cream—so plain."

"How come?"

"I was raised in church. My parents took me to my first service when I was less than a week old. My preschool Sunday School teacher told me about Jesus, and I believed in Him. I got baptized when I was ten. Sure, I've weathered a few hard things, but I've never walked away from God."

"So, your parents are Christ-followers?" Tyler asked.

"Yes. How about yours?"

"Nope. So, what'd you think of the chicken?" Tyler asked, quickly changing the subject.

"Delicious. It's hard to believe we're not at KFC."

"Oh, we'll get there, too. They have some unique menu items I want you to see."

Claire laughed and shook her head. "Nothing in this country is as it seems."

The party at Ethan's was underway. Jezmeen had purchased a nice buffet of appetizers, drinks and desserts. V.J.. Mark, and their new girlfriends, the ladies from the bar, had already loaded their plates and were seated in the sunroom when Ethan spotted them. He was moving to say hello when Jezmeen called him over.

She was in the dining room talking with a man in his fifties. He had wavy hair, like his own, with gray starting to highlight the edges around his face. Dressed in khaki pants and a white polo, he was one of the more casually dressed guests.

"Ethan," Jezmeen said with glee. "I'd like you to meet someone special tonight. Wayne Copeland."

Wayne Copeland. The name was so familiar-. She didn't. She couldn't have known. Ethan began to break out in a perspiration. The first night he met Jezmeen, the infamous night of his greatest drunken binge, he had shared with Jezmeen he'd never met his dad...Wayne Copeland. He had shared the name. The full name. How had she tracked him down? Did Wayne know who he was?

When Ethan didn't say a word, Jezmeen continued. "Wayne and I met at Finnegan's when I first started working there. I hadn't seen him in a while, and I thought you might want to meet him. He does electrical work."

Ethan felt like the possum he'd caught last fall in his hoop house. The possum played dead. Ethan nearly wished he was.

Jezmeen looked disgruntled at Ethan's lack of conversation. "You would have been quite the man to have on the job when Ethan had the electric line run to his greenhouses."

"You have more work to do, right?" Wayne asked. "That's why Jezmeen said she wanted me to stop by."

"Don't you want to run electricity to the future storefront?" Jezmeen asked, tipping her head to the side and giving Ethan a dirty look.

Ethan stared at Wayne. Lean but muscular. Tan but not dark. And he seemed confident—totally unlike himself.

"Umm, yes," Ethan stammered. "Someday that's the plan."

"Why don't you take Wayne out to the greenhouses and show him around, then you can bring him back, and I'll fix him a drink. What are you having tonight, Wayne? I know you used to like Jack and Coke, but I haven't seen you in a while."

"I've been busy. Can you believe I have a thirteen-year old daughter? Her mom's not in the picture, so I have her when she's not at her grandma's."

Ethan could barely contain his astonishment. He had a half-sister.

"Well, it sounds like you have your hands full," Jezmeen said kindly. "I'll go fix that drink. Go ahead and give him a quick tour." She shooed them with her hands.

"Just make it a Coke, Jez," Wayne shouted on the way out.

"You've got quite the operation here," Wayne said as they exited the fourth hoop house, moving onto the fifth. "And I like your catchy names." He read the sign above his head, "Regal Rose Grove, contained all the roses, and now we're at the Berry Backwoods. How'd you come up with all these?"

"I used a thesaurus," Ethan said honestly.

Wayne's easy nature made Ethan relax a little, even though he still couldn't believe he was in the presence of his dad. Why in the world had Jezmeen invited Wayne without telling him? It certainly wasn't strictly business.

"Who ran your electric in here?" Wayne asked.

"Ruby Electric," Ethan replied, remembering who Claire had hired.

"They're good," Wayne said.

"Do you work in town?" Ethan asked, curious how far Jezmeen had to track him down as he led Wayne through the rows of tiny strawberry, raspberry, blueberry, and blackberry plants.

"Yeah. When I first started out, I worked for Timberlane Electric. Now I work for myself."

"So, you know how tough it is to run your own business, too," Ethan said, liking that they had something in common.

"You're growing herbs in Berry Backwoods?" Wayne asked. They were walking down a row that held small black containers of parsley, basil, oregano, and other savory edibles.

"I figured I'd put all the things you could eat in one building," Ethan replied.

"Good thinking," Wayne said.

Ethan couldn't believe he was walking down rows of plants, hearing words of encouragement from the man who didn't even know he had a son. He wanted to tell Wayne the truth, but he didn't know how. What could he say? I never came to see you because I was born with port-wine stains, and I found myself hideous?

As they stepped back outside, the night air was cooling. Even though it was half-past seven, the sky was still bright. The calendar was nearing the summer solstice, and the light of day was long.

"So, where is it you'll be putting the storefront?" Wayne asked.

"Over here," Ethan said, walking towards the space he'd mapped out in his mind. "I think it'll be 40 foot by 40 foot. Jezmeen thinks it would look better if it was built out of wood, but I'm still looking into metal buildings."

"It's always good to please the lady," Wayne chuckled.

"You married?" Ethan asked, sincerely curious, although he already noted Wayne wore no ring.

"Nah," Wayne said as they stood facing the empty land where the future storefront would go. "Never been. Just know how the ladies are, that's all." Wayne swatted a mosquito away from his arm. "Well, I'll be happy to give you a quote for the job," Wayne said. "Don't know why Jez called me to do this on a night of a party, but when you get a call from that gal you don't refuse."

Ethan knew it was time to head back to the house, but he felt the growing intensity of his secret needing to get out.

"I think I know," Ethan said softly, looking into the distance, eyes set towards the "grand mansion."

"Know what?" Wayne asked.

"Why Jez called you," Ethan said. "I mean, I'm not sure about the timing of it all, but I know why she picked you to run the electric."

"My good rates?" Wayne chuckled.

"It's a bit more than that," Ethan said, feeling like his heart would beat out of his chest. "You're my father."

# Chapter Twenty-One

"You'll need to repeat that. It sounded like you said, 'I'm your father.'" Wayne laughed nervously.

"You heard correctly," Ethan replied, still not making eye contact.

"You seem like a nice young man, but you must be mistaken. I only have one child— Izzy...Isabella- and she's with her Mom's mother, her grandma, tonight."

Ethan took a deep breath. His stomach was beginning to hurt from anxiety, but he plowed ahead.

"Do you remember a woman named Suzanne Adams? Petite. Dark haired." Ethan searched Wayne's face, squinted in thought.

"Suzanne Adams. Suzanne Adams," he repeated. Then a truthful reality settled upon him, and his countenance fell. "Oh my-"

"She said she met you at a bar, Charlie's Lounge. I guess it's closed now."

Wayne exhaled and ran a hand through his hair. "How old are you, Ethan?"

"Thirty-three, coming up on thirty-four this October."

Wayne paced a few steps forward, thinking, and then walked back. "Suzanne and I only knew each other for a few months."

Ethan remained silent. He didn't dare say it was long enough to conceive a child.

"If this is all true, why didn't Suzanne ever tell me?" Wayne didn't seem angry, just confused.

"I was born with port-wine stains on half my face." Ethan heard music coming from the house as he waited in silence for Wayne to say something.

"Purple birthmarks?" he asked for clarification.

"Yeah."

"What happened to them?"

"I had laser surgeries two summers ago."

Wayne went back to pacing, and Ethan longed to know what he was thinking.

Wayne came back and stared into Ethan's face. Ethan was about an inch taller than him, at six feet. "My head is reeling, Ethan. What you're saying could be true. But I'd like to talk to your mom. Is she still in Springfield?"

"Yes," Ethan replied softly, turning away from his intense gaze, and wishing Wayne would take his word on the matter. He couldn't even begin to think about how his mom was going to react to this sudden development.

"I guess we better go-" Ethan said, still frozen in place, but knowing there wasn't much more he could say.

"Wait," Wayne said with concern, laying a hand on Ethan's arm to delay his movement. "If you are my son, Ethan, and I believe that you are, then I'm going to work hard to make up for all the years I've missed out on your life. I've made a lot of mistakes, but you're not one of them." Wayne pulled him in for a tight hug, and Ethan couldn't help but let out a sob, as he felt his dad's arms around him for the first time.

It was dark in the master bedroom. The clock read midnight, and sleep was eluding Ethan just as it had the past three nights. He hadn't talked to Jezmeen since the party. She knew why, and begged him to open up, but he was too angry. They'd slept in separate beds until tonight. He was still awake when she got home from work, and she pleaded with him to lay by her.

Ethan wondered if just being near another warm body would help him relax enough to go to sleep, but the hope was in vain. As he stared at the ceiling and thought about his dad, he heard

Jezmeen muffle a sob.  This was a first.  He'd never heard her cry.

"Please forgive me," she whispered, knowing he was awake.

Ethan remained on his back, picking out the distant hum of the ceiling fan.

"I should have told you I knew your dad." She sniffed a few times, holding back another sob.  "Inviting him to the party was a mistake.  I just thought you'd be so happy..."

Ethan felt his anger bubble and resisted the urge to yell.

"The poor man was dumb-founded.  You should have seen him, Jez."

"I wish he would've come back for his drink," Jezmeen sobbed.

"That was the last thing on Wayne's mind."

"But I could've explained why I did it."

"Why did you do it?" Ethan asked, rolling over unto to his side.  He wanted to see Jezmeen's face as she explained her reasoning.

"I wanted to connect you to each other.  I realized I held a missing piece, and I really believed you would be-"

"Be what, Jez? Thankful? That I'd kiss your feet? Give you money for a new piece of artwork?"

She sobbed again.

"Were you thinking of me or just yourself when you called Wayne?"

She sat up, reaching for a tissue. "That's a mean thing to say. You, of course. Always you," she lied.

Ethan noticed the change in the pitch of her voice and how she moved away.

"Whatever, Jez. The damage is done."

"You still haven't even told me what he said to you when you were out there," she sniffled.

"He said he was going to talk to my mom."

"Did he?"

"Yes, the next day."

"And?"

"And he went to her apartment. They talked. He believes I'm his son, but he still wants to do a DNA test to make sure."

"Do you want to?" Jezmeen wiped her eyes.

"My mom said she explained she's never been with anyone else. So, it seems like a waste of time, but if Wayne wants to, I'll go along."

"That's hopeful," Jezmeen said with renewed cheer.

"I guess he wants me to go to dinner this Sunday. He thinks I should meet my half-sister."

"See, it's all going to work out."

"Jez, I hope that's the case. But you *never* should have planned this the way you did. It was wrong. Deceitful. Sneaky."

She began to cry again.

"My mom was right," Jezmeen said between sobs. "Men never appreciate anything you do for them."

"Goodnight, Jezmeen," he sighed, and rolled over to face the door.

"How long do we have to entertain the little nose-wipers?" Tyler asked.

Claire and Tyler were sitting at Claire's kitchen table, cutting shapes out of felt for the children's Bible study.

"Nose-wipers?" Claire laughed.

"Yeah, isn't that what most kids do?  Rub their noses on the sleeve of their shirt?"

"Not all of them, and we only have to entertain…I mean teach… them for an hour."

"After we finish the shapes for the felt board, we need to practice the skit," Tyler said.

"I can't believe you gave me the part of wise old grandma."

"Well, the story needed a narrator."

"And you still think it's a good idea for you to play both Adam and Eve?" Claire asked, raising an eyebrow with mock concern.

"Don't forget I'm also performing the role of God, the water, the sky, and all the rest of the days of creation."

"I can't wait to see this," Claire chuckled.

"Oh, it will be *good*."  Tyler boasted in jest.

"Do you miss doing plays?"

"A little, but to tell you the truth, I get to do some acting with my classes.  I read parts of stories in different voices.  And I like to be "high energy" when I teach, so I guess it feels like acting at times."

Tyler set down the fish and picked up a red piece of felt that had a sketch of a bird on it.

"Do you miss anything from your former life?" Tyler asked.

Claire thought for a second. Her family, former students, Adams Landscaping and Ethan came to mind.

"Sure. I miss my mom and dad, my sister, and definitely my mom's baked zucchini casserole with tomatoes and garlic. This time of the year, my mom harvests fresh produce from our garden."

"You eat so healthily," Tyler noted. "When I think about American food I miss, it's a good slice of pizza or a great burger. I've only seen you eat junk food when I've made you."

Claire chuckled. "I grew up eating that way, so I guess it's just natural now."

"Wow. My mom, being a nurse, always wanted us to make good food choices, but I just gravitate to chips and cookies," he teased.

"My sister, Gretchen, does too, but she stays amazingly slender for someone who eats the way she does."

"So, you were the unique child."

Claire felt an opening to tell Tyler about her diabetes, but that was a big step. She wanted Tyler to treat her as he had so far, but managing her disease was a huge part of her life. Rarely did fifteen minutes go by, during her waking hours, where she wasn't analyzing her condition.

She could have a smoothie and eggs for breakfast one morning, and then the next day have the same exact thing and her numbers could be different. Or her numbers could climb high, and she'd give herself insulin only still to have the numbers continue to rise. Diabetes seemed to defy logic.

True to his word, in one short month, Tyler had become her best friend and constant sidekick. There had been times that she wanted to tell him. Now she felt secure enough in their friendship to let her guard down.

"One out of 400," she said, in answer to his question.

"What?" Tyler replied, confused.

"You said I was a unique child. I was one out of 400 young people to develop type one diabetes as a child. It's a lifelong condition with no cure." Claire busied herself cutting out a tree, not looking up from her work.

"Wow. I had no idea."

"Good, then 'operation seem normal' worked."

"Does diabetes run in your family?" Tyler asked, stopping what he was doing to concentrate on Claire.

"No. No one else in my immediate family has it."

"Then how'd you get it?"

"I inherited a predisposition to the disease, and then something triggered it when I was four."

"What?"

"Doctors don't know for sure. Maybe I had a viral infection. Maybe it was a change in the environment—diabetes seems to be diagnosed more in the winter."

"How'd you find out you had it?"

"My mom said I was really thirsty for a few weeks before she took me to the doctor, and I was constantly hungry and tired."

"And once you were diagnosed you had to take insulin?"

"Yep. You haven't noticed my insulin pump?"

"No, where is it?"

She pulled back her chair from the table and pointed to the left side of her waist.

"I've got to try something," he exclaimed, suddenly. "Stand up."

"What?" she laughed.

Tyler had already risen from his chair and gone to Claire's side.

"Please stand up," he repeated, taking her hand, and pulling her out of a seated position.

He grabbed her around the waist and drew her near to his body. Feeling his frame against hers, she wasn't sure if she should draw back or nestle into his hug.

"I can't feel it," he declared, deciding for her, as he pulled away.

"That's because the pump is in my pocket," she giggled, and then she pulled out the small black device, revealing her slender stomach, to show Tyler. The tubing trailed with it. "Crazy, right?"

"I wouldn't call it crazy. I'd call it amazing. That little thing is helping keep you alive."

Tyler watched her tuck the device back into her pocket.

"What?" she giggled with nervousness, as he continued to gaze at her, even after the pump was put away.

"You're really beautiful," he said, looking into her eyes.

Claire felt embarrassed and diverted her eyes to the table.

He gently tipped her chin up, so she could see him.

"I've wanted to do this from the moment I met you."

He bent down and kissed her lightly on the lips.  When she didn't resist, he pulled her back into his body, kissing her more passionately, and for the next fifteen minutes she easily forgot about being a type one diabetic.

# Chapter Twenty-Two

Claire stared at the pile of clothes, still on hangers, that she'd laid on her bed. Trina had declared, earlier in the week, that Claire was taking too long to get a style make-over. So, she persuaded Claire to block out Saturday afternoon, and it became their girl's spa day. First, Trina talked Claire into coloring her hair. Within two hours, her copper-brown locks became brighter— more of a sun-kissed red—with loads of shine. Trina gushed that she could model for Clairol.

After the salon, Trina dragged her to a make-up counter, and the sweet saleslady did a good job lightening Claire's wallet. New foundation, blush, mascara, eyeshadow, and brushes for each, had already been neatly tucked away in the bathroom drawer.

Finally, they'd spent the last of her week's pay on clothes. Trina purchased a few new outfits for summer and helped Claire select three feminine tops in jewel tones—sapphire, amethyst, and emerald— and two pairs of dress pants for work or church.

Claire began humming a praise song while she hung her fashionable wardrobe on the rack in the closet. The last time she felt this happy was when she was setting up her first classroom in Springfield. It had been a few days since Tyler first kissed her, and Claire knew their budding relationship was bolstering her mood.

Tyler was nearly perfect, she thought. Handsome, a Christian, funny, a fellow teacher. And he had taken the news about her diabetes in stride. After their kiss, he'd asked her appropriate questions, wanting to learn more. She appreciated his concern and interest. Even more, she welcomed his long embrace at the end of the night, confirming he was on board with where they were headed—health diagnosis included.

She'd talked with her mom a day earlier, but she didn't open up about what had transpired between her and Tyler. If they became really serious, she'd let her know. Connie, however, shared that she and Jed attended a one-year anniversary celebration for Adams Landscaping at Ethan's new home.

Connie said Ethan wasn't to be found when they arrived. But Jezmeen mentioned he was giving someone a tour of the greenhouses. After that, Jezmeen began to ask her parents strange questions about their home, like did they have a mortgage, and would they ever want to move? She also asked if she could tour their farmhouse sometime.

Her mom, in kindness, had agreed, but wondered why Jezmeen was suddenly so interested. Claire would've liked to hear more about Adams Landscaping. The days in Tianjin had flown by, but she still thought about Ethan from time to time and prayed for him and his business.

Claire hadn't told Tyler much about her former summer job or the employer she used to have a crush on. Maybe she would—if it ever seemed necessary. Since she'd spent the day with Trina, she wouldn't be seeing Tyler until church the next morning. And she missed him— even though it had only been a day since she'd seen him last. Was this love, she wondered?

"You're going to love their rib strips," Isabella declared. "Make sure to dip them in the sauce. That makes them better. I could eat a whole plate all by myself."

"Truer words have never been spoken," Wayne chuckled.

The summer night was humid, and the windows inside James' Home Kitchen had condensation around the bottom edges. Ethan was thankful Jezmeen had to work. This was one dinner he was happy to attend alone.

However, he almost called it off because he was so nervous, but after he talked with his mom, he knew he wanted to meet his half-sister and get to know his dad. So, he pushed through his fear. When he arrived, Wayne and Isabella were already seated, but as he approached the table, Isabella hopped up and gave him a spirited hug.

He'd only just met Isabella, and besides learning her preferred name was Izzy, he also realized they were complete opposites. She was spunky, theatrical, and talkative. Maybe talkative was an understatement. Her lips ran a marathon. With her blue eyes, straight blonde hair, and glasses, they also looked different, except they both had the same heart shaped upper lip.

"So, Ethan, my dad tells me you grow things for a living," Izzy bubbled. "One time, I planted some watermelon seeds at my grandma's house, and I actually got like five watermelons that summer. They were full of seeds, and I hate seeds. But my grandma *made* me eat them. Of course, I picked out the seeds, but that took forever. I'd love to see your greenhouses, Ethan. Would you let me come over?"

Ethan was amused at how many words Izzy could say without taking a breath.

"Sure, you're welcome anytime."

"That's awesome! Dad, can I go tomorrow?"

Wayne looked at Ethan to see if he actually meant what he said. Ethan smiled and nodded approval.

"I'll have to talk to your grandma," Wayne replied.

"I still can't believe I have a brother. I bet you still can't believe you have a sister. We're so far apart in age. I'm only thirteen, and you're how old again, Ethan? My dad told me, but I forgot."

Wayne sat back in amusement, obviously enjoying Izzy's interaction with Ethan.

"I'm thirty-three. I'll be thirty-four in October."

"So, my dad—well our dad—was twenty when you were born," Izzy replied, quickly doing the mental math. "Dad you were so young."

"I know, and Ethan can't take credit for any of these gray hairs, so where do you think they're all coming from?" he teased Izzy.

"Hey," Izzy replied. "Ethan's going to get the wrong idea about me."

"Izzy's actually a really good kid," Wayne smiled at Izzy.

"What? I am not a *kid*!"

"Sorry," Wayne said, "Teenager."

"What were you like when you were my age?" Izzy asked Ethan.

Ethan cleared his throat. "Kind of a loner," he replied.

"Dad told me about your birthmar-"

"Izzy," Wayne interjected, "Ethan might not want to talk about that."

"Oops, sorry, Ethan. My dad says I don't have a filter. Whatever I think, I just blurt out. Dad says that it's a bad habit, but it's impossible to correct."

"It's okay," Ethan said kindly.

"So, Ethan," Wayne interjected, stepping in to steer the conversation, "tell us more about your business."

For the next few minutes, until their dinners arrived, Ethan told them about Adams Landscaping, fielding many questions from Izzy. After their meals came, Ethan was surprised when Wayne asked if he could say a blessing before they ate. When they bowed their heads, Wayne softly gave thanks for Izzy and Ethan, and asked God to direct their conversation.

As they collectively looked up, Izzy's eyes met Ethan's. "That embarrassed you, didn't it?"

"Nah," Ethan lied.

"It embarrassed me at first, too. You'll get used to it," she said.

Izzy did most of the talking after that, which was fine with Ethan. Initially, when Wayne told him Izzy would be coming, Ethan felt disgruntled. He wanted time with his dad—alone. But as the evening played out, he was grateful she'd come. She was a pleasant buffer, and there were no awkward silences with her around.

After the bill was paid, Wayne asked if they could make Sunday dinners a weekly tradition, and Ethan readily agreed. As he drove home, he turned on the radio and sang along softly. The night had cooled, and he opened the windows. A refreshing breeze blew through the car, and Ethan chuckled to himself at something Izzy had said. Then he wondered if she'd show up at the greenhouses tomorrow after work, like she promised. He secretly hoped she would.

Jezmeen chose a respectable looking outfit for the farmhouse tour with Connie. As a future bed and breakfast owner, she'd have to change her bartender image. She hadn't told Ethan her ideas yet, partially because they were still barely speaking and because she was fairly certain he wouldn't like the plan. Afterall, he and *Claire* had nixed her idea to open a winery on the property.

Her new vision was to open a bed and breakfast. The new house didn't have the charm or character needed, so she began eyeing the Rogers farmhouse. When she attended the Christmas party, there was a warm and cozy atmosphere—one she'd rarely experienced. And the white siding, black shutters, and long porch were welcoming.

Jezmeen envisioned people coming to stay overnight in the beautiful home, which she would decorate until her heart was happy. And she'd prepare the guests a hearty breakfast. It would require a break from bartending, and the little challenge of learning *how* to cook, but it could be a positive change. And the job would certainly be more wholesome.

In her mind, she saw visitors checking out Ethan's greenhouses and storefront. It would bring in more revenue, and the B & B could become a tourist attraction. *She* loved her ideas, but wisdom told her the Rogers would not agree to sell their home. Jed's family had owned the land for years. But Jezmeen didn't want the farmland, just the house.

"Connie, this is just lovely," Jezmeen gushed, as they looked around Claire's bedroom loft. "This space is bigger than the master bedroom. And I love that there is a full bathroom up here."

"We wanted Claire to feel independent living at home," Connie replied. "Of course, I think that worked too well, now that she's flown to China," she chuckled with a hint of sadness.

"How is Claire doing?" Jezmeen asked, moving towards the large windows that faced the road.

"Good. She's made some nice friends, so that's helped."

"I love the view," Jezmeen said, staring at the tall corn stalks across the road. Then she caught sight of a work truck kicking up dust from the gravel drive as it pulled into the Adams Landscaping parking lot. She saw Ethan get out. Jezmeen looked at her watch. It was only five. She was surprised Ethan was already back from the job site. Maybe he needed to pay Hannah.

"It must be hard to take care of such a big house," Jezmeen said. She walked back to Connie's side and followed her out of the room.

"Jed and I only use a few rooms, so I don't have the upkeep I did when the girls were here. It's not too bad," Connie said. They began the descent to the first floor.

"How long before Jed retires?" Jez asked, nonchalantly.

"Well, he doesn't have anyone to pass the business to, so I guess he'll work until he can't anymore. He loves to tend the land."

Jezmeen's heart sank. This was going to be more challenging than anything she'd attempted in the past. "Thanks for the tour, Connie. Ever since we came over last Christmas, I have wanted to see the whole house."

"You're welcome anytime," Connie said, not knowing her words would be hard to keep.

# Chapter Twenty-Three

"How do you survive out here?" Izzy asked Ethan as he led her around "The Green Jungle."

"You think it's hot?" he teased.

"Not even those fans help," she groaned.

"You should have been here in June last year when we didn't have *any* fans," Ethan smiled.

Taking in his grin, Izzy reached over and spontaneously grabbed him around the waist. "I'm so glad I have a brother."

Ethan exhaled, as the wind got knocked out of him temporarily. "And I'm so glad I have such a strong sister."

"I'm not that strong, actually," Izzy babbled. "Exercising and sports have never been my thing. I'm more into plays and musicals."

"Have you ever been in one?" Ethan asked as they rounded the corner of boxwood containers.

"Mostly just school productions, but next year I might try out for the Muni."

"That's the outdoor theater in Springfield, right?" Ethan asked.

"Yeah," Izzy said, stopping to look at the thermometer hanging on the support pole of the greenhouse.

"It says it's 88 degrees in here," she muttered.

"I'll have to tell Wayne to take you on a camping trip or something. You need to get used to the outdoors."

"Don't even! If I'd be forced to do something like that, I'd prefer glamping. You know 'glamorous camping.'"

They exited "The Green Jungle" and headed to "The Eternal Forest."

"Ah, a cool breeze," Izzy said, lifting her nose to the sky and breathing in the air.

"Does Wayne take you on vacations?" Ethan asked out of curiosity, wondering what he'd missed out on all these years.

"You can call him Dad, you know. Your DNA tests came back, and it's official."

Ethan wasn't ready to call him Dad, but he didn't want to tell Izzy that. He opened the swinging door to the second hoop house, and they stepped inside.

"What are these?" Izzy asked, fingering the trailing green plant in front of her.

"Silver falls dichondra," Ethan answered. Hannah didn't make signs for the plants like Claire had.

"Pretty," she said. "Dad didn't take me on many vacations until the past two years. He's changed a lot- for the better."

Izzy used her foot to push a potted plant back into line, as it jutted out into the walking path. Hannah also didn't keep the place in pristine condition like Claire did, he noted.

"My grandma always says she doesn't know how I turned out so well. My mom, well, ...she's in jail. Drugs. Dad used to have a drinking problem. He wasn't a mean drunk. He just watched television and drank beers all night. I would hang out in my room most of the time when I was at his house."

"So, what made him change?"

"He passed out one day at work, and the doctor ran a bunch of tests. I guess his kidneys weren't really working that well anymore, and so Dad decided to quit cold turkey. But it didn't last more than a couple of weeks. Around that time my mom got arrested for drug possession, and dad just kind of fell apart. Whenever I would go over, he'd be drinking a lot. I actually told my grandma I didn't want to visit him anymore. When she spoke with him, I guess he decided to get serious. He started going to AA meetings and then he began going to a church that's not too far from our house. I'm glad you met him now and not two years ago."

Izzy watched Ethan pull a small trimmer out of his pocket and snip a couple of dead flowers off of a purple plant.

"He seems really glad to have met you," Izzy said sincerely. "And why wouldn't he be? I mean look at all these plants and your big house. I kind of saw it from the road."

"You mean the grand mansion?" a voice said from the doorway.

"You must be Izzy," Jezmeen said as she approached.

"And I bet you're my brother's girlfriend. My dad told me you were really pretty," Izzy said.

Jezmeen extended her hand towards the young girl, but Izzy wrapped her in a hug.

"We're practically family," Izzy said while squeezing Jezmeen tight.

Jezmeen let out a genuine laugh, but Ethan bristled at the sight of Jezmeen. She always seemed to intrude.

"Why, thank you. I'm Jezmeen," she said as they pulled away. "I heard you talking about our new home. Would you like a tour?"

"Absolutely," Izzy gushed. "My dad said it's amazing. I bet you even have a bathroom with a separate tub and shower. One of my friend's has a bathroom like that at her house. Well it's actually her parents' bathroom, but you know what I mean."

"We do have a bathroom like that, and sometime soon you'll have to spend the night and take a bubble bath in the big tub."

"That would be so fun," Izzy replied. "We could rent movies and make popcorn. I would even help out at the green houses, if you'd let me," she asked, drawing Ethan into the conversation.

"Uh, sure," he said. He'd have to think of a job to give Izzy.

"But," Izzy began, "maybe renting movies is really boring for you. You two probably do that all the time."

Jezmeen chuckled. "Not really. Ethan's in the midst of his busy season, so he's wiped out when he gets home."

"Well, if Ethan can't make it, you and I can hang," Izzy said.

"I'd like that," Jezmeen said genuinely.

"You look so professional," Izzy said, eyeing Jezmeen's white slacks and short sleeved red sweater. "Did you just come from work or something?"

"No, just the neighbors."

"What do you do, Jezmeen?"

"Let's show Izzy the next hoop house, Ethan. It's hot in here," Jezmeen said.

"Thank you," Izzy replied, looking at her brother with pride. "I told him that," she said to Jez.

As they exited, Jezmeen replied to Izzy's question. "I work at Finnegan's Taphouse."

"Oh, that restaurant downtown," Izzy said. "Are you a waitress?"

"No, I'm a bartender."

"Wow. I've never met a bartender. Is it a fun job?"

Jezmeen smiled. No one had ever asked her that.

"I make good money," she replied, then regretted it. Ethan would probably wonder if her "loan" was paid off.

"I bet it's hard to stay up so late," Izzy replied. "I used to go to bed at midnight or one when I was at my dad's. Now he's gotten a lot stricter. Sometimes I miss the old days, well not really, but that part of it at least."

"Must be nice to have a dad," Jez replied, walking ahead with Izzy at her side and Ethan trailing behind.

"You don't have one? I mean, I know you have one, but you don't know him or something?"

"Never met him," Jezmeen said.

"What happened? Did he die? Maybe I shouldn't have said it like that. I just put my foot in my mouth, didn't I?" Izzy put her hand to her lips. "I have to tell you, Jezmeen, I just say what I think. I need to stop, but it's hard."

Jezmeen put her arm around Izzy. "I like you just the way you are."

"Oh, that is *so* nice of you," Izzy bubbled. "I think people either love me or can't stand me."

"Well, I love you already," Jezmeen continued.

Izzy leaned her head against Jezmeen, as they walked. They headed into the "Once Again Woodland."

"My dad didn't die," Jez said. "He just left before I was born."

"Don't you know where he went? Did you ever try to find him? I still can't believe Ethan never tried to look for my dad- well *our* dad. If it hadn't been for you, Ethan and I never would have met," Izzy looked into Jezmeen's eyes with admiration.

Ethan observed how taken Izzy was with Jezmeen, and he was also dumbfounded that Izzy could get Jez to talk about her past.

"My mom didn't know much about my dad," Jez replied. "All I know is that his name was

Efrem. My grandmother lives in Colombia and my grandpa was African American. Hence the brown skin," Jez said holding out her arms, as if to show her color.

"Well, maybe Ethan can help you find your dad since you helped him find his," Izzy said.

Jezmeen looked back at Ethan who had been quiet since she got there.

"Maybe," she replied softly.

Jezmeen had been looking forward to Izzy's overnight since it was scheduled. Ethan said he'd hang out, as long as he could stay awake. With the hours he'd been putting in landscaping, it probably wouldn't be that long, but she'd take what she could get.

Wayne dropped off Izzy at six, and he stayed to visit with Ethan for a few minutes about the storefront project. Jezmeen showed Izzy the movies she'd rented while they talked. Ethan invited Wayne to stay for their pizza dinner, but Wayne politely declined, saying Izzy would be furious if he intruded on her special night.

After Wayne left, they loaded up paper plates with pizza and took their food and cans of soda into the family room. Izzy chose a comedy, thinking it might keep Ethan's interest. Then Jez loaded it into the DVD player and took a seat on the couch by Izzy. When the previews began to roll, Izzy insisted they play them, just like they would in a regular theater.

"Is this what you did when you were my age?" Izzy asked Jez, half-heartedly taking in the previews.

"Not really," Jez said. "You're almost a freshman, right?"

Izzy nodded, her mouth full of pizza.

"My freshman year of high school I met a boy. We got pretty serious, and I just spent all my time with him."

"High school sweethearts," Izzy sighed. "What happened to him?"

"He kind of bailed," Jez said disdainfully.

"Well, if he hadn't, you couldn't have met my brother," Izzy said. She looked over at Ethan, who was sitting in the black recliner, listening. "How did you two meet?"

"He came into Finnegan's and talked my ear off," she laughed, trying to help Ethan recall how much he used to like her.

"That's surprising," Izzy replied. "He's usually so quiet."

"Let's just say alcohol can make people act differently."

"Tell me about it," Izzy said. She wiped her mouth on her napkin. "So, did he sweep you off your feet?

Jezmeen stopped to think. Ethan had been romantic—until she moved into the trailer.

"When we first met, he bought me some really beautiful flowers, and he gave me a book about plants. Oh, and there were some very sweet notes," she said, recalling a few of the letters he had written.

"I bet it's great to be in love," Izzy swooned. "I've never been in love. I've been in "like" before, but not love. There's this boy, Preston, who I think is cute, but dad says no boyfriends until high school."

"That's good," Ethan interjected. "Maybe you should wait until college," he said seriously.

"Oh, Ethan," she said, throwing a pillow at him. "Don't even give dad any ideas."

"Does Wayne date a lot?" Ethan asked curiously.

"Not since he began going to church, but there is this lady there who I think likes him. She's always coming up after church and talking to us."

"So, Wayne makes you go to church?" Ethan asked.

"No, I wanted to figure out what made him change so much, so I just started going with him. It's kind of nice to spend time with him there."

"So, you and your dad go to church?" Jezmeen asked, and Ethan realized he'd never told her about his conversation with Izzy about Wayne's conversion.

"Yeah, but since I'm staying the night here, I'm just skipping tomorrow morning."

"Well, you two can sleep in. I'll get us breakfast," Jez said, knowing it would be a good alibi for her Sunday jaunt.

# Chapter Twenty-Four

Ethan fought the dread of being overwhelmed. He'd spent the last fifteen minutes listening to a disgruntled customer. Hannah had forgotten to call the Johnstons to let them know their project was being pushed back, and unfortunately, this was the second time it happened. It didn't matter that it had rained the week before, and all jobs were rescheduled, the Johnstons decided to go with a different landscaper.

Losing the income was disappointing, but Ethan cared more about his reputation in the community, and he hoped it wasn't getting tarnished. Sadly, Hannah had done this before, but Ethan couldn't do his job and hers, too.

As he drove into the parking lot of Adams Landscaping, he backed up the truck and slowly maneuvered to the empty space intended for the storefront. Then he hoisted out the drill and some sill seal. He was thankful Wayne had agreed to help him install the sill seal around the concrete foundation that had already been poured.

When he talked to Wayne about the storefront project, he had been eager to help, although Ethan said there was no rush to get started. Ethan would have felt less stressed if they weren't building during the peak of summer sales. He also would've chosen to begin after the heat of the season had passed, but Wayne offered to be available every Sunday after church. Ethan wondered if he was trying to make up for lost time.

Thankfully, Jezmeen was still gone to wherever she went on Sundays. Ethan used to care, but lately he felt no emotion. He'd become distrustful of her. When he had more time or energy, they would have to have a serious talk about where their relationship was headed, he reasoned. Grabbing the blueprint of the construction plan, he stepped out of his truck to see Wayne approaching.

"Izzy was disappointed that Jezmeen had to work today," Wayne said, as he neared.

"I think Jez was sad, too," Ethan replied. "She can't wait until the next overnight."

"I didn't take Jezmeen to be the kid-type," Wayne said.

"Me neither, but she sure likes Izzy."

"Izzy says that people either love her or hate her, but I've never met anyone in the second camp." Wayne said with a smile. "So, where do we begin?"

Ethan showed Wayne the drill, and they got to work sinking anchor bolts into the cinder blocks every four feet. By noon, they had finished overlaying the sill seal, so they stopped to take a break.

Ethan had bought sandwiches and bags of chips, and after a short walk to the house, they were seated at the bar stools in the kitchen ready to eat. Wayne asked to pray before the meal, and Ethan complied.

"Izzy told me how the whole praying thing came about," Ethan said, as he unwrapped his sandwich, avoiding a lag in the conversation and not knowing what else to say.

"Oh, did she?" Wayne asked, raising an eyebrow. "What'd she tell you?"

"Just a little about your past," Ethan said self-consciously.

"I've been sober 457 days," Wayne said, with a hint of pride.

"That's great," Ethan said, thinking back to his shot of bourbon the night before and wishing he didn't need a drink to put himself to sleep. Why had he ever let Jezmeen get him hooked on the stuff, he wondered?

"I guess A.A. has helped," Ethan said, taking a bite of his sandwich.

"Step number one is admitting you are powerless over your addiction, and step number two is that you believe a Power greater than yourself can give you back your sanity. But it's step number three that changed my life," Wayne said.

He dumped a few corn chips onto the napkin in front of him before continuing. "You turn your life and your will over to the care of God.

Ethan, I'd tried many times in the past to stop drinking. I could go for a day or two, one time even a few weeks, but I'd always slip up. When that happens so many times, you begin believing you can never be free."

He rubbed his hand over the graying stubble on his chin.

"When Izzy's mom got arrested, I felt like a semi crashed into me. Suddenly, I realized I had to clean up my act. Izzy didn't deserve to have two parents who were totally messed up. And, while I am thankful for her grandma, she's almost seventy, and raising a teenager is hard work."

Wayne took another bite of his sandwich.

"One Sunday morning I woke up, depressed and desperate. So, I looked up service times for a church next to my house, got dressed and went. My palms were sweaty, and I felt like I wanted to run, even though I walked in and sat down. The preacher gave a sermon about how God provides the only foundation that will stand the tests of life. He said some people build their lives on things that won't hold up under stress. I was carrying a lot of shame and anxiety, and instead of turning to God, I turned to the illusive comfort of alcohol."

Ethan listened closely, not touching his food.

"As I sat in the pew, I knew that fifty-two-year-old Wayne Taylor Copeland needed a new

Captain of his ship. And that was the start of living out step number three."

Ethan's defenses went up. His old neighbor and friend, Danielle, had told him that he needed to do the same thing his dad did—surrender. He remembered how he had prayed that Danielle would become his girlfriend. She was so sweet and kind—not like the manipulative and selfish woman he lived with now. If there was a God, He hadn't answered *that* plea.

"So, did life magically become better?" Ethan replied, not even trying to hide his sarcasm.

Wayne turned to look at Ethan, ignoring the tone. "For a few weeks the urge to drink was completely gone. I thought it had been a miracle, but then the desire came back. The difference was, I wasn't steering the vessel. Every time I was tempted, I talked with God. I began saying scriptures aloud that spoke about self-control and strength. I tapped into the tools God gave me by seeing a counselor and calling my mentor. It hasn't been easy, but I've never felt so free."

Ethan was surprised at Wayne's answer. He thought he'd talk about instant change, not hard work.

"Even though we're just getting to know each other, I can see a lot of my old self in you. You live with insecurities, just like I did. My addiction was fueled by emotion. If I was sad, I drank. If I was anxious, I drank. If I was down, well you get it."

Ethan saw a similar pattern in his own life and knew he needed to make a change with his nightly habit.

"Do you still attend A.A. meetings?" Ethan asked.

"Yes, and I might need to for the rest of my life. I've found the accountability helps and so does the support." Wayne looked down at his sandwich. "Finding out I had a son, well that was a surprise."

Ethan felt bad for any turmoil that was caused by his sudden appearance.

As if he knew Ethan's thoughts, Wayne continued. "Don't get me wrong, I am thrilled to have a son," he said, his voice getting husky. "I just wish I had watched you take your first step, ride a bike, come home with an A on a spelling test."

Wayne sniffed. "But I talked with my mentor, and he reminded me that God is in control. He knew when, and how, we would connect. He made you and has been taking care of you since you were born. I only pray I don't let you down, now that we've found each other."

# Chapter Twenty-Five

The taxi driver announced they had arrived at Italian Style Town, and Claire and Tyler exited out the back doors. The Sunday afternoon weather was pleasant, and Tyler had been looking forward to showing Claire a piece of Europe all week.

"Welcome to Marco Polo Square," Tyler said.

Claire stared at the fountain that sprayed streams of water at a tall statue labeled 'The Goddess of Peace.'" The circular plaza was relatively crowded, and she was thankful for Tyler's arm, holding her close.

"It doesn't even seem like we're in Tianjin," Claire said, amazed.

"I know. This city is a collision of cultures. At the turn of the nineteenth century, the Second Opium War brought in waves of foreign troops. Even the United States got involved. After the war, sections of Eastern China were divided and given to other countries. Hence, the Europeanization of China in Tianjin. And that, my dear, is your history lesson for the day."

Tyler took Claire's hand. "Let's head to Anghiari. There are little shops down that street," he said.

Claire stared at the quaint brick buildings that mimicked an authentic Italian town.

"I can't get over how different this looks from the architecture one block from here. We went from contemporary Chinese buildings to this."

They passed a black wrought-iron fence and stepped onto a cobblestone street.

"If we hadn't just eaten with the Wangs, I would have suggested that we stop at one of these Italian restaurants," Tyler said, as they passed a few. "How are your numbers, by the way?"

Claire pulled out the insulin pump and read the screen. "A little high, but walking should help with that." She felt relieved that hiding her pump was no longer an issue with him.

"Can you tell when something's off?" Tyler asked.

"Absolutely. I get really thirsty, or tired...or irritable. My poor parents, especially my mom, got the brunt of that last one. I shudder to think of all the mothers dealing with hormonal teenage girls that are type one diabetics."

"I bet your parents miss you," Tyler said.

"My mom was really worried about me living on my own. It's hard enough for someone with my condition to manage it in their home country— let alone abroad. How about you? You don't talk about your parents much.  When was the last time you went home to visit?"

They walked past a petite Asian lady sitting on a stool next to the colorful scarves she was selling.

"Ah, but where is home truly, Claire?" Tyler teased philosophically.

"That will be my next essay, Professor Stephens," she teased.  "But really…when was the last time you were stateside?"

"Two years ago," he replied, nonchalantly.

"What?" Claire exclaimed.  "You haven't gone home once?"

"I like it here, especially now that you've arrived."

Tyler raised her hand to his lips and kissed the top of it.

"Do you talk with your family?"

"Sure, every now and then I talk with my dad, but he's not much into words.  And my sister and I Skype occasionally.  She puts my niece and nephew on sometimes."

"You didn't mention anything about your mom."

"That's because I don't talk with her," Tyler said.  "Hey, look at those music boxes." He pointed to a window display. "Let's go inside that shop."

Claire didn't know if Tyler sincerely liked music boxes or if he steered away from the conversation on purpose, but for the next ten minutes they perused the tiny space.

"How's your blood sugar now?" Tyler asked, as they exited the shop.

Claire checked her monitor.

"Better. But you don't have to ask all the time."

"Now that I know, I just want to help."

"I really appreciate that," Claire said, looking up into Tyler's brown eyes. "I feel really blessed that you care so much."

Claire thought about how her mom would constantly text her throughout the day, while she was in college, to check her numbers. Finally, she set some boundaries. If her numbers were abnormally low or high, she'd let her mom know, and follow-up when it was remedied. As much as she appreciated Tyler's concern, she didn't want him to feel like he had to manage it, too. "I'll let you know if something is really off," she said.

"Other than your boyfriend," he laughed.

"Boyfriend?" she asked.

Claire saw Tyler's face fall when she questioned the word.

"I thought that's where we were at…with us."

"So, you want me to be your girlfriend?" They walked past a bronze statue of a woman holding a basket of flowers above her head.

"You are somewhere I have never traveled, gladly beyond."

Claire looked at Tyler, confused.

"E.E. Cummings."

Tyler stopped walking, and Claire followed suit. She looked at his face, and he held her gaze.

"I was searching for a lot of things when I came to China. I found new life, and then I found new breath."

He took her hands in his and rubbed his thumbs against her soft skin.

"I want you to be my everything…but we'll start with girlfriend." He searched her eyes hoping to see she felt the same way.

Claire hadn't hesitated when Tyler asked her to be his girlfriend. Every day she woke up joyful, and when she laid her head on the pillow, she didn't feel fear, like she used to, about being alone with diabetes. Having Tyler in her life felt like a gift. She still thought about Ethan, but only when her mom brought him up.

Lately, Connie had been talking more about Jezmeen. She'd taken a tour of the farmhouse and asked a lot of questions. Something felt off, but Connie didn't know what to make of it. However, Connie was pleasantly surprised when Claire informed her about her relationship status. She hoped to meet Tyler in February, when Chinese New Year brought Claire home.

But he hadn't been back to visit his family for two years, and Claire wasn't sure if he'd head to Iowa—or Illinois for that matter. Maybe he'd make the trip back to meet her family, but she wasn't going to count on it.

Claire took the steps to Tyler's office two by two. She'd finished teaching her classes and had taken the bus to Nankai University so they could work out details for the children's Bible study, and she was anxious to see him.

As much as Tyler insisted that he disliked kids, he was fantastic with them. He loved to joke and tease. He brought popular trading cards to hand out each time. And whenever he started the skit, they got silent. It was their favorite part of the lesson.

Claire pulled the monitor out of the pocket of her new black slacks, as she walked down the hall. She was wearing her new emerald green top, and she had done her hair and make-up. Glancing at the device, she saw her blood sugar was stable, and she felt good. Tyler would probably ask about her numbers, and even though she told him he didn't need to help regulate her health, he still wanted to know how she was doing. He even watched her change out her cannula the last time she switched the site.

"Don't you look gorgeous?" Tyler said, as she entered his small office. He was seated behind his desk, which was laden with papers.

She smiled appreciatively and took a seat across from him. The sun had set, so the sky outside his window painted a navy background. Behind him, the soft glow from the tall lamp was inviting. He leaned across the desk to kiss her, and she welcomed his lips.

"I missed you," he said, sitting back down.

She laughed. "We saw each other last night."

"I know," he smiled warmly. "How were your classes? Were the kindergartners well-behaved?"

"Yes, much better than usual. It's a long day for those five-year-olds...going to school and then tutoring."

"That's the culture here. Families want their children to learn English, as soon as possible. It opens doors for them."

"How was your class tonight?" Claire asked.

"Fine. Everyone was well-behaved," he teased. "Here, I can do this later," he said, setting aside the papers he was grading. "We have a lesson to plan." As he reached down to put the papers inside his briefcase, he knocked it over. Claire bent over to help him pick up the contents of the bag and grabbed the first book she saw.

"Managing Type One Diabetes," she muttered, reading the title.

Tyler, who had crouched to help, looked sheepish. "I wanted to know more."

Claire's heart melted. She stuffed the book into the case and sat back up.

"So, what's D.KA.?" she asked, quizzing him.

"That's easy. Diabetic ketoacidosis which is where you aren't getting the glucose you need, and it can be serious."

"Correct," she said. "And hyperglycemia?"

"Too much glucose in your blood."

"Wow," she said, sitting back in the chair with a smile. "You have done your research." She noticed a stray paper on the floor and bent down to retrieve it.  When she sat back up, Tyler had moved to her side of the desk and was leaning against the surface.

"Ask me another question," he said.

"Well, Professor Stephens, what are ketones?"

"Chemicals made by the liver when your body doesn't have enough insulin."

He opened his palm for a high-five.  Claire obliged.

"Very impressive, Professor."

"I'm just glad you didn't ask me about medications.  I haven't gotten to that chapter yet."

"Thanks," she said softly, looking up at him from the chair.

"For what?" he asked, still leaning against the desk.

"For caring so much."

He pulled her upward into his arms and let his lips linger near hers.

"I couldn't sleep last night.  You were on my mind." He kissed her gently.  "You've been there a thousand times before." He kissed her again.  "I love you, Claire."

Jezmeen was curled up in a black leather recliner in the family room, laptop resting on her legs. Ethan had taken to reading the Bible, thanks to Wayne's influence, and he was holed away in his office. So, Jez was alone.

She had just finished reviewing a few legal documents online. One of her loyal customers was an estate lawyer, and she asked him to help her look into loopholes on how to get possession of the Rogers' farmhouse. The lawyer had done her a favor and taken a trip to the assessor's office. He looked at the property records, including detailed maps of the boundary markings.

When he reported back that the land lines were accurate and there was nothing to stake a claim on, he said she'd have to acquire the farmhouse the old-fashioned way—by waiting for it to come up for sale. Jezmeen knew that wasn't going to happen any time soon, and she needed more anchors in Ethan's life.

It had been awhile since they'd been intimate, and they barely talked. If life with him wasn't so lucrative, she'd leave willingly, but now that Izzy was in the picture, Jezmeen felt the desire to stay grow even stronger. Izzy was a ray of sunshine.

For days she stewed about what to do. Bringing Wayne into the picture hadn't made her a hero, even though Ethan seemed to enjoy time with his dad. Her usual seductions weren't doing the trick either. The lawyer hadn't told Jezmeen what she wanted to hear, but she didn't give up that easily.

Jezmeen planned to switch the property documents at the Accessor's Office with forgeries, and then she would "hire" a lawyer to represent her case. If a *real* attorney wouldn't take the job, she would. The Rogers didn't know her number, so she'd create a fake name and give her cell phone a new voicemail message. If the Rogers called, they'd reach attorney Cassandra McCabe. Now all she needed was a formal letter to evict them. She opened a Microsoft Word document and began to type.

*Dear Jedediah and Connie Rogers,*

*Our client, Jezmeen Williams, a legal resident of Sangamon County, presently residing at 2770 Farmingdale Road, is desiring to execute a POWER OF JURISDICTION, over property at 2790 Farmingdale Road. After surveying the land and accessing the records at the City Clerk's office, a land line encroachment has been identified. Your house falls on property rightfully owned by Jezmeen Williams and Ethan Adams.*

*Our firm represents Williams, and we are prepared to file a trespass lawsuit, unless the house on which the land lies is sold to Williams at a fair market value. You have thirty days to initiate this transaction, at which time legal action will be initiated.*

Jezmeen stopped and corrected a few spelling errors, then finished the letter by signing it with Cassandra's name and adding her cell phone number.  As she pressed save, she wondered what was the worst thing that could happen.  Ethan could find out and break up with her.  That didn't seem so bad, they were headed that direction anyways.

Or the Rogers could see through the scheme and have her tried for impersonation.  But the Rogers seemed too kind to press charges.  If they found out, they'd be angry and scold her.  Neither consequence was frightening enough to make her change her mind.

The best outcome would be acquiring the farmhouse and turning it into a bed and breakfast.  Decorating a house, with Izzy at her side, seemed like a slice of heaven.  She'd use her nest egg to buy it.  Ethan wouldn't need to be brought into the transaction.

Using her large savings account was the hardest pill to swallow.  Jezmeen had been stockpiling her income so she could buy a beachfront property and never again have to bartend.  She didn't want to rely on men forever.  That was work, and she wanted to retire...someday.

For a brief moment she doubted her own plan.  If the Rogers learned the truth, that there was no property line issue, she would be sunk.  Everything rested on her ability to successfully switch the documents.

The hot July morning started out full of hope. Jezmeen dressed strategically in tight fitting blue jean capris, a snug short sleeve sweater and wedge heels. After she ate a bowl of cereal, she addressed and stamped the letter to the Rogers and set it on the counter. A trip to the Accessor's Office was in order. If all went as planned, she would slip the envelope into the mailbox in the afternoon.

As she drove to the County Building, with a manila folder of fake documents riding in the passenger seats, she felt a pang of guilt. Her scheming would devastate the Rogers, and they seemed like such a nice family.

If only Ethan loved her, Jez wouldn't have to go to such lengths. She thought about her very first boyfriend. The one she spent all of her high school years devoted to. The one who would never leave her. She knew men couldn't be trusted, and securing her future was her job.

Once inside the building, Jez was gravely disappointed. Instead of being met by a male employee, like she envisioned, a portly lady with glasses and a light mustache grimaced at her from behind the counter. All of her hope deflated like a balloon.

If there had been any sparks of faith left, they were extinguished when the portly woman told her that files were kept electronically as well as in paper form. Even Jezmeen's resourcefulness had its limits. Even if she could get away with switching the paper documents, she knew she couldn't manipulate the electronic copy. She felt sick with grief over the ruined plans.

The kids were putting the final touches on their craft project, as parents started to arrive at the Wangs' apartment. Eight little bodies were squeezed around the kitchen table gluing animals onto their arks. Claire hovered over a dark-haired girl, helping her stick two elephants next to each other.

Bingquin held LiNa against her shoulder, and the young baby was entertained by all the activity.

"How are things going at the training school?" she asked Claire.

"Very well," Claire replied. "It's different from my work back home. With my first-graders, I taught all different subjects. Now I teach the same subject but all different ages of students."

"And living on your own is going okay?" Bingquin asked.

"Surprisingly, yes. Don't get me wrong, the first week or so, I had a lot of anxiety—especially at night, but now that's gone away."

"Does that have to do with a certain someone?" Bingquin asked with a twinkle in her eye, as she stared at Tyler who was talking with Li Wei and a parent in the living room. The open space made both rooms accessible.

Claire felt warm happiness just talking about Tyler. She'd spent part of the previous night journaling about all the things she loved about him, and then looked at a map online to figure out how long it would take to get from Bloomfield, Iowa to Springfield, Illinois. Claire desperately hoped he'd be willing to make the trip back in a few months with her.

Seeing her smile, Bingquin continued. "He's a great guy, Claire. Two years ago, we saw the hunger in him to know about God. He's becoming mature in his faith."

"We've been praying together," Claire said. "I've never done that with a guy."

"That's a great foundation for your relationship." Bingquin bounced LiNa back and forth. "I'm glad that you have found each other, especially since Tyler has expressed a desire to become an official ex-pat."

"Ex-pat?" Claire asked.

"An expatriate. He wants to live in China."

"Really?" Claire's face darkened. He'd never told Claire he wanted to make Tianjin his permanent residence.

Bingquin noticed the change in Claire's expression, and she backtracked. "That was a while ago though, before you came. Maybe he's changed his mind." A new parent walked in the door, and Bingquin went to greet her. Claire began cleaning up the scraps of paper on the table.

"Your theater presentation this afternoon was highly enjoyable," she overheard Li Wei say to Tyler in the next room.

"Thanks, it's been fun to put them together," Tyler replied.

"How did you get into acting?" Li Wei asked.

"It was always something I enjoyed, but my mom really encouraged me when I got to high school. She had done plays and musicals herself and talked about what fun she had being on stage."

"How is your mom doing?" Li Wei asked with concern.

"I still haven't talked to her," Tyler said dispiritedly. "And she's stopped calling."

"But have you forgiven her?"

"I pray about it, but I'm not sure if I have. Whenever I think about that day, I feel so angry. Does that mean I really haven't forgiven her?"

"At some point you're going to have to let go of your resentment. I don't think you'll be truly healthy until you are able to do this. But forgiving doesn't mean you forget. You can pray that God will soften the memory, or erase it, and He may. But in the end, forgiveness is often a process, Tyler, not just a one-time decision. When the hurt comes in waves, and it will, just keep praying to extend your mom mercy."

Claire was so intent on eavesdropping, she didn't see Bingquin return to her side.

"Will you hold Li Na for a minute?" she asked. "I need to get something out of the bedroom for one of the neighbors."

"Sure," Claire said, taking the baby into her arms. As Bingquin walked away, Claire took in the weight of both conversations. Was Tyler planning on becoming a Chinese resident? And why did he need to forgive his mother?

# Chapter Twenty-Six

"Two, please," Tyler said, passing 140 yuan underneath the circular opening in the plexiglass. After paying, Claire and Tyler walked hand-in-hand to the fully enclosed passenger capsules of the Tianjin Eye, a 120-meter tall Ferris wheel mounted on a bridge.

"It might not be as cool as watching fourth of July fireworks stateside, but—You okay?" he asked Claire, who looked ashen. "Too much standing in line?" They had waited over an hour.

"No, I'm just trying not to get cold feet," she replied.

"You'll be fine," he reassured her. "It's only a half hour, and it moves really slowly. Plus, we have snacks," Tyler said, patting his pocket stuffed with candy and granola bars.

She kissed him on the cheek.

"What was that for?"

"Just for being you," she smiled.

They stepped into a capsule, and the operator closed the door.

"I'm really doing this," Claire said, breathlessly.

"You've done so many brave things this year. What's one more?"

Sitting down on the cream-colored cushioned seat, Claire said, "You must not be scared of anything."

Tyler sat down next to her. "No, I'm scared of one thing."

"What's that?"

"Messing up what we've got going."

He laced his fingers through hers.

"Do you have a poor track record?" she asked curiously.

"Not really. All my relationships have ended with good reason."

The pod began to glide upward, and they looked out at the river in front of them. A tourist boat passed by, and its lights blinked red against the inky black sky.

"Are you doing okay?" he asked as they traveled further towards the top.

"Yes," Claire said, standing up to look out. "I'm actually starting to relax. I guess we just had to get going. Sometimes the anticipation is worse than the thing you fear."

"Wise words, Miss Rogers," Tyler said, coming to put his arm around her waist.

They stared out at the Tianjin skyline, observing towering hotels and high rises. Tyler pointed to a particularly bright section of the city.

"That's the Italian Style Town, over there. And that's where we live," he said, pointing in a different direction.

"Do you see yourself staying here for a long while?" Claire asked.

"Well, the ride is only a half-hour, and I think they kick you out," Tyler joked.

Claire laughed. "Seriously, how many more years do you think you'll teach here before you go back to Iowa?"

Tyler removed his arm from around her waist and went to a different lookout point.

"I don't know if I'll ever go back to Iowa, Claire."

"Really?" Claire replied, trying to play it cool but feeling her heart sink.

"There were reasons why I left, and to my knowledge nothing has changed. Plus, I like it here. My students are enjoyable, I love my job, and I've found that city life suits me."

"But don't you want to have a family one day?"

"I'm not sure. You know how I feel about the nose-wipers," he winked. "Plus, look at the Wangs, they're raising a family here in the city."

"I guess growing up on a farm makes me think every kid should have acres of land."

They were quiet for a moment, contemplating their differences.

"We've reached the top," Tyler declared triumphantly.

Claire sat down. "I don't think I want to look out right now."

Tyler sat next to her.

"Then let me distract you," he whispered, pulling her into his body and kissing her tenderly.

"I'm so sorry you're sick," Tyler said, touching Claire's forehead. "At least your fever seems to be gone for the moment."

"Thanks for coming by," Claire said with a scratchy throat. "I'm sure it's just a cold."

"One of the little hooligans probably gave it to you," he teased, sitting down on the chair across from her couch in the living room.

"I don't want you to stay," Claire insisted.

"Oh thanks. That makes me feel really welcome," Tyler joked.

Claire gave a half-hearted smile. "I don't want you to get sick."

"I'm not worried," he replied. "I've only been sick once since I got here. I must have a strong immune system."

"Or it's because you teach grown-ups," she laughed and then coughed.

"Do you want me to get the soup I brought?"

Tyler ran a hand over his beard, and Claire looked at him with love. He was so handsome, and not just because he was good-looking. He was so kind to her, and that made him attractive.

"No, I'm okay for now."

"How are your numbers? I read that when you're sick, they can really get out of whack."

"They're definitely off-track, but that does seem to happen every time I catch something."

"Hopefully you'll be well in time for our Friday afternoon children's Bible study. I don't want to do it alone."

"Let's pray I'm better by then. I feel badly that I had to call in sick to work. But, if you did have to run the whole thing, you could just make up a really long skit. They love your theater presentations."

"When I was a kid, I would write plays and make my mom and sister do them with me. So, it's not all that different."

"Your dad must have been gone a lot," Claire said, noticing he'd omitted his father from the list of actors.

"Yeah, sometimes people say they feel bad for me because of that, but I didn't really know any differently."

"I bet it was hard on your mom."

Tyler paused, picked up a wooden coaster off the table, and began rolling it around in his hands.

"She never really complained when we were growing up. Even though she had to be a single parent during the week, she always told us our dad worked hard to provide for the family. But maybe-"

"What?" Claire asked, confused.

"Maybe that was just something she said to make us feel better. I don't know if she meant it."

"Why wouldn't she?"

Tyler sighed. "I knew this would come up eventually. But it should wait until you're well enough to have this conversation."

"It's okay," Claire replied with intense curiosity. "I'm not doing anything but laying here."

Tyler paused, mentally debating whether he should continue or leave. Claire's pleading eyes made it clear.

"When I told you I came here because one of my college buddies made it look so fun, I was telling the truth, but only half of it. I had put in my application for the job at the university and was still deciding what I would do if I got the position when I went home one night, unexpectedly, to talk it through with my mom. I found her on the couch making out with another man."

"I'm so sorry," Claire said softly.

"The man, some doctor from the clinic she works at, left quickly. I would have too, but my mom pleaded with me to stay, then proceeded to tell me how lonely she had been since my sister and I moved out. I asked her if my dad knew about her 'extra-curricular activities.' and she said it would break his heart. She begged me not to tell him. She said she'd let him know on her own time frame."

Tyler stood up and walked over to the big window that overlooked the road below.

"I haven't talked to my mom since that day. When I left, my friends and family threw me a party, but even than I avoided her. Can you believe she still hasn't told my dad? Well, at least from the conversations my dad and I have, it doesn't seem like she's told him. Who knows if she's still involved with someone else or not?"

He turned around and faced Claire. "Now you can see why I don't want to go back. I can't imagine how I would sit at a family dinner, acting like everything was normal. And I think if I was around my dad, I wouldn't be able to keep my mom's secret."

"She shouldn't have asked you to do that," Claire said.

"I agree," Tyler replied. "But what should I do now? It's been two years. I don't want to be the one to ruin their marriage."

# Chapter Twenty-Seven

Claire was thankful that the virus was short-lived, and she was able to attend church at the Wangs' apartment on Sunday morning. Being the first weekend in July, it was warm out, so she wore a sundress with spaghetti straps. She enjoyed Tyler's arm wrapped around her shoulder, touching her bare skin.

As she listened to Bingquin read a scripture passage, baby Li Na smiled at her, and she grinned back. Claire would love to have kids one day. If a future with Tyler was at hand, she wasn't sure that would happen. He always talked like he didn't like children—although his actions proved otherwise. But it also wasn't clear if he would return to the United States, and Claire hadn't intended on raising a family in a foreign country.

When Li Wei began his sermon, Claire silenced her ponderings. "Where is home?" he asked the small congregation. Not waiting for a literal response, he continued. "Bingquin and I have lived in many places. Bingquin grew up in Danshui. I grew up in Humen. We met at Bible college in Shenzhen. We moved to Chicago, Illinois for more education, and now we are here in Tianjin. Home is where you hang your hat, some say," said, first in Mandarin and then again in English.

Li Wei sat in a simple wooden chair as he spoke, and his gentle voice captured the room.

Even Li Na made no noise but bounced on her mother's lap.

"Jesus said that foxes have holes and birds have nests, but He had no place to lay His head. Once He entered ministry, He lived a nomadic life, moving from town to town. Does that mean we all should travel spreading the gospel? Some may be called to that, but there is also a great need for many to share the good news in the place where God plants them. So, how do we know where home is?"

Li Wei seemed to look directly at Claire and Tyler, but Claire wasn't sure if it was her imagination.

"Paul says in Second Corinthians that we have an eternal home in heaven, not built by human hands. I challenge us all to recognize that Christ followers are aliens in this world. Our home is heaven. So, when we feel the discomfort of this life, have hope that this is not all there is. But for now, how do we know where to make our earthly home? I implore you to recognize that our true earthly home is found within ourselves. Last night, before I went to bed, I looked in the mirror...and I shaved. Can you tell?"

Li Wei rubbed his hand under his chin. Little ripples of laughter rode through the room.

"This morning, when I went to the bathroom, I brushed my teeth, and I was still there—in the mirror. There's only one person you can't escape from...yourself. Do you like the person you live with? Are you at "home" when you're alone?  When you find Jesus the Christ, you get an address in heaven.  When you live in the center of God's will for your life, cultivating His character and becoming one with Him, you find home on earth."

Li Wei continued his sermon, but Claire became caught in thought.  Maybe it didn't matter which city she lived in.  Perhaps Li Wei was right.  Anywhere could become home, if she was striving to be who God asked her to be and live where he wanted her to reside.  Months ago, she'd prayed to have direction, because she was dissatisfied in Springfield, and the plans for working in Tianjin came through.  Now, snuggled in Tyler's arm, she made a new determination to stay put until God moved her elsewhere.

The afternoon weather was hot and humid.  Clouds to the west indicated storms, but Ethan kept working.  He'd left V.J. and Mark at a job site in town, pouring a cement patio, while he went to dig out and replant three dead boxwoods in the neighboring city of Riverton, at a house where he'd planted bushes the previous fall.  Claire had started a policy to call clients six months after the job had been completed to see how they liked the work.

Ethan had Hannah continue the practice, in order to keep customer retention high, and he'd learned about the diseased shrubs from a customer satisfaction call. With every plant he sold, he promised a one-year guarantee.

As he pushed his foot against the shovel, wedging it around the dead shrub he thought about the sermon he heard the day before, when he went to church with his dad and Izzy. It was as if the pastor knew he was coming. He'd talked about seeds. The part that hit Ethan the most was when he said that the cares of the world and the greed of wealth would choke out what God was doing in a person's life.

Over the course of the last ten months, since Jezmeen had moved in, he'd felt the heaviness of his burdens grow. The mortgage payment on the new house was strappingly high, and he hadn't been able to purchase equipment for his business due to Jezmeen's lavish tastes.

He was stretched too thin with landscaping and building the storefront, and as he read the Bible, he didn't really seem to match up with what a man of good character would look like. He drank too much, didn't really think of anyone besides himself, and he had a woman living with him. That bothered him the most—especially now that Izzy was in the picture. He wanted to be a good influence for her.

The preacher said that God's Word could also be choked out by weeds. Since he'd moved into the new home, he had to pull out bindweed growing around the air-conditioner twice.

Bindweed was also known as Creeping Jenny, but when he thought about his own life, he felt like he was being overpowered by Creeping Jezmeen.

The horizon to the west began to darken considerably, and Ethan felt the weight of the heavy, still air against his skin. His phone buzzed. It was Hannah.

"Ethan," she said breathlessly. "My husband called. A twister touched down five miles from here. What should I do?"

Ethan heard the blare of tornado sirens in the background of the call.

"Head to my house," he said then changed his mind. "No, wait, it's locked up. Jezmeen's not there right now. She's working a double shift. Try the Rogers, Connie is usually home."

"The Rogers?" she asked, confused.

"The white farmhouse right next door," Ethan said with worry. "I'll be there as quickly as I can."

As the call ended, he grabbed his shovel and ran to the truck. It felt odd to head towards the charcoal sky, but he knew that by the time he arrived, whatever damage may occur would be done. He felt hopeless.

He'd felt the same way when his old neighbor, Danielle, didn't want him, but at that time, he picked up and changed directions. He was the master of his life.  Now, someone Sovereign was in control, and he was powerless.

With the windows down, he headed onto the interstate, an eerily cool breeze flowed through the cab.  Papers he had on the floor blew in a spiral motion.  He hadn't prayed since he'd left the old house, next to Danielle's, but now he was desperate.

"God, please get Hannah to safety.  Help the Rogers be home.  And if you really love me, please spare my business.  It's all I care about."

*"Things of this world will pass away, Ethan,"* a Voice replied.

"But God," he pleaded, "I've never had much.  This is my greatest accomplishment.

*"Store up your treasures in heaven, where moth and rust do not destroy."*

"This conversation isn't happening.  I'm talking to myself," Ethan said aloud in his head.

*"Ethan, it takes faith to believe in One you haven't seen."*

"Faith hasn't been my strong suit.  I deal in logic," Ethan replied.

*"I created logic, Ethan.  You don't have to chose one or the other."*

Light rain began to fall on his windshield, and he turned on the wipers.

*"Return to me with your whole heart, Ethan, my very beloved son, and I will shelter you all the days of your life,"* the Voice said.

Claire's cell phone jolted her from a deep sleep. She groggily looked at her insulin pump thinking it was making the noise. Becoming more alert as the ringing continued, she reached for her phone on the nightstand, and the clock's neon blue numbers read 5:25 a.m. She put in the phone's password and saw that it was her mom calling.

"Is everything okay?" she asked with a froggy throat.

"I'm sorry to bother you so early in the morning. I'm at the emergency room with your dad. He's had a stroke."

"Oh my goodness," Claire said, suddenly becoming wide awake.

"About an hour ago, a tornado ripped through our area. Your dad was out in the fields making sure they were ready for the chemical application this week. I had the television on, and the news station broke into the show saying we were under a tornado warning. I texted Jed to get home. Everything happened so fast, Claire."

Connie muffled a sob. "He had just gotten down into the basement where Hannah and I were listening to the radio."

"Hannah?" Claire asked.

"Your replacement at Adams Landscaping."

"Oh," Claire said, remembering.

"Then we heard it," Connie said. "When you were a baby an EF-1 touched down. It sounded just like it. I don't think it was overhead for more than a minute, but it felt like a lifetime. The power went out, so I couldn't see your dad, but after it passed, he said he didn't feel well. I tried to walk him up the stairs, but his body was so rigid. Hannah had to help me. When we got into the kitchen, his eyes didn't look right, and the right side of his body was limp. I didn't know if an ambulance could get through, so Hannah and I got him into my car, and I drove to the hospital."

"How is dad right now?"

"They took him back to do an MRI."

Claire hesitated, not wanting to ask her question, but knowing it would burn away at her if she didn't. "Is he going to be okay?"

"I got him here quickly. The doctor said it's a good thing I did because there's a small window of time with strokes to get the best outcome."

"Mom, I'm so sorry.  As soon as we're off the phone, I'll call the airlines.  I'll be on the first flight home."

"You've only been in China ten weeks, Claire.  Your dad wouldn't want you to leave."

"Is Gretchen coming home?"

"I haven't called her yet.  But with her internship this summer, I can't imagine she'll be able to."

"Then there's no question.  I'll be there tomorrow."

# Chapter Twenty-Eight

Rain fell steadily as Ethan pulled onto Farmingdale Road. The forty-minute drive to get home felt excruciatingly long. After he finished praying, he turned on the radio and listened to the weather reports coming in. When the reporter announced a second report of a tornado touch down happening south of Route 97, Ethan felt his heart sink.

Slowing down, to avoid splintered lumber on the blacktop, he observed that a ranch-style home was missing its roof. The next house fared a little better with only a large section of roofing missing, but a thick tree laid across the driveway, crushing a red pick-up in its path. Only one more house before he'd see his own estate. He felt numb.

Ethan didn't want to look until he knew Hannah and the Rogers were safe. So, he kept his eyes on the road, swerving around siding and wood as he attempted to pull into the Rogers' driveway. But there was too much debris. A quarter of their roof was missing, and the silo was flattened. One of their trees was pulled out of the ground, exposing its roots.

Not hesitating, Ethan jumped out of the truck and ran to the front door, feeling the rain against his skin. Ignoring proper etiquette, he wiggled the door handle. It was locked. It took all his will power to resist looking over at his hoop houses. He sprinted to the back door and found it unlocked. Barging inside the dark mud room, he tried the light switch. No power.

"Hannah, Connie," he called.

There were no responses. He hurried into the kitchen, yelling their names again. The first floor of the house looked fine. Surprisingly, nothing seemed damaged. Eyeing the open door to the basement, he bellowed down into the dark space. Again silence.

Ethan sighed and pulled the cell phone out of his pocket. There was a message from Hannah. *I'm okay, but Connie's husband isn't. She took him to the hospital. Call me.* Ethan quickly dialed Hannah only to get her voicemail box. He exhaled and ran a hand through his wet hair. He couldn't wait any longer. He had to see how much damage his property incurred. Running back out of the house into the light shower, he dared to let his eyes drift to the five greenhouses.

"No... it's not possible," he whispered aloud.

All five structures were intact.

One of the tarps was flapping in the breeze, hanging on by a few nails, but he could see the plants inside remained untouched. He jogged to the gravel parking lot. Then, one by one, he toured each space. Every single plant was standing upright, except in the structure where the tarp was flying.

When he got to "The Once Again Woodland," he stopped in his tracks. A brown leather Bible was laying on the grass, getting soaked by the rain. He stooped down to pick it up. Flipping to the front, he saw the name Claire Rogers written in black ink, on the inside cover. Below her name she had penned a scripture, "*I have loved you with an everlasting love. I have drawn you with unfailing kindness.*" Isaiah 31:3

Ethan fell to his knees, sinking into the wet grass outside the greenhouse. The sun was trying to peek out from behind the clouds, but droplets still fell onto his outstretched face.

"Thank you, Lord," he breathlessly muttered. "Thank you." He squeezed the Bible to his chest. "From this day on, I will try to become the man You want me to be."

"I really don't want you to stay in the house alone," Connie said in a whispered tone as she and Claire sat in the hospital room watching Jed sleep. "I appreciate that you came right here from the airport, but you haven't seen it yet. The roof was partially ripped off, and it's only covered with tarps, thanks to Blackhawk Roofing."

The July afternoon was sunny and hot, but the air-conditioning was keeping the room cool.

Claire had traveled twenty-five hours, then rented a car and drove straight from the St. Louis airport. When she arrived, her dad was awake, but after attempting to visit for a half-hour, he slurred a few words about wanting to take a nap.

Claire thought he looked ten years older, but what concerned her the most was his broken speech. Her mom explained, during one of Claire's layovers, that the stroke had been mild, but it had affected the part of his brain that deals with language. The doctor assured Jed and Connie that with therapy and effort much progress could be made.

"I can sleep in the guest room on the second floor, or the basement," Claire replied, not sure why her mom was fixated on not wanting her in the house when they had so much going on.

Connie sighed. "It's just that I'm nervous about everything structurally, and I won't feel comfortable having anyone sleep there until the construction company takes a look. I wish they could fit us in today, but they can't get to it until tomorrow."

"Okay, fine, I'll stay at a hotel tonight," Claire said, trying to be agreeable because she knew her mom was under so much stress. "At least you have a cushy hospital chair for a bed," she smiled, trying to lighten the mood.

"The doctor said one or two more nights, and then your dad can go home."

"I still don't understand why dad had a stroke. What caused it? Was it the tornado?"

"Well, honey, I didn't want to tell you this, but your dad and I have been under some intense stress the past few days...and it's not just due to the tornado. Someone's trying to get us to sell our home."

"Who?" Claire whispered.

"Jezmeen and Ethan...Well, the letter said Jezmeen hired the lawyer, but Ethan's name is mentioned, too."

"No," Claire uttered.

"Supposedly our property line isn't accurate. The house falls on their land. So, it's either sell the house or get into a lawsuit."

"I can't believe Ethan would do that to you. He never showed any interest in your home, or your property lines, when I worked for him. Have you talked with him?"

"Not yet. We just got the letter on Friday afternoon, before the tornado. Monday, we were going to go to the County Clerk's to look at the records ourselves. Actually, the plan was to go when your dad got back from the fields."

"So, dad was carrying that burden, and then he raced home to avoid a tornado."

"The doctor said his stroke was caused by a clot in a blood vessel in his neck. The clot caused the blood flow to be cut off, which in turn, damaged the section of his brain that helps him speak."

"Will he be able to talk normally again…I mean without slurring his words or having so much trouble forming what he wants to say?"

"Since his stroke was so mild, the speech and language pathologist said there's a great chance of him making a full recovery. It will just take time."

"I'm going to discuss this whole thing with Ethan," Claire fumed. "I can't believe he would sink so low."

"Don't worry about it, honey. When your dad is better, he and I can take care of it. You don't need to fight this battle. Afterall, you'll be going back to China in a few days, right?"

"No, I bought a one-way ticket."

"Why?" her mom asked, wide-eyed.

"I knew you needed me here. I'm where I'm supposed to be."

Connie reached across the chair and hugged her daughter.

"Oh, Claire," she said, drawing her into her arms.

Claire's shoulders relaxed for the first time in over a day.

"I'm going to go check out the house," Claire said, as they withdrew from the embrace. "I need to see how much damage we're dealing with."

"Okay, just be careful, and please promise me you won't go into your room. It could be really dangerous up there."

"Do you need me to get you some clean clothes or a toothbrush? Have you even left this place since dad got admitted?"

"I haven't," Connie said, sheepishly. "Both would be nice." She smiled warmly at Claire. "I'm so thankful you're here. Gretchen said she'd come on Saturday."

Claire stood up to go, and Connie rested her hand on her arm. "In all the whirlwind of your arrival, I forgot to tell you how nice you look. Your hair, your make-up, your clothes...you look quite beautiful."

"Thanks, Mom. My friend Trina got a hold of me."

Claire pulled into the driveway, as far as she could. She was shocked at the amount of debris in the front lawn and she saw her comforter was stuck on a branch in one of the trees in the backyard. Her mom was right. A good portion of the roof had been torn off, and she could see the triangular beams that held the wood and shingles in the place for so many years.

A few of the windows on the second floor were broken, and she was careful to avoid the shards of glass, as she walked in the back door and up the stairs to the second floor. After she packed a bag for her mom and dad, she walked down the hall to the stairs that led to her room. Curiosity was eating at her. She looked up and saw the door had been blown off, so sunlight was streaming in from above. The steps were littered with wood, glass, and a few pieces of clothes. All it would take to go up was...

"Claire," she heard a voice bellow.

# Chapter Twenty-Nine

The voice sounded familiar. Claire headed back down to the first floor and found Ethan entering the living room, about to yell her name a second time. He looked awestruck when he caught sight of her, and a large grin broke across his face.

Claire stared at Ethan. He was wearing one of the brown work shirts she had printed for all employees, a pair of blue jeans, and his fedora. He seemed awfully happy for a man who was trying to steal her house.

"Claire, I thought I saw you when I was at the greenhouses. When did you get home?"

"This afternoon."

"How's your dad doing?"

"He had a stroke, and it affected his speech, but all things considered, we're thankful his impairments aren't worse," she said curtly.

"Yeah, Hannah told me she thought he had a stroke, but that's all I knew. I should've called your mom," he replied, sounding genuinely sorry.

"So, you'd call her to ask about my dad, and then chit-chat about how many days she has until you give her the eviction notice," she sarcastically, leaning against the wall next to the stairs.

"What are you talking about?" he asked.

"Oh, sure, act like you don't know that your girlfriend...or is she your wife now...has hired a lawyer because she wants this house."

"Jezmeen is not my wife," he said emphatically. "And I don't understand what you're saying."

"You mean to tell me you have *no* idea that Jezmeen says *your* property line falls on this estate. Supposedly, after all these years we've owned this land, it's not really ours."

"That doesn't make any sense," Ethan said, frowning. "I have a copy of the plot I purchased and its dimensions."

"Well, show it to your girlfriend," Claire said, still fuming.

"I will, but I want you to go with me. We need to clear the air."

"I can't," Claire stated. "I have to take a bag to my mom, and then I'm staying in a hotel tonight."

"Why?"

"My mom doesn't think it's safe to stay here, until she hears otherwise from the construction company tomorrow."

"Please don't stay in a hotel. Come to my new house. We have plenty of guest rooms. It's the least I can do given the circumstances. I want to make this right."

Ethan sat at the kitchen table waiting for Jezmeen and Izzy to get home from their shopping trip. He texted Jez that there was a matter of urgency needing her attention, and she said they were headed back with Chinese take-out.

Izzy had moved in days earlier. She was shaken-up by the news of the tornado and asked if she could stay with Ethan during her grandma's weeks for the remainder of the summer. She said that knowing Ethan could have been killed made her realize she wanted more time with him. Izzy's grandma agreed to the arrangement, and Jezmeen thought it was a great plan, so Izzy took over the guest room down the hall from the master suite.

Ethan picked a callus on his hand while he stewed. Jez never mentioned wanting to acquire the Rogers' farmhouse. Why would she want it, and what would make her hire a lawyer? He hadn't *really* talked with Jezmeen in weeks, but surely she wouldn't keep a secret this big from him.

On a happier note, Claire was back, Ethan mused, and she was...beautiful. He remembered how lovely she looked at the Christmas party—when she announced she was leaving. Would she be staying?

He needed a new administrative assistant. Hannah called and said her husband asked her to get a new job. He didn't think it was safe enough for her to work in the hoop houses. Maybe Claire would want her old job back—and not just because she was good at it. Ethan shook his head. It wasn't right to think about Claire when he was living with Jezmeen. Even without knowing scripture, he knew it was wrong.

"We're back," sang a young voice. Izzy came bounding into the house, swinging two bags. "I got three new school outfits."

"And we brought orange chicken and fried rice," Jezmeen said, following happily with a white plastic bag of food.

Ethan remained seated, looking glum.

"Well, it looks like someone had a bad day," Izzy observed.

"Hey, Izzy, would you mind eating in the family room? You can watch tv in there. I need to talk with Jezmeen in the sunroom...privately."

"Uh oh," Izzy said, looking at Jez. "You're in trouble."

Jezmeen laughed nervously. "Here, take the whole bag, and find your dinner. We'll be in shortly."

Ethan and Jezmeen moved to the wicker furniture in the sunroom, and she turned on the fan.

"It's hot in here," she said, sitting down at the glass table, across from him.

"Claire's back," Ethan said, not mincing words.

"Oh, good," Jez said bitingly. "How's the little thief?"

"Don't call her that," Ethan retorted. "She's going to stay the night here."

"Why?"

"Her dad and mom are at the hospital."

"Oh right, he had a stroke…Why can't she stay at her house?"

"Part of the roof is torn off, and her mom isn't comfortable having her sleeping there until someone can come to look at the house tomorrow. She was going to stay at a hotel, but we have all the extra space upstairs."

"Sure, fine, what's one more guest," Jez replied, coolly.

Ethan heard crickets chirping outside the windows.

"That's only part of what I wanted to talk to you about," he said, setting his folded hands on the smooth table.

"Our dinner's getting cold."

Ethan ignored the comment. "There's more. Claire mentioned something about a letter, a lawsuit, property lines, us trying to acquire their house. Do you have any idea what that is all about?"

Jezmeen felt her stomach turn. She hadn't planned to continue with the deception, once she realized there wasn't anything she could do to permanently alter the property records. But to her surprise, Izzy had mailed the letter while Jez was at the Accessor's Office. She had been helping Ethan in the greenhouses, and he asked her to feed Chewy. When Izzy saw the envelope on the counter, stamped and addressed, she told Jezmeen she had wanted to be kind and take it to the mailbox down the long driveway for her.

After Izzy went back to the greenhouses, blissfully unaware of what she had done, Jez ran to the mailbox to see if the letter was still there, but it had already been picked up. The damage was done, and Jezmeen had been waiting for it to catch up to her. She knew it was only a matter of time.

"I have a lawyer friend at the bar who showed me our property documents, and it appeared as if their house fell on our rightful land," she lied.

"Jez, I have a copy of the plot I bought. I *do not* own their land."

"Are you sure you read it correctly?" she said, desperately.

"Before I started building the house, I had to get a permit for it. It was zoned for farming and the greenhouses. When they surveyed the property, the boundaries were reconfirmed. I know it's accurate."

Jezmeen played the game Battleship once in junior high school. She knew her ship had been hit on all sides, and it was sunk. So, she rose to the surface of the water waving a white flag, and she wasn't about to indict Izzy.

"I love their house, Ethan," she said, pleadingly. "I have since the first time I went inside for the Christmas party. Ever since you told me you wouldn't plant a vineyard, I thought about other ways I could contribute to the business. Then, I came up with the idea to run a bed and breakfast. The Rogers' farmhouse seemed perfect. Customers could stay overnight and then shop at the greenhouses and storefront."

"So, you wrote them a dishonest letter?"

"Yes, but—" she looked away from his eyes.

"What?"

"I didn't really intend for them to see it."

"I don't understand."

"I wasn't going to mail it…" Jezmeen replied, knowing she couldn't blame it all on Izzy. She would have sent it if she had thought she could have pulled off the plan. "Never mind," she sighed.

Ethan stared at her, wondering what she was hiding. "Who did you hire as your lawyer?"

"Myself," she said, coming clean. It would be easier to tear the whole band-aid off at once.

"But Claire said you hired a lawyer."

"I made one up."

"So, you lied about the property lines, and you pretended to be a lawyer?"

"Yes."

"Did you include me in the lie?"

"Yes."

He held his tongue, waiting for her to reveal more. Jezmeen exhaled.

"I said that we both owned this land. I made it seem like you were in on the whole thing."

Ethan seethed with anger.

"If they *had* agreed to sell their home, how were you planning on paying for it?"

"Your royalty checks," Jezmeen shrugged, lying again. She didn't want to admit she had a nest egg.

"You're going to have to explain this all again—when Claire gets here."

"Fine," Jezmeen said with an air of haughtiness. "I'm a big girl. I can handle it."

Ethan ran his hands through his hair.

"This really embarrassed me, Jez. For someone who's been saying it's so important that I make a good name for myself in the community, you certainly are likely to ruin it with one rash decision."

Jezmeen could see the worry etched on Ethan's face, but after accepting so much blame, she felt the need to justify herself.

"Maybe if you didn't make it so hard to live with you, I wouldn't have had to—"

"You think I'm hard to live with? Who's the one spending all my money, having parties all the time, and lying to the neighbors?" Ethan retorted.

"If you showed even the littlest bit of appreciation for all I've done—decorating your house from bottom to top, connecting you with people of influence, hanging out with *your* sister—"

"I thought you liked doing things with Izzy?"

Jezmeen cooled. "I do. I shouldn't have made that sound like a chore— I adore Izzy."

As Jezmeen's flare died, so did Ethan's. "Jez, I've been thinking about "us" for a long time. You know we've been drifting apart for months-"

"Don't go there, Ethan. Not right now. Let's get through this thing with Claire, and then we can talk."

Ethan exhaled. They sat in silence for a moment. "Okay, but know this conversation isn't done."

# Chapter Thirty

While in the shower, Jezmeen replayed the conversation she'd just finished with Claire and Ethan. Claire had arrived from the hospital looking exhausted. But sparks of anger had flown from her eyes as they discussed the letter—once again.

Jezmeen should have called the Rogers as soon as the note had been sent, but a small part of herself wanted to see how it would all play out. Jez wished she could rewind the whole situation, especially when he saw the way Ethan looked at Claire.

The six weeks in Tianjin seemed to turn the girl into a woman, with hair swept into a French twist and clothes that flattered her petite figure. Claire had been surprisingly forgiving, even though Jez could tell she wasn't happy. Claire didn't outrightly say that letter added to the stress that caused her dad's stroke, but she implied it. Jezmeen took no blame for Jed's health crisis though. She hadn't caused the tornado to swirl through Farmingdale Road.

Ethan had told Izzy it was a miracle that his business was still standing. Supposedly he'd given his life to Jesus Christ, whatever that meant. Izzy was happy for him, but Jezmeen didn't care so much about his spirituality.

Her concerns were focused on losing the connection with Izzy...and being homeless. She thought about Ethan's ominous words...the conversation wasn't done. They were drifting apart. Jezmeen turned off the water and grabbed the towel that hung over the top of the shower door. After changing into her pajamas, she slipped into the dark bedroom. Ethan had already turned off the light.

"Claire forgot her shampoo. I told her you'd bring her ours," Ethan said stoically from the bed.

Jezmeen didn't respond, she just turned and went back in the bathroom. Then she headed down the hallway, passing Izzy's closed door. Izzy had been so patient, since neither Jez nor Ethan spent much time with her that evening. The door to the room Claire was using was also shut, and Jezmeen knocked quietly.

"Come in," Claire said.

Jezmeen entered to see Claire propped up against the headboard, pillows behind her back, reading the Bible in the light of the lamp next to the double bed. Claire had already washed her face, and without the make-up, she looked less sophisticated—and more tired. For a brief second Jezmeen felt sorry for her. She'd traveled all day, gone straight to the hospital, and then had their "meeting."

"Here's the shampoo," she said curtly, placing it on the dresser. "Need anything else?" she asked to be polite.

"Actually, I think I left my water bottle at the hospital. Could you let me know where I could get a glass? I know it's late. I'm sorry for the inconvenience."

"No trouble," Jezmeen replied. "I'll bring you one."

Jezmeen saw a pack of fruit snacks, a granola bar, and a few pieces of candy on the bedside table, and she smirked inwardly at Claire's sweet tooth. Jez closed the door behind her, and started down the hall to the kitchen, when Izzy popped her head out of her room.

"Jez," she whispered.

"You okay?" Jezmeen asked with genuine concern.

"Yeah, I just heard you talking to Claire, and I wanted to check on you. I know you and Ethan didn't want me eavesdropping on your conversations tonight, so I didn't, but I can't stand not knowing what's going on."

Jezmeen headed into Izzy's room. Izzy had chosen the white guest room to be hers for the remainder of the summer. The walls, comforter, throw pillows, and lamps were all white. The only pop of color came from the green plant she'd taken from one of the hoop houses. Ethan told her what it was, but she couldn't remember, maybe a hosta? She sat down on the edge of the bed, as Izzy curled up under the covers.

"Can you tell me *anything*?" Izzy pleaded, with all the hunger for gossip a young teen girl could muster.

Jezmeen sighed. "Well, I made a mistake, and we're all working through it."

"Whatever you did couldn't be that bad."

Jezmeen knew if she told Izzy the whole truth, she might like her less.

"I said I wanted to buy Claire's parents' house."

They had introduced Izzy to Claire after their "meeting" had ended.

"That's all?"

"I guess I said it a little too forcefully," Jezmeen ran her hand through her wet hair, untangling the loose strands, resisting the urge to say Izzy had a part in it.

"So, why's Claire spending the night?"

"Her mom and dad are at the hospital, and her mom didn't want her staying in their house until someone came to look at it."

"That makes sense. I wouldn't want to stay in a house if the roof was ripped off. I bet the wind would howl the whole night, and I'd be so scared." Izzy stopped talking and stared at Jezmeen. "You look sad."

"I just hope I didn't mess up too badly," Jezmeen said, running her hand against the comforter, smoothing invisible wrinkles.

"Now that Ethan's a Christian, he'll forgive you. Jesus is all about forgiveness. And, of course, I forgive you, even if I don't know exactly what you did."

"Thanks, Izzy," Jez said.

After they talked for a few more minutes, Jezmeen turned off the light and said goodnight. As she gently closed the door, she realized she still had to get water for Claire. Claire probably thought she was delaying on purpose. She hurried down to the kitchen and filled a glass from the refrigerator's dispenser.

She gently knocked on Claire's door. When there was no response, she pushed it open a crack. The bedside lamp had been turned off, but the light from the hallway revealed Claire was asleep.

Jezmeen carefully carried the water to the bedside table and pushed aside the snacks to make room for the glass. As she was about to leave, Jezmeen caught sight of a small black device on the extra pillow next to Claire. An alarm clock? Jezmeen wondered. For a brief moment, Jezmeen was tempted to change the time.

Claire had mentioned she'd be getting up early, so she could see her dad as soon as visiting hours started. She'd be eating breakfast with Ethan. Jezmeen decided Claire needed a few hours of extra sleep. Afterall, she'd just gotten off a plane from China. She grabbed the little black rectangle.

That's odd, she thought. It felt like it had something attached to it. She couldn't see clearly, but she hit a button that made the letters "BG" appear on a neon green screen. Up and down arrows ran along the side of the black box.

Maybe this was the type of alarm they used in China, she reasoned. Not knowing what to do, she pressed the up arrow. 100. 125. 150. 200. 225. 250. A red screen flashed "High BG." Jezmeen stopped. The screen just kept blinking. So, she hit a circular button that read "ACT."

The words "enter food grams" appeared. What was this thing? A weird dieting device? Afterall, Claire kept food by the bed. Maybe she needed one. Jez hit the up arrow a bunch of times, but the numbers still didn't make sense. She didn't want to mess with the device anymore, so she hit the circular button, but another screen flashed the word "bolus."

Jezmeen knew she needed to leave it alone, but the screen wouldn't stop blinking, and she didn't want Claire to wake up and realize someone had messed with it. Jezmeen pushed the up arrow a few more times, hit the ACT button, and it stopped flashing. Gently setting the strange thing back on the pillow, she tiptoed out of the room, and closed the door behind her.

It was dark when Claire awoke to a racing heart. Where was she? Ethan's house, she realized foggily. Was there a clock in the room? She looked around. Not seeing any light, she reached over to the floor and groped for her phone. She'd placed it near the edge of the bed.

As she pulled it up, she felt nauseous. She knew she didn't feel well, but why? Had she contracted some virus on the plane home? It was four o'clock in the morning, she gathered, as she unlocked her phone. Claire felt parched, like she had been sunbathing in the desert.

She wished she could remember if Jezmeen had brought her a glass of water. Claire reached for the bedside lamp and turned it on. She saw a glass on the side table, and with a quivering hand she grabbed the cup and downed the whole thing. Yet, she still felt thirsty. What was wrong with her? She couldn't think straight, which only heightened her anxiety.

Maybe she should go wake someone, but she dreaded being a troublesome guest. Think, Claire, think, she told herself. She sat up and felt the tubing at her waist tug. Yes, she thought. I need to check my insulin pump. She reached for the device. Why did it say her blood sugar was so low?  That didn't make any sense.  Before she went to bed, she was in the normal range.

She was thankful she had put two cinnamon candies by her bed.  She reached for one, unwrapped the red cellophane, and popped it into her mouth.  Claire felt so tired, like she had to go back to sleep, but she also instinctively knew something wasn't right.  She was so disoriented.

I need to take my blood sugar reading, she thought.  Looking around for her bag, she saw it under the window.  As she tried to get up, she felt vomit burn her esophagus, so she made her way to the bathroom in the hallway.

The yellow bile scorched her throat as it hit the sink.  She felt sweaty and weak. Even though she wanted to clean up, she didn't have the energy.  She needed more water.  Dragging herself back to the bedroom, she retrieved the glass and then filled it from the bathroom sink.

"Claire, are you okay?"

The deep voice startled her, and she turned around to see Ethan in the doorway.

"I don't think so," she uttered, grateful to see another human.  She would have even been glad to see Jezmeen.

"What's wrong?" he asked, with concern in his eyes.

"I don't know.  Something's wrong with my blood sugar."

"What do you mean?"

"I need to get the testing supplies out of my bag."

"Are you diabetic?" Ethan asked, remembering some of these terms from his medical transcribing days.

"Yes," Claire replied.

"Okay, let me help you."

Ethan held her as they walked back to the guest room. Then he rummaged through her tote, locating the clear plastic bag containing the supplies. He watched her poke her finger, wipe the first drop of blood, then put the testing device against her finger for the next drop.

"54," Claire exclaimed. "I don't think it's ever been that low."

"What did you eat for dinner?" he asked, dropping to his knees beside the bed where she sat.

"A salad and some chicken from the cafeteria at the hospital. I had a roll, but it wouldn't do this to my blood sugar," she said, opening the bottle of glucose tablets found in her supply bag. She needed fast-acting sugar.

"Do you have any strips to test if you have ketones?" Ethan asked, recalling something he'd typed about a patient.

"Back at the house, in my bathroom, but the loft is destroyed." She laid back down, unable to hold herself up.

"I'll go look," Ethan replied quickly.

"Don't risk it, Ethan," Claire replied. "It's dark…and dangerous."

"It's either that, or I'll call you an ambulance—I may have to do that either way," he said, taking in her wretched appearance.

Claire didn't want to be taken to the hospital. That was the last thing her dad and mom needed.

"By the time I get back, we'll see if the glucose tablet helped. We need to get your numbers up," Ethan replied.

# Chapter Thirty-One

Ethan was thankful he had brought a flashlight. Ethan had never been to the second floor of their home. Where there should have been a door, leading up to the converted attic, there was only a door frame and flowing air.

The white beam of the flashlight revealed broken glass, splintered lumber, and clothing littering the steps. He pointed the light upward. A dresser drawer rested on the top two stairs, but besides the debris, the stairway looked stable.

Even though he hadn't slept much, he was wide awake, and adrenaline coursed through his veins. Carefully treading up the mess, Ethan arrived at the top and forced himself to focus. He couldn't waste any time. Something was seriously wrong with Claire.

Using the flashlight to scan the room, all he saw was rubble. He couldn't make-out where a bathroom could be. To the right, there was what remained of a wall, and to the left just debris. If he tried to walk into the room, he would be met with a sagging pile of splintered boards, roofing, and furniture.

He groaned. It didn't look like he would be able to find a box of test strips in the clutter and driving to a twenty-four-hour drugstore in town would take too long. Ethan kicked at the boards in front of him, and one started to edge closer to his face.  Thinking better of that choice, he knelt down and began rummaging through the things he could reach.  He brushed aside soft pink insulation from the attic, books, and even a pillow.  Then he crawled on his knees, as far into the mess as he could go.  He could see the bed frame hidden under a pile of lumber, a sweater, and a lamp shade, but there were no boxes of ketone strips.

*Where, God?  Where should I look?*  Ethan prayed.  It had only been two days since the tornado, and nothing felt normal, especially now that Claire was back.  But talking with God, through short, whispered conversations had become part of his new routine.

*Turn around.*  He pivoted and crawled back to the steps.  Now he was right where he began, and again he saw nothing.  He didn't want to fail Claire.  He'd read about ketoacidosis while typing a transcription, and he knew the body could start to shut down if blood sugar levels didn't get under control.

It's hopeless, he thought.  With frustration he started down the stairs, nearly tripping over the dresser drawer.  His near fall moved the drawer a half-inch and laying there, crushed, was a box of ketone strips.  Ethan yelped with joy and grabbed the lost treasure.  When Ethan got back to the guest bedroom, he found Claire looking comatose against the headboard.  He ran to her side and began to shake her shoulders.

"Claire," he shouted.

Her eyelids fluttered, and she mumbled, "I was just taking a cat nap."

Ethan's heart felt like it would burst out of his chest. He had thought...

Claire reached for her insulin pump. "The glucose tablet and candy are bringing up my blood sugar. I just feel so tired," she said reassuringly.

"Do you still want these?" Ethan asked, extending the box towards her.

"What's going on in here?" Izzy asked, rubbing her eyes, standing in the doorway.

"Claire isn't feeling well," Ethan said.

"Oh," Izzy replied. "I heard someone yell."

"Sorry," Ethan said self-consciously.

Claire took the box from Ethan and shakily got to her feet. "I'll go do this," she said, walking slowly to the bathroom.

"Is Claire going to be okay?" Izzy asked with concern.

"I hope so," Ethan said.

"Maybe she's pregnant," Izzy said.

"Why do you say that?" Ethan asked, cocking an eyebrow.

"You gave her a box," Izzy replied. "And then she went to the bathroom."

"How do you know about pregnancy tests?"

"I saw my mom take one once. She wasn't pregnant though."

"Claire isn't sick because she's pregnant, Izzy. She has diabetes."

"What's that?"

"It's a condition where your pancreas doesn't make insulin or can't use insulin as well as it should."

"So, you gave her some insulin?"

"No, she's taking a test to see if she has ketones in her system. If she does, that means her blood sugar is too low, and she may need to go to the hospital."

"Yikes, that doesn't sound good."

"You don't have to stay up, Izzy. Sorry that I woke you."

"Why don't we pray for her, Ethan?"

"Good idea, sis," Ethan said, with a small smile.

They stood in the doorway, and Izzy said a prayer for Claire. Then she wrapped Ethan in a big hug before heading back to bed, making Ethan promise to wake her if Claire took a turn for the worst. Ethan had just sat down in the oversized gray chair in the corner of the room when Claire returned.  She made her way to the bed, as if she was forging through quicksand.

"So?" Ethan asked.

"Well, the bad news is that I have a small amount of ketones in my system, but the good news is that I figured out why."  She pulled the comforter over her body and leaned against the pillows.  "Somehow my pump was programmed to give me a large bolus dose.  When I was in the bathroom, I scrolled through the dosing history, and it's no wonder I feel so sick.  I have too much insulin in my system, and it caused my blood sugar to drop really low."

"Do you need me to take you to the hospital?"

"No, now that I know why this happened, I can treat it.  I've already reprogrammed my device."

"Did you bump it in your sleep or something?"

"No, a programming error like that was the result of someone manually setting the device."

"Who would've done that?" Ethan asked, regretting the words, as they both sat silently thinking of the same name.  "What can I do for you now?"

"Do you have a few water bottles?  I'll need to keep flushing out my system."

"Sure, I'll go get you some."

"And if you could hand me my tote, I'd appreciate it. I have some extra snacks in there. I'll keep eating every hour or so until my numbers are up."

Ethan retrieved her bag and set it on the floor beside her.

"Thanks," she said.

As he was exiting, she called to him. "Hey, Ethan, thanks for getting the test strips. I can't believe you found them."

"I had some help," he replied.

Claire knew she'd need to stay awake to monitor her blood sugar level and eat glucose tablets every fifteen minutes until her numbers started reaching a normal reading. She still felt sick to her stomach and very tired, but she knew who she could call for support.

Reaching for her cell phone, she pulled up Tyler's number. It was nearly five in the morning in Springfield, and her brain was still too foggy to compute the exact time in Tianjin, but she knew it was probably afternoon.

When she left for the Midwest, Claire was too rushed, and burdened with details, to talk with Tyler, but she texted him before the plane took off. She attempted to call him at the first layover, but it went straight to voicemail, and she knew he was teaching during the second layover. It had been three days since they'd spoken, and she longed for the comfort of his voice—especially now.

He answered on the first ring. "Claire," he exclaimed, with a mixture of relief and worry.

She wanted to cry, as she felt the love in his voice at just the exhalation of her name.

"Is your dad okay?" he asked.

"He will be," she said wearily, wondering if her quick decision to call Tyler was a good one. She felt so miserable.

"What's wrong? I don't know if it's the connection, but you sound sick."

"I'm having a little issue with my blood sugar, but I'll be okay," she replied, hoping she sounded reassuring.

"I wish I was there to help."

"Me too," she said. Claire missed Tyler so much her heart ached. He truly had become her best friend, just as he declared he would. "I don't have a lot of energy, but I needed to hear your voice," she said. "And I need help staying awake."

"Claire, maybe you should call your doctor," Tyler said. "This doesn't seem right."

"I'll call my doctor in a few hours, when his practice opens. Everything's going to be fine, but could you just talk to me? I'm too tired to make the effort."

"Sure, sweetheart. What do you want me to talk about?"

"Anything," she replied, laying back on her pillow and resting the phone next to her ear. Even her arm felt fatigued holding the phone.

"Okay. I'll tell you about-" Tyler began.

"Hold on a second," Claire said. Ethan had entered the room with water bottles and containers of orange juice."

"I did a search on my phone, and it said fruit juice can raise your blood sugar. All I had was orange," Ethan said.

"Thanks," she said softly, putting her hand over her phone.

"Oh, are you talking to someone?" he asked, quizzically.

"My boyfriend, Tyler."

Ethan looked surprised, but he didn't say anything. He set the drinks on the crowded bedside tabletop. "I'll be in the office, down the hall, if you need me." Ethan gently shut the door on his way out.

"Who was that?" Tyler questioned, once Claire got back on the call.

"Ethan."

"Who's Ethan?"

"My neighbor. I couldn't stay in my house tonight. I'll explain when I have more energy."

"Okay," Tyler said, hesitantly. "Let's see," he continued. "I was going to tell you a love story."

"My favorite," she mumbled.

"There was this man, a twenty-seven-year old college-professor, with a well-maintained beard."

Claire giggled weakly.

"A very handsome young man, I might add. And this man flew across the ocean to escape from his problems, only to find himself very lonely and lost in a new city. The man found love when he found God, but he still longed for a companion. So, his friends told him to pray, and that's what he did."

Claire reached for the juice and opened the cap.

"The man prayed for a year with no answers, but then a girl with a very heavy suitcase came into his life. She was so cute and kind, he liked her instantly. As the weeks passed, he found he wanted to spend all of his time with her. Then one day, this young lady was playing with a baby after church. She was making the baby laugh by playing peek-a-boo, and even though this very good-looking man claimed children were a nuisance, he wanted a few one day, and this beautiful woman adored them. And she adored God. So, what was the man to do but confirm he was in love right then and there."

Claire smiled. She looked at the insulin pump, and her blood sugar had risen again. Tyler, or the orange juice, maybe both, had a good effect, and she praised God silently.

# Chapter Thirty-Two

Ethan drummed the kitchen table with his fingers. He'd finished his bowl of cereal and was debating what to do about his day. V.J. and Mark were finishing a concrete patio, and he was supposed to be putting plants around the fence line at the property. He really couldn't afford to take time off, especially since he was already two weeks behind schedule. But he didn't feel right leaving Claire, and he definitely needed to talk to Jezmeen.

He checked his watch. Seven a.m. He'd hoped Claire would come to see him, while he was studying the Bible in his office, but she hadn't. While he was upstairs, Ethan prayed and read. He was so troubled about all the events that had transpired over the last twenty-four hours, he needed Divine wisdom. But, when he didn't hear anything directly from God, he restlessly began working on tweaking an upcoming landscaping design until he went down to breakfast.

And now he sat, trying to decide if he should stay home or go to work. Could he trust Jezmeen and Claire under the same roof? Jezmeen admitted to her wrongdoing with the Rogers' house, but would she really have messed with Claire's insulin pump? Certainly, Jezmeen wouldn't have stooped so low.

Ethan needed to know if Claire was stable, and he needed to find out if Jezmeen had a part in

all that transpired.  So, he trudged up the stairs.
None of the sleeping beauties stirred as he walked
down the hallway.  When he reached the guest
room, he knocked quietly on the door.  Given no
answer, he opened the door a crack and peeked
inside.

Claire was asleep.  Why hadn't he noticed
how lovely she was when she found him tangled in
the tarp so long ago?  He didn't know whether he
should wake her or let her get some rest.

He stood there mentally debating what to
do for minutes before deciding he needed to know
if she was doing any better.  Ethan softly walked to
her side and touched her on the shoulder.  When
she didn't respond, he whispered her name.

Her eyelids fluttered open.  "Hey," she
uttered.

"Sorry to wake you."

She looked at her insulin pump.  "I'm almost
back to normal."

"That's great."

"I'm still feeling really tired.  Do you mind if I
stay until this afternoon?  I'll just tell my mom I had
really bad jet lag and couldn't sleep all night, so I
wanted to rest.  I already planned to meet the
person from the construction company at three, so
I'll set my alarm."

"Sure, that's fine.  I'll get you some
breakfast.  And Izzy will be here, if you need

anything, once I go to work. You're welcome to rummage through the pantry and fridge anytime."

"Okay, thanks."

"It's the least I can do...after all that's happened."

"None of it was your fault," Claire said, giving Ethan a weary smile.

"Well, I take responsibility for the company that I keep, and indirectly this does come back to me." Ethan reached down and touched her shoulder. "And for that I am truly sorry."

After Ethan left the room, he stood outside the door wondering if he should deal with Jezmeen now or take care of it later. If Jezmeen had messed with Claire's insulin pump, then he couldn't leave.

Without knocking, Ethan entered the master bedroom. Jezmeen's beautiful brown hair was fanned out on the white pillowcase. She looked so peaceful. Ethan strode to the side of the bed, and sat down, inching her body over to make room. Jezmeen felt the movement and stirred.

"I need to talk to you," Ethan said gruffly and then regretted his tone. He was trying to live like a new man, with a changed attitude. "Good morning, Jezmeen."

"Hey," she croaked, rolling to her side. "What time is it?  Is everything okay?"

"It's a little after seven. Sorry to wake you." Ethan didn't want to jump to accusations. "It's been kind of a wild night." Jezmeen's eyes opened, and Ethan was reminded again how striking they were. "Claire got really sick."

"Oh no," Jez said, pulling her body to a sitting position. "Something she ate?"

"I don't think so. Claire's a diabetic. Somehow her insulin pump got reprogrammed. She got too much insulin and her body started to go haywire."

"Is she going to be okay?"

"I think so. Thankfully she woke up and figured out her pump was continuously dosing insulin. If she hadn't, I would've taken her to the hospital."

"Wow," Jezmeen whispered.

If she had done anything wrong, Ethan couldn't tell from her expression. "Do you know how that could have happened?"

"What? Do you mean did I mess with her pump?" Jezmeen said defensively.

"Yes."

"I didn't even know she was a diabetic. How would I have done something like that?" she huffed.

"When you brought her the shampoo last night," Ethan recalled, "did you touch anything in the room."

"No," Jezmeen answered honestly. She hadn't touched anything when she delivered the bottle.

"Did you see her insulin pump?

"I don't even know what an insulin pump looks like," she said, her voice raising.

Ethan took a deep breath and exhaled. Nothing was clear. Somehow Claire's pump had been recalculated, and Jezmeen claimed to be innocent. Maybe Izzy had touched it by accident.

"Well, I guess it was Izzy, if it wasn't me, and it wasn't you. I'll have to call Wayne and have him come and talk to her along with me. She's got to know, even if it was in naivete, she can't do things like that."

"Wait," Jezmeen interjected. "Izzy didn't do anything."

Ethan pursed his lips. "How do you know?"

Jezmeen couldn't believe she was about to come clean for the second time in twenty-four hours to protect Izzy. "After I dropped off the shampoo, Claire asked for a glass of water. Izzy and I got talking. When I finally brought her the glass, she was asleep. I thought the thing on her pillow was an alarm. She looked so tired, and I heard her say she was going to get up early."

Ethan frowned.

"I was just trying to be kind," Jezmeen lied. "I had no idea that it wasn't an alarm clock."

Ethan sat silently, trying to forge through all his thoughts to figure out what to do next.

"Jez, I think it would be best if you left," he said deliberately and slowly.

"What? You're kicking me out?" she cried.

Ethan remained calm. "I think it would be the best for both of us."

"Forcing me into homelessness would be the best for me?" she retorted angrily. "You know I don't have any place to stay."

"Well, you did tell Izzy you made good money bartending," Ethan said, remembering an earlier conversation. "I imagine you will be able to find something."

"After all I've done for you, you're just tossing me to the wind. Really nice. And Izzy said you'd be forgiving. So much for the love of God," Jezmeen said angrily. Then she scooted across the bed and locked herself in the bathroom.

When Ethan came home with lunch, he saw Izzy in the family room watching television. She waved, and he promised to be right back down with her sandwich as soon as he delivered Claire's salad.

Claire's door was partially open, and she was on the phone when he got there, so he left the bag on her bed. She waved a thank-you, and he exited. Ethan headed downstairs and plopped down next to Izzy on the sofa.

"Jezmeen wouldn't like you sitting on the clean couch with your dirty work pants," Izzy sang.

"I know," Ethan sighed.

"Where is Jezmeen, by the way?" Izzy asked as Ethan handed her a plastic bag with a sub sandwich inside.

"No clue," Ethan said.

"I checked the whole house when I woke up. I mean, I didn't just barge into the master bedroom. The door was wide open. No one was in there. She wasn't anywhere to be found. Not even at the greenhouses. I looked there, too. Of course, no one was at the greenhouses. Now that Hannah has quit, and *you* won't let me work there, they are all just locked up."

"Well, you're too young to work out there alone, and I really don't know where Jezmeen went."

Ethan unwrapped his sandwich.

"She told me about the Rogers' house," Izzy said. "I could tell she was sorry, and I told her we'd both forgive her. I mean, the Bible talks all about forgiveness. It's just something we have to do."

"That's not why she left," Ethan said casually.

"Then why did she leave?"

"You know how Claire was sick last night? Well, someone messed with her insulin pump, and that's what caused her to be ill. Jezmeen admitted to it."

"That doesn't make any sense. Why would Jezmeen do something like that?"

"She said she thought it was an alarm clock."

"Well, then it was just a mistake, and you need to forgive her."

"It's not as easy as that."

"Why can't it be? Doesn't the Bible say to turn the other cheek and seventy-times seven and all of that? Jezmeen doesn't have anywhere to go, she's told me that before. She doesn't have any really close family. We're all she's got. You have to call her and tell her to come back," Izzy begged.

"I'll think about it," Ethan said, not wanting to push the issue. "Claire's going to be here through the afternoon, and I don't feel comfortable with both of them in the house together, so I'm not doing anything about it today." With that, Ethan picked up his sandwich and left the room. He needed some time and space to clear his head.

# Chapter Thirty-Three

Jezmeen drove around all Thursday morning, trying to work out a plan. She didn't cry, or even feel, she just kept pressing forward. The only person she could think to contact was Nick. She hadn't talked to him since their break-up, but she believed he still cared for her. When she called to see if she could crash at his place after work on Thursday evening, he agreed hesitantly.

Parading the diamond necklace he'd bought her, as she walked through his apartment door that night, he greeted her with reservation at first. But after sharing a modified version of all that transpired between her and Ethan, she had him feeling sorry for her. Sorry enough to share a bed together.

When Ethan called on Friday, offering her a chance to come back until she had a proper place to stay, Jezmeen told Nick goodbye for the second time. He seemed to take it well, maybe knowing one night was all they would have.

The best sight was Izzy waiting for her on the front porch, when she drove up on Friday afternoon. Izzy explained she convinced Ethan to take her back. Izzy's confidence that the relationship could be restored gave Jez hope, but when she went into the master bedroom, she found a note on the bed. *I washed the sheets in the guest room after Claire left. It's all yours until you find a place to stay.*

So, she took her suitcases to the guest room and avoided Ethan all weekend. She hadn't planned it, but their work schedules made it so. When she left the house on Sunday morning, Ethan wasn't around.

That was okay, she needed to see *him*. Pulling into the parking lot at 8:50 a.m., she ever parked in the same spot, just the same area. In the back corner, she had a perfect angle to watch him walk in. The first Sunday morning, after she found out where to look for him, he was in a baby carrier. All she could see was the "plastic boat" being heaved into church by Sarah or Terrence Harris, *his* adoptive parents.

She had chosen Sarah and Terrence because they were a couple who seemed grounded in their faith. Even though Jezmeen didn't care much about it for herself, it felt right for her son. She also picked the Harris' because they were a bi-racial couple. Sarah had white complexion while Terrence's skin was dark brown. Her son would look like he could have come from Sarah's womb and not her own.

When Jezmeen chose to have a closed adoption, meaning she'd never contact the Harris', she truly thought that was the best option. After she gave birth, postpartum depression, shame, and guilt became companions she wished she could shake. She longed to see her baby. Finding out, during the conversation she overheard at the bar, that Sarah and Terrence attended Cornerstone Christian Church with Ace gave her a weekly purpose.

Of course, Jezmeen knew Ace was the name *she'd* given him. The Harris' called him Owen, but she still thought of him as Ace. He was her firstborn baby, her only son, and Ace seemed to suit him.

She might hear the name Owen being called today by Sarah or Terrance, she thought, as she rolled down the window. Jezmeen rarely left the car running. On hot mornings, like this scorcher, she would revel about how much Ace had grown, what he was wearing, or if he looked happy.

Then, after the fleeting few minutes of observation were up, she would scroll decorating websites on her phone, flip through a magazine, or lay her seat back and nap until he came out again at the end of service. Many times, she fell into such a deep sleep that she didn't awake until she heard doors slam on the vehicle parked next to her.

This morning, she had a peach tea and an egg sandwich from a drive-through to enjoy, but she would wait until after he was inside to eat. Only a few Sundays a year were the Harris' gone from church- presumably due to illness or vacation- but Jezmeen never knew when those absences would occur, and she always anxiously awaited the next Sunday, so she could get a glance at her son.

Jezmeen eyed the Harris' dark blue minivan pulling into the parking lot, and she hunched down in the seat. Sometimes she'd pretend to be putting on make-up or act like she was bending down to reach something. She never wanted to be spotted. Jez had met Sarah and Terrence only once, after selecting them from a big binder of interested couples. Jezmeen didn't know if they'd recognize her, but she didn't want to chance it.

Since Ace's adoption ten years ago, the Harris' added to their family. Sarah gave birth to a baby girl when Ace was four. Long ago, when Jezmeen read Sarah and Terrence's file, it said they couldn't have children due to Sarah's endometriosis. However it happened, she was thankful Ace had a sibling, and it warmed her heart when brother and sister walked into church holding hands.

After Terrence parked, Ace got out of the back seat and waited for his dad. Terrence put his arm around Ace, as they walked into the building, and Sarah and the little girl followed. Ace wore khaki shorts and brown sandals. The baby blue polo shirt looked good with his light brown skin and dark hair, she thought, and he seemed content. Even though Jezmeen was tired from work, she was satisfied and could rest easy until next week.

Jezmeen usually stayed until the end of the service, so she could soak up a few more glimpses of Ace. If it was unusually cold, she would leave because running her car the whole time would draw attention. A few times she was afraid Terrence had seen her. Those days she'd drove off quickly. Today neither event occurred, so she would wait.

Only once had she thought about going inside. That particular morning, she was very depressed, and she was desperate enough to consider anything. But being spotted was a higher concern, so she never went in.

By 9:15 the noise from the parking lot had quieted, and Jezmeen shut her eyes. The sound of the crowd leaving the church service awoke Jezmeen. Men, women, and children dressed in everything from blue jeans to sundresses headed to their cars. Jez watched for Ace. She was so absorbed she didn't notice Izzy, Wayne, and Ethan walking right towards her car until it was too late. Izzy ran to the driver's side.

"Jezmeen," she said, elated. "Did you go to church?"

"Yeah," she lied.

"Dad, Ethan," she called to the men who were still twenty feet behind, "Look who's here."

Ethan eyed Jezmeen curiously as he approached.

"Hi, Jez," Wayne said, walking to Izzy's side. "Are you a regular attender here at Cornerstone?"

"Kind of," she mumbled, not showing her tension.

"I usually go to the late service, but Ethan wanted to come with me, and he has to meet a client now," Wayne said.

Ethan saw the opening to leave, and he took it. "I better get going," Ethan said. "See you all later."

Izzy whispered something in her dad's ear, and Wayne nodded in approval. "Do you want to go to lunch with us? My dad says it's okay."

"Sure," Jezmeen replied, looking out of the corner of her eye, to make sure their conversation wasn't drawing attention from the Harris family.

"Can I ride with Jezmeen?" Izzy asked her dad.

"Is it okay with you?" he asked Jez.

"Absolutely. Where are we headed?"

"Charlie Parker's Diner," Izzy bubbled. "It was my day to pick. Did you know that restaurant was featured on the Food Network? It was on the show called *Diners, Drive-Ins and Dives.* I love their pancakes. Have you been there?"

Wayne interrupted. "Slow down, Izzy. Save some words for the car ride."

"Dad," Izzy groaned. "You know I never run out."

Wayne smiled. "See you ladies there."

When Jezmeen arrived home, she was surprised to find Ethan sitting in the family room on the black leather recliner with no entertainment— just silence.

"Charlie Parker's was offering free muffins with breakfast. Do you want it?" she asked, as she carried the white restaurant container into the room.

She felt nervous being alone with Ethan, and she hadn't felt anxious about sharing a space with a man in years.

"What did you think about the choir this morning at church?" Ethan asked, looking up as she came in.

"I liked the choir," she said, setting down the box on the coffee table before choosing a middle cushion on the couch.

"What were you really doing there?" Ethan sighed.

"Same thing as you."

"The choir didn't sing today, Jez. They had the week off."

Jezmeen wondered how she could fake her way through a church conversation with Izzy and Wayne but blow it so quickly with Ethan. She mentally debated what to do. Even her mom didn't know where she went on Sundays. No one did. Why let Ethan in on the secret? As she tried to think of a lie, she realized she was tired. Not just from bartending the night before, but a bone-weary, soul-heavy exhaustion from hiding lies and constantly trying to make her world work.

"I have a son," she declared curtly.

"What?" Ethan exclaimed in surprise. "What's that have to do with church?"

"His adoptive parents go there, and I like to see him...not that you care," she said defensively.

"Of course I care. Why would you say that?"

"It's not like we've ever had a heart to heart," she said sourly. She was letting her guard down, and it felt like she was standing on the edge of a cliff.

"Well, we haven't been on good terms for quite a while," Ethan replied.

"But even before that, you never really seemed to be interested in my life."

"I'm sorry," Ethan said, sincerely. "You know I'm not the best with people. Watching your interactions has helped me get better, but the art of conversation is not my strong suit."

Ethan leaned forward in the chair. "So, you have a son," he said gently.

Jezmeen softened. "His name is Ace. That's what I call him, anyhow. His parents named him Owen."

"How old is he?"

"Ten."

"So, you had him when you were just seventeen," Ethan said softly, recalling Jezmeen's age.

"Let's just say, giving birth my senior year of high school didn't earn me any special titles in the yearbook."

"I'm not sure if this is appropriate to ask, so forgive me if it isn't, but where's the boy's father?"

"I haven't seen Steven Reeza in years. I met Steve when I was a freshman, and he was a senior. We both came from, how should I put it?" Jezmeen stared at the field of poppies painted on a canvas hanging behind Ethan's chair. "Troubled homes."

Leaning back into the couch, making little eye contact, she continued. "After he graduated, he got a job doing oil changes at an auto repair shop. My junior year, he got an apartment and asked me to move in. After I got pregnant, he stayed around for a couple of months. By then, I already had the baby's room decorated. We had planned to keep Ace. One afternoon, I came home from school, and there was a note on the counter. Steve said he couldn't handle the stress. He was moving to the west coast. I had till the end of the month to get out of the apartment, and he asked me to give the baby up for adoption."

Jezmeen picked up a throw pillow and held it on her lap. "So, there I was, four months pregnant, with no place to go. When I moved back home, my mom convinced me to go through with an adoption. She didn't want to help me raise a baby. On Sundays, I go to see him. It's a closed adoption, so it's not like we've actually met, but I've watched him grow up…the only way I know how."

Jezmeen finally looked at Ethan. "You know what I learned about men? Even when they tell you they love you they might not mean it."

Ethan didn't know what to say. He'd never told Jezmeen he loved her, except when he was intoxicated. Maybe the comment was intended for him, as much as it was for Steven. For the first time, he looked at Jezmeen and saw beyond her exterior. Below the surface, her wounds were so fatal only a truly skilled Surgeon could repair them.

# Chapter Thirty-Four

Ethan knocked on the Rogers' front door. In his hands he held a brown bag, and he hoped Claire hadn't eaten breakfast yet. It had been three days since she left on Thursday afternoon. He'd watched the construction crew begin the process of repairing their roof, on Friday and Saturday, and they pounded away, above him, as he waited on the porch.

Claire arrived at the door dressed in shorts and a t-shirt. With no make-up, she looked like the girl he first met over a year ago.

"I brought you some steel-cut oatmeal," Ethan said, handing her the bag.

"My favorite," she exclaimed, stepping outside.

"I remembered," Ethan said, recalling a conversation they had months earlier. "I wanted to see how you and your parents were doing. I brought them some bagels," he said, pointing to a sack that was on the floor by his feet.

"That was really thoughtful. I'm sure they'll appreciate it. My mom took my dad to speech therapy this morning."

"Will he be able to work in the fields?"

"Yes. He can't stand to sit around, but the doctor told him he still has to wait two weeks until he's able to get on a tractor."

"Is there anything I can do to help?"

"My dad has a friend— a retired farmer. He's agreed to help us out for a while, and my mom and I can pitch in, too."

"That's great," Ethan said listening to a shout from the workmen above.

"They're noisy, aren't they," Claire smiled.

"Is the damage as bad as it looks?"

"It's pretty extensive, but the insurance will cover everything after the deductible."

Claire swiped a fly away from her face.

"How are you feeling?" Ethan asked.

"Oh, fine. It took a few days to get my energy level back to normal, but I just told my parents it was jet lag."

"For what it's worth, Jezmeen admitted to messing with your pump. She thought it was an alarm clock. Supposedly she was doing you a favor—letting you sleep in."

Claire decided to take the high road and not respond.

"I'm sorry for all the trouble she's caused you and your parents."

"Thanks. I told them that the letter was a fake. They were so relieved that it wasn't real and that they didn't have to deal with fighting a lawsuit on top of my dad's recovery, I doubt they'll press charges."

Ethan and Claire's conversation came to a lull. Claire picked up the bagels. "Thanks again for stopping by. It seems like it's going to be a hot day. It's a good thing you have fans now in those greenhouses, so Hannah will stay cool," Claire chuckled, remembering her summer days under the tarping.

"Hannah quit last Monday," Ethan said.

"Oh no! How come?"

"Her husband was spooked because of the tornado. He asked her to get a safer indoor job, and I don't blame him."

"What are you doing in the meantime?"

"Losing clients," he said matter-of-factly. "I can't deal with all the phone calls and scheduling right now. I'm in the midst of finishing a big job and starting another. Hopefully, I'll have time to get an advertisement for the position posted to a few job sites tonight after work."

"Don't," Claire practically shouted. "I'll help you out."

"But your dad?"

"I can't really do much for him. My mom's taking him to appointments. The family friend is helping out with the land. So, I'm mostly here for moral support."

"You're not going back to China?"

"I put in the official word with my employer in Tianjin, last Friday, that I'm not returning. At least not anytime soon. My mom and dad don't need me here for the physical help, but they both just feel better having me close, and I don't want to add an extra burden of stress by leaving right now."

"You'd really be willing to take on the job?"

"Sure. I can be right next door to my mom and dad all day, set my own hours…if you'll still allow me that privilege, and help you out at the same time."

"Well, this is the best news I've heard all week," Ethan smiled.

"It's only Monday," Claire giggled.

Claire took the oatmeal to the kitchen table. She was thankful she'd heard the doorbell, with all the pounding upstairs. Ethan had remembered her favorite breakfast, and he had come to check on her. Those two things wouldn't have happened a year ago. He seemed different. Through the debacle with her blood-sugar, he was kind and attentive. She still couldn't believe he risked his own safety to get the ketone test strips.

Hopefully saying yes to returning to Adams Landscaping was the right choice, she thought as she took the hot container out of the brown bag. The night before, she and Tyler prayed together, over the phone, that she would be able to find a job. Claire didn't want to be locked into a full-time teaching position, in case her dad made such a quick recovery she could return to Tianjin, possibly after Christmas. She planned to substitute teach in Springfield when the school year started.

Her life in China seemed like a distant memory, but it had only been a week since her departure. So much had transpired, including nearly ending up in the emergency room like her dad. She dumped a small plastic container of walnuts and blueberries onto the top of the oatmeal.

Now that Ethan verified it was Jezmeen who caused her to be so sick, she had double the reasons to be upset with her. Truthfully, she was angry at the emotional distress that Jez caused her dad and mom. She didn't want to dwell on the fact that she could have been seriously injured, if she hadn't woken up. Claire was resentful, but she also felt pity. Jezmeen lacked a moral compass—a woman adrift.

She didn't have any close family, her last boyfriend had kicked her out, and it was obvious she and Ethan were on the rocks. Claire knew that beauty was fleeting, and Jezmeen was a walking illustration of what it looked like to be an empty vase.

Claire hoped that Jezmeen wouldn't visit the greenhouses. Ethan's little sister was a different story. On Thursday, when she met Izzy, the talkative teen gave her a rundown of her unification with Ethan. Claire was thrilled Ethan found his dad—and Izzy. She would be welcome to help her anytime.

Scooping the first bite of creamy porridge, Claire wondered why Ethan would bring her breakfast on a Monday morning at nine. She knew he started work between seven and eight. If he'd made a special trip just for her, she was flattered.

Almost three months ago, she would have swooned. She had liked Ethan immensely before he met Jezmeen. Even the note she'd given to Jezmeen, before flying to Tianjin, left the door open for communication, when she shared her address in China. Of course, she'd never heard from him, but now she had Tyler, or rather, Tyler had her heart.

All that she'd ever desired in a relationship, she had with him. However, maintaining their connectedness, while living oceans apart, would take effort. Claire prayed they would be equally committed to doing everything they could to make it work.

Ethan sat in the sunroom, taking in the summer sunset. Jezmeen was at work, and Izzy was at Wayne's. It had been a long day, and he relished the feeling of clean skin and hair, after taking a shower.

Nearly two years ago, he had stood outside the Arctic Fox observing the pastel pinks, blues and oranges painting the horizon for the first time, as the proud owner of twenty-three acres of land off of Farmingdale Road.

With his hands, he had built five greenhouses and begun construction of the storefront. Those structures meant more to him than his new house, but he was thankful to have a roof over his head – especially when so many were ripped off by the tornado. It had only been one week since the twister passed over, and he was still immensely grateful for God's grace.

He took a drink of water. Giving up bourbon—and all alcohol for that matter—was part of his "live like a new man" plan. Being kind, and thinking of others above himself, was another prong.

After his talk with Jezmeen, he realized he didn't really know her at all. Manipulation, selfishness, and greed seemed to define her. She had a son, and she'd given him up. Her first love had abandoned her when she needed him the most, and she lived with guilt and shame. If he learned all that from one conversation, how much more was there still to uncover?

Ethan looked at the empty field outside the sunroom windows. He had wanted to plant trees for the past two years, maybe this fall he'd actually get around to it. With Claire at the helm, the business-side of Adams Landscaping should have stability. It had been another good year of revenue, and a Tryton royalty check would come through again shortly. He'd have to make sure to give Claire that raise he promised.

During their morning conversation he had wanted to find out about her boyfriend, but an opening hadn't come. He didn't understand women nearly as well as he would have liked, but he also didn't sense that Claire had any special feelings for him. When he delivered the breakfast, she was cordial, but that was all. He did not hold her heart. If it ever had been available, he'd missed his chance.

Jezmeen would be home early, he thought, seeing it was Monday night. Home. It was hard to believe that the huge house was all his. He'd lived at many different addresses growing up and a few as an adult. When he left the small bungalow, he had owned for ten years, and moved to the countryside, he thought he had found home.

But if home was safety, peace, and love, he hadn't found his true dwelling until a week ago when he surrendered his life to the Lord. The weights he carried—building the store, managing the business, dealing with Jezmeen, getting to know his dad and sister—were still there, but he'd changed. Ethan no longer felt the need to handle it all himself. God was in charge, and that made life feel lighter. Farmingdale Road was his earthly address, for the moment, and wherever he traveled God would be with him.

Jezmeen was used to driving home in the dark. The difference tonight was the lack of noise. Usually she played country or rock music on the radio. Now, she savored the quiet. Even though she had gotten plenty of sleep the night before, and the shift at the bar was easy, she felt fatigued.

Her life had always been fueled by momentum. Growing up in such a fluid atmosphere, Jezmeen craved change. It was when the chaos in her life came to a crashing halt that sadness crept in, and that's where her emotions rested, as she drove away from Finnegan's.

Fingers of depression threatened to pull her down. In the past two years, she'd shared a bed with three men, lived in two apartments, a house, and a trailer, crafted many lies, stolen plenty of money, and made one person very sick. Most of the things on the list were common for Jezmeen, but the last item was a first.

Even if her intentions weren't exactly upright when she messed with what she now knew was an insulin pump, Jezmeen hadn't meant to harm Claire. Jezmeen wondered if that was what was weighing her down. Yet, Claire had gotten better.

Maybe she didn't want to leave Ethan's place, she mused. The house was nearly perfect. It just needed landscaping, and a pool would be nice. No, it was more than that.

Jezmeen often wondered if she really could be a mother. After all, she'd given up her firstborn, and she was an only child. But being around Izzy made her realize she did have a nurturing instinct, and that she could love and be loved.

Izzy was three years older than Ace, but she felt like a mixture of child, sister, and friend. The light turned green, and Jezmeen gently pressed the gas. No, Jezmeen, told herself. It wasn't even Izzy that was burdening her. She'd let her guard down. After Stephen, not even her next boyfriend knew about Ace.

Jezmeen determined that she wouldn't let her past define her relationships. She didn't want to be judged by anyone. Long ago, when her pregnancy got too far along to hide, she had dropped out of high school. After she gave birth, she earned her G.E.D. Sure, there were rumors, but only her mom, Steven, and her mom's boyfriend at the time, knew the truth. Now Ethan knew as well.

This vulnerability was new. Jezmeen felt like she was standing in the field behind the grand mansion wearing nothing. Why had she even told Ethan about Ace? Maybe it was because she'd just gotten through coming clean about the letter to the Rogers and the debacle with Claire. Or maybe it was because she really wanted him to know why she was at church on Sunday morning. She did a lot of things that rightfully earned his disapproval but sitting in the parking lot, looking at her son wasn't one of them.

When Jezmeen pulled into the driveway and neared the house, she saw the lights in the kitchen were on. Usually Ethan shut everything off except the light over the sink when he went to bed. So, when she went inside, she wasn't too surprised to see him in the family room.

"You waited up?" Jezmeen called, as she set her keys on the counter and walked into the family room dressed in her bartending uniform.

"I was working on a landscaping plan," Ethan said, looking up from the laptop computer.

"Must be for an important client. You don't usually stay up this late." Jezmeen looked at her watch. It was 10:30.

"Our talk yesterday got me thinking. You were my first girlfriend, and you were right. I don't know you—at all."

She sat down on the couch next to him reflecting on his word choice. He referred to her as his former girlfriend.

"I know you'll be moving out when you find a place, but that doesn't mean we can't be friends. And friends know each other." Ethan shut the laptop. "I'm not really good at asking questions, but I wrote a few down to help me get started."

Ethan pulled out a piece of paper from his pocket. "Let's see. Number one. What is your middle name?"

"Of all the things you could ask me, you want to know my middle name?" Jezmeen smiled. "It's Marie—carried down from my mom and grandmother."

"Can you believe we've lived together for ten months, and I never knew that?" He looked down at his list and read, "Okay, number two. What was your favorite school subject?" He looked up. "Were you a good student? Did you like school?"

"Whoa," Jezmeen laughed. "That's three questions." She felt flattered by his effort. "I loved art class. I've always liked to see how colors can come together to create something beautiful...like your landscaping designs. And I was a good student. I always cared about my grades. My senior year I only got one B—in Pre-Calculus. When I was in elementary school, I liked going, but once I got to junior high let's just say the boys started to notice me, and well," she paused, "that made the girls hate me. So, school became a nightmare, thanks to the bullying."

Ethan was surprised that she had been harassed, too. He had been teased because he was too "ugly," and she had been ostracized because too pretty. The paradox seemed great. He continued with his list of ten questions, and when they were done, they headed upstairs.

"You want me to join you tonight?" Jezmeen asked, feeling happy about their connection.

Ethan hesitated on the stairs, thinking. "No thanks," he replied. "I'm working on being a better version of my old self, and I think that would include refraining from some fleshly desires right now."

"Okay, suit yourself," Jezmeen replied, a hint of frustration in her voice.

"Goodnight," he said softly, as she headed to the guest room.

# Chapter Thirty-Five

## AUGUST 2013

Claire missed Tyler so much there were times she could barely concentrate. If she had doubted that she was in love, there was no confusion now. Each daily conversation with Tyler, whether over the phone or Skype, ended with three beautiful words, *I love you.*

Her parents saw how happy she was and hoped to meet him. Claire didn't want to put pressure on Tyler to visit, but she knew his summer semester was only days away from ending, and she hinted that flights to St. Louis had dropped a few hundred dollars in price. He hadn't taken the bait, and Claire knew he couldn't come all the way to the United States and not visit his parents, so she rested knowing God's timing was not her own.

Claire had already put in two full days substitute teaching, which was surprising since school had just begun. But she was grateful for the work. Managing Adams Landscaping was a lot easier now that she didn't have the preparation of lesson planning, grading, and communicating with parents as a full-time teacher.

Everyone seemed pleased that she had returned. Even V.J. and Mark stopped by to tell her they were glad she'd come home, and Jezmeen stayed away. And her dad's speech was improving. Jed was able to recall words more easily and did less slurring. Claire still had to practice patience waiting for him to respond, but he was making progress. Jed seemed to enjoy being in the fields more than ever—maybe because they didn't ask him to speak.

Claire had just begun to fill a black container with a potting mix in the "Berry Backwoods," one Friday afternoon, when Ethan walked in.

"Wow, you've gotten a lot done today," Ethan said, as he observed how many empty tables there were in the greenhouse.

"I just consolidated all that you had left. We'll have more room for these blueberry plants," she said pointing to the containers by her feet. "Oh, and I checked the drip-irrigation system for the mums. Everything looks fine."

"Good. I thought that row on the far right wasn't getting watered," Ethan replied.

"I like that you are growing them outside this year. You've got the land to do that."

"They do better out there, and I can spread them out. We have double the inventory from last year." Ethan grabbed a pot to start filling.

"Did you get done early today?" Claire asked, noting it was only four forty-five.

"Wayne and Izzy are coming over tonight for dinner. Izzy wants to tell me about her first full week at school."

"Oh, that's great," Claire replied. "I wonder if I'll ever get to sub at her school this fall. She's at Grant Middle School, right?"

"Yeah, you haven't been there yet?"

"No, I'm trying to stick with elementary jobs, if I can help it. Hey, I met someone who knows you. Danielle Patton. Does that name sound familiar? She said she used to live by you."

Ethan instantly recalled the beautiful blond neighbor who drew him out of his shell and introduced him to Jesus. She was Danielle Davison then. She must have gotten married to James Patton, the congressman she had fallen for.

"How's she doing?"

"She was completing some observation hours at Owen Marsh Elementary School for her teaching degree. I met her in the break room when I was subbing there two days ago. Somehow, we got talking about what I do, and when I mentioned I worked for you, her eyes lit up. She said she and her husband have been following your career, and they are glad you're doing so well. She said to say hello and tell you that your old house is going back on the market. They plan to move to a bigger home in Springfield to raise their family."

"So, she stayed on the path towards teaching," Ethan said, mostly to himself.

"What did she do before?"

"Social work."

"Ah, that would be hard, especially with a baby on the way."

"What?"

"Oh, she's pregnant. I guess she got married last winter. The baby's due in a few months."

"Wow," Ethan replied. Life continued for Danielle and James, and he was happy for them.

"Is Jezmeen going to join you for dinner tonight?" Claire asked, changing the conversation.

"No, she has to work, much to Izzy's disappointment."

"That girl loves Jezmeen."

"She sure does, but she also really enjoys working out here with you. Thank you for letting her help."

"No problem. She's fun to have around— makes the hours go by quickly with all her stories and chatter."

Ethan smiled knowing how Izzy could fill a space.

"She'll be here to help with the mum sale in a few weeks, right?" Claire asked. "We can use every pair of hands we can get."

"Izzy will be here and so will my dad," Ethan paused, catching himself. He'd used the word "dad" aloud when referring to Wayne, and he was taken aback. He continued again, trying to sound controlled. "Both Izzy and Wayne will be here, and they said you could put them down for any job you need help with."

"Great," Claire said, dusting off her hands and pulling a notebook out of her apron. She flipped a few pages. "I think I'll put Izzy down to help with refreshments, and Wayne can run a cash register. I don't trust myself around those things the day of the sale," Claire said, recalling the mysterious loss of money the previous fall. "I'm just glad I was able to pay you back."

"What?" Ethan said, halting his work transplanting a cutting.

"I just had to set a little out of each paycheck before I went to China," Claire said, putting the notebook back into her apron.

"I didn't get any money from you, Claire."

"What do you mean? I gave the note with my new address and the cash to—"

They both said "Jezmeen" at the same time.

Gretchen's old room had been repurposed into a guest space even before the tornado hit. Now Claire claimed the room, since the loft was inhabitable. She laid on the plaid comforter, laptop resting on her legs. Nighttime in Springfield meant morning in Tianjin.

"Can you believe she never even gave him all that money?" Claire complained to Tyler over Skype.

"I don't usually like to think the worst about people, but Jezmeen seems pretty wicked," Tyler said as he moved around the kitchen in his apartment, his phone in hand.

"I just hope she doesn't volunteer to help with the mum sale," Claire said.

"When is it again?"

"Two weeks. Why? Do you want to come?" she teased.

"More than you know."

"You don't want to miss a children's Bible study, do you?" she chuckled.

"You've got me all figured out," he smiled.

"I still can't believe you've continued leading it without me there."

"Well, you know Shui would miss me too much," Tyler said.

"Shui and all the other kids." Claire adjusted the pillow behind her head. "How's your summer break going? Are you still looking forward to spending a week in Hong Kong?"

"I wish you were here. We could go to Hong Kong together."

"You'll have fun with…what are their names again?"

"Yu Yan and Zhang Wei." Tyler grabbed a bottle of water from the refrigerator. "And, sure, it will be a lot of fun tagging along with a young married couple," he said sarcastically.

"Then why'd you agree to go?"

"Because we're staying at Yu Yan's aunt's apartment. I can couch surf for free."

"You could always come to Springfield and couch surf at my parent's house," Claire proposed, not for the first time.

"Maybe at Christmas. I'm praying by then I'll be ready to do the whole reconciliation thing with my mom."

"I'm praying for that, too. I never thought I could miss someone so much."

"What? You miss my mom? You've never even met her," Tyler joked.

"You know what I meant," she smiled.

"I do," he said, turning serious. "I rolled over in bed this morning and envisioned what it would be like to wake up holding you."

Claire wanted nothing more, and hearing Tyler's deep voice saying those words only made her miss him more.

Jezmeen had another early night at work. Tuesdays were often as slow as Mondays. When she pulled into the driveway, she saw lights on in the kitchen again. Maybe Ethan was waiting up to talk. When had that ever happened in her relationships, she wondered? Men stayed up, but not for conversation.

As if yesterday was on repeat, she threw her keys on the counter and greeted Ethan, who sat on the black recliner in the family room. She had brought home a container with a burger and fries from Finnegan's.

"I should have texted to see if you wanted me to bring you something," she said, entering the family room with her dinner. "I just didn't think you'd be up this late two nights in a row."

"No worries, I already ate. I guess I just had some more questions for you," Ethan replied. He'd thought, all afternoon, about how he'd handle the accusation that Jezmeen had taken eight-hundred dollars Claire had intended for him. Sometime during the afternoon, he sensed that he should learn more about Jezmeen's past. He felt it would shed light on her behavior.

Jezmeen opened the lid and picked up a fry. "This reminds me of when we first met, and you'd stay late at the bar. I was so worried you would fall asleep on your job one day."

"That would be hard to do in my line of work," Ethan smiled.

"So, do you have another list of questions tonight?" Jezmeen wriggled her body back into the sweet spot of the couch.

"Kind of. I'm curious about your mom," he said boldly.

"My mom?" Jez stopped eating, a quizzical look shadowing her face.

"You've never told me about her."

"Her name's Sherry. She was a hairdresser. Still is, as far as I know. We don't really stay in touch."

"How come?"

"She did her job. I'm an adult now."

"Most people don't tend to 'outgrow' their parents," Ethan replied, studying her striking eyes and noted they were clouded with sorrow.

"Well, she's not really the mothering type," Jezmeen huffed. "Never was."

"So, you practically raised yourself?"

"You can say that."

"Did she ever marry?"

"Twice, but neither time for very long." Jezmeen liked yesterday's questions about middle names and favorite school subjects. These were getting deeply personal.

"Did you ever feel unsafe when you were growing up?" Ethan asked softly, beginning to steer the conversation where he wanted it to go.

Jezmeen didn't say anything but picked up another French fry.

"Was there ever a time your mom wasn't able to provide for you?"

Jezmeen stuffed the potato in her mouth. "Where are you going with all this?" she asked defensively.

"I just see two different sides of you at times, Jez, and I'm wondering who you really are. I thought asking about your past may help me figure it out."

"Well, was I homeless? Yes, a few times. But Uncle Eddie or Kenny or Robert would put us up until Sherry could snag a long-term relationship. And, just like most teenage girls, I had to defend myself in the shower from pervs a few times before I remembered to lock the door," she said sarcastically. "But that's just page one of my very long novel, and I'm sure you'd rather sleep."

Ethan didn't know exactly what ran through Jezmeen's head when she pocketed the money many months ago, but these small glimpses helped him realize what he suspected. Beyond her stunning exterior, there was a hurting woman. Ethan heard as much as he needed to, for the moment, and didn't want to push her.

"I would like to hear more, but I don't want you to feel like you have to share your life story in one night." Ethan moved to sit next to her on the couch. "I'm sorry," he said, as they both looked at the still fireplace.

"For what?" she asked, as if she didn't know.

"I'm sorry that Jezmeen Marie Williams has felt alone most of her life—without a safe place to land." He set his hand on hers for a moment and let it rest there in the silence.

# Chapter Thirty-Six

**SEPTEMBER 2013**

Claire had turned down two substitute teaching jobs on Friday so she could prepare for the mum sale. The weekend forecast predicted sunny skies and upper seventy-degree temperatures. By giving up a week of his own work, Ethan's father had called in the help of every friend who could swing a hammer, and his team managed to get the storefront finished by Thursday afternoon.

Wayne, Ethan, Izzy, Connie and Jed, along with Claire, all pitched in on Thursday night to set up displays of mums, plants, and a refreshment station in the new building. Jezmeen had to work, but that was fine with Claire. The less contact they had the better.

The biggest day of the sale would be on Saturday, but they'd be open for a few hours on Friday afternoon. Claire's blood sugar had been up and down all day, but she attributed that to stress. Her memory associated with last year's money mix-up only added to her concern.

When she arrived at the new storefront at four-fifteen, Izzy was already there arranging containers of roses, and Ethan and his dad were finishing up the installation of the credit card machine.

"Your hair looks really nice like that," Izzy said, as Claire neared.

"Thanks, I thought it would be good to have it out of my face," she replied, patting the clip that held her locks in place.

"You look good in brown," Izzy said, putting a container on top of a bale of hay. "I told Ethan I was only wearing this brown shirt because everyone at the business wears them, but I hate brown. I know hate is not a nice word—well at least that's what my grandma says—but I really do hate brown."

Claire laughed at Izzy's rant. "Well, I picked the color last year."

"Why?" Izzy exclaimed. "What's wrong with sapphire blue or cardinal red or lime green?"

"Nothing," Claire smiled. "I just figured that Ethan's team is always dealing with dirt, so brown would look the cleanest, even when it wasn't."

"Well, you got me there," Izzy giggled.

Ethan and Wayne approached Izzy.

"Looks good," Ethan said, inspecting the display.

"Do you like how I'm making them look fuller by grouping them closely together?" Izzy asked, pleased at her work.

"Absolutely," Ethan replied. "I also have to thank you for making that amazing advertising video for our Facebook page. You worked really hard on that."

"She did," Wayne replied. "It took her two weeks to get all the video footage she needed and another week to edit it."

"If you don't want to go into theater," Ethan said, "you could definitely have a career as a news anchor. You were so professional when you were interviewing Claire and talking about what we do at Adams Landscaping."

Ethan opened his arms, and Izzy freely enjoyed his embrace.

"How about we pray, since we're all standing here, and the sale is going to begin in forty-five minutes," Wayne said.

Wayne reached for Ethan's hand, Izzy took his other one, and Claire connected the circle. *"Father, I thank you for bringing Ethan into my life. I'm so grateful to have him as my son,"* Wayne stopped momentarily, fighting back emotion. *"Thank you for helping everything come together for this day. I pray you bless the hard work that went into the preparation, and guide Ethan as he makes decisions for his business. Help him thrive and flourish and be generous with the fruitfulness You've given him."*

As they opened their eyes, Ethan's were moist. Izzy squeezed his hand and smiled. "If only Jezmeen didn't have to work," she said.

The storefront's barn doors were open, and a customer walked in carrying a large mum in front of his face. Claire looked down at her watch. It wasn't even five yet, but it wasn't unusual to have an early customer.

"We have shopping carts now, sir," Claire said, pushing one towards the customer.

"Thank you," the man said, setting the mum in the basket.

"What?" Claire exclaimed, taking in the sight of Tyler.

"Your stellar advertising worked," Tyler said with a grin. "I heard about this sale all the way in Tianjin, China."

Tyler pulled her into his arms and wrapped her tightly in a long embrace. Pulling away, Claire's eyes were filled with tears, and Tyler's were too.

Claire reached up and ran her hand over his cheek and beard. "Oh, Tyler," she said.

"I've missed you more than words could say," Tyler replied. He bent down and kissed her tenderly.

As if the whole world faded, Claire became lost in the moment until Izzy couldn't contain herself any longer. "Aww, you two are so cute," she blurted.

"Izzy," Wayne reprimanded.

"What? It's just so sweet," Izzy exclaimed.

Claire laughed, and put her arm around Tyler's waist. Then she gave proper introductions all around before asking to be excused to talk with her boyfriend. Claire didn't know where to take Tyler. There were benches in front of the store, but the parking lot would be filling soon. She decided to head to the "Berry Backwoods." They had moved all the items that were saleable to the storefront, and the hoop house was closed to customers.

"I can't believe you're actually here," Claire gushed, as she led him to the greenhouse. "What about Hong Kong?"

"I realized there was only one person I really wanted to spend time with during my last weekend before school starts again—and that was you," he squeezed her hand.

It was warm inside, so Claire turned on the fan.

"Here," she said, leading the way. "We can sit on the tarp." There was a blue plastic covering on the floor in the back of the building. "I work here putting potting soil in containers. Sorry there's really no other place to go."

Tyler sat down and Claire followed, both sitting cross-legged, face-to-face. Claire ran her hand over his beard again. She just wanted to confirm he was really beside her.

"When did you get here? Did you fly into St. Louis? How long are you staying?" she asked, like a rapid-firing machine gun.

Tyler laughed.  "I just got into Springfield, but I flew into St. Louis two days ago," he said sheepishly.

"What?  You've been in the states for two days, and I didn't know!"

"Well, I wanted to surprise you, and I think it worked."  He smiled.

She intertwined her fingers with his.  "Did you see your parents?" she asked with hesitant hopefulness.

"I did."

Claire bent her body towards his and kissed him and said, "I'm amazed by you."  Claire settled back on the palms of her hands and asked, "How did it go?"

"A week ago, I sent my mom an email letting her know I would be coming home, and that if she hadn't told my dad about...well you know the story...that I wouldn't keep her secret any longer.  I didn't sleep much on the flights.  I was too excited about seeing you—and talking with them.  After I got into the St. Louis airport, I rented a car and drove to Bloomfield."

He shifted positions, uncrossing his legs and leaning back on his arms.  "When I got to my parent's house, I saw my sister's van.  My niece and nephew made signs to welcome me home, and my grandparents were there, too.  It was a nice afternoon."

"Was your dad there?"

"He was," Tyler replied. "I had called him, a few days before, to let him know I was making a trip home, and he rearranged his schedule to take time off."

"So, did your mom have the guts to do what she should have done years ago?"

"After everyone left that evening, my mom, dad, and I talked in the living room. My parents sat by each other on the couch, and they seemed cordial, so I launched into how the summer semester had finished up, filled them in about you and your family," he grinned, "and when we exhausted all those topics, the elephant walked into the room."

"Did it sit down?"

Tyler chuckled. "You look good in brown," he said, reaching up and tucking a loose strand of red hair behind her ear. "Do you realize it's been six weeks since I've seen you?" He leaned near.

"You're stalling," she whispered, their lips touching.

"Some authors drag out the ending to make it more dramatic," he said breathlessly, kissing her.

"Does this story have an epic conclusion?" Claire asked.

"Not really," he said, leaning back again. "When I said I was going to head to bed, my mom told me to sit back down. She then explained she informed my dad of what happened two years ago and promised she'd never strayed since. My dad admitted he was upset about everything, but through the course of their conversation he realized he hadn't been investing enough in their relationship. Once the kids were gone, my mom got lonely. He seemed to take some responsibility for the whole thing."

"Do you think he should?"

"I don't know. He wasn't the one who did the cheating, but I guess when there's a void you look for a way to fill it."

"Do you think they're going to be okay?"

"I hope so. They said they're looking into counseling, and I told them about a good church they could try not too far away." Tyler picked up an empty black container. "So, you sit here and plant things?"

"Let me show you," she said, grabbing him by the hand and pulling him from the floor. She led him to a table of blueberry starts.

"I love blueberries. Think they'd let me through airport security with one of these little babies?"

"Probably not," she smiled, "but I'll take care of one all through the winter just for you, and I'll plant it outside next spring."

"Do you think you'll be here that long?" he asked with reservation.

Claire patted down the dirt around one of the plants. "I don't know for sure. You know I'd love to get back to you—and China, but I can't guarantee anything."

"I'm going crazy, being apart from you for just six weeks. I can't imagine going four months before I see you again."

"You're going to come back for Christmas?" she exclaimed.

He shook his head affirmatively. "I want to give you an early gift, so you have time to find something to match it, since I know my parents will want you to come to their holiday party."

Tyler dropped to one knee, in front of the wooden table holding rows of plants and reached for the pocket on his khaki pants. Claire's hands flew in front of her mouth, and they began trembling.

"There were forty-three sunsets since our last kiss, but I was able to manage because I knew I would see you again. When you called, telling me your blood sugar was off, it was obvious something wasn't right, and I went from loving you to never wanting to be apart. I will wait until you're ready, but I want you to have this ring as a symbol of my commitment to this relationship, because I want to be with you forever." Tyler opened the plush maroon box he was holding. "Will you be my wife?"

Still shaking, Claire breathlessly whispered, "Yes."

He slid the beautiful, round diamond ring mounted on a white gold band onto her finger. Standing up, he drew her into his arms and held her. "I love you so much, Claire," he spoke softly, as he felt her head against his chest and her hair against his chin.

"I love you, too, Tyler," she replied, tears streaming down her cheeks. When she pulled away, she looked at her outstretched hand, admiring the ring. "My parents are going to be shocked."

"Maybe not as much as you might believe," he smiled mischievously. "Before I got to the storefront, I stopped by your house. Remember when you gave me your mom's number a month ago, so I could text her my concern for your dad? Well, I called her and let her know I was going to be coming this weekend. And I asked for your dad and mom's blessing when I got here this afternoon."

"That means so much to me," she replied, holding him tightly. "I can't wait to show this to everyone," she said, staring again at the ring.

Ethan set out for home. He carried a money box under one arm and a golden mum for Jezmeen in the other. Wayne convinced Izzy that Ethan needed some downtime before the sale again tomorrow and dragged her to his house. Ethan smiled remembering how Izzy promised she'd get some good footage in the morning for another advertising video.

As he reached the front porch, he noted he'd have to schedule some time, on a less busy weekend, to pull weeds in his own yard. It didn't seem right for a landscaper to have such an unkempt property. Jezmeen hadn't nagged him about it for a while, but it needed to be done.

One thing he could count on was that weeds would return. He put down barrier paper, rock, and mulch to keep them out in his client's yards, but as the wind blew, they carried and buried.

Ethan had been working to uproot weeds in his own life since he became a Christ-follower. Every day, as he read the Bible, he learned new ways God wanted him to live as a man after His own heart. Undoing the crutch of alcohol hadn't been difficult. He was thankful he hadn't gone down the dark path of addiction, like Wayne.

Becoming less selfish and thinking of others above himself was much harder. It wasn't until he really began examining his motives that he saw how inwardly focused he was. Today was a good day, however. He rose above his insecurities to offer words of gratitude to Izzy, Wayne and Claire. He even told his dad he loved him. It wasn't the first time, but the words rolled off his tongue with greater ease.

Without Izzy, Wayne, and Claire, the mum sale wouldn't have gone as well as it had. He'd sold about a fourth of his inventory in the two hours they were open, and they expected their biggest crowd on Saturday. To honor God, he decided to close and rest on Sunday. Resting one day a week was new to him, and he didn't know if he enjoyed it—yet.

Jezmeen was still looking for an apartment, but she seemed to have an unusually long list of requests. It had to be on the first floor, the closet had to be a walk-in, the bathroom had to have a separate tub and shower, and the kitchen had to have granite countertops. Where she would come up with the rent money for those demands was not a mystery to him. He knew, now, the type of parasitic relationships she'd been in, and he'd realized she must have a nice savings account.

In the meantime, he'd begun praying for Jezmeen and continued to spend time getting to know her. Ethan thought about Claire's ring, as he set down the money box and mum, so he could unlock the front door.

Tyler had gotten her a beautiful diamond, and she radiated happiness. There were a few times he looked at Claire, like Tyler looked at her. But the difference was Tyler said he couldn't live without her, and Ethan had let her go without too much trouble.

No, Ethan thought, he had never been in love with Claire, and he was thankful she'd found someone who desired her and saw her worth—because she had so much to offer. Ethan opened the door.

Jezmeen had hung a mirror in the hall, and as he passed it, he glanced at his reflection. His signature fedora was still on his head, and, as always, his eyes zoned in on the pink spot next to the bridge of his nose. Daily, he checked his face for the return of port-wine-stains. Now that it was the end of summer, he noticed a little pink blotch on his cheek, and he knew it was time to schedule another laser treatment.

Those would always be part of his life, he reasoned, but he also knew his outward appearance wasn't what made him content. It was all about the health of his inner man. Ethan set the mum and cash box on the counter before going to wash his hands at the kitchen sink.

He looked out the window at the fields as he lathered soap between his fingers. His heart was grateful, satisfied, and peaceful. He dried his hands on the towel by the sink and turned to get a drink from the refrigerator. An envelope on the counter caught his eye. His name was written in Jezmeen's script. He pulled out the note, bumping his finger on something inside.

*Dear Ethan,*

*I hope the sale went well this afternoon. I'm sorry I couldn't be there to help. I know you and I have had our ups and downs, and I know we're*

*working on creating a friendship in the place of*
*animosity. I hope what we've built so far is strong*
*enough for the news I have to share with you.*
*Take some time to think about it. I know I need to*
*do the same. We'll figure it out—together.*

*Jezmeen*

Ethan shook the envelope. What news was
Jezmeen talking about? Out tumbled a long
plastic strip with two pink lines in the middle of a
circle. Jezmeen was pregnant. For all he knew,
Ethan Adams was going to be a dad.

# Discussion Questions

1.  Ethan wanted to move to the country to change his lifestyle. Does living in the country appeal to you? Why or why not?

2.  Do you know anyone with type-1 diabetes, like Claire? What makes it difficult to manage?

3.  Jezmeen ends up living a lifestyle similar to her mother's, even though she didn't want to go down that path. Why do you think she went that direction?

4.  Claire quotes part of 1 Corinthians 1:18, "For the message of the cross is foolishness to those who are perishing, but to us who are being saved it is the power of God," in Chapter Thirteen. What do you think this scripture means, and how have you seen this to be true in the lives of people around you?

5.  Have you ever been to China? Did anything in the chapters about Tianjin strike you as interesting?

6.  Pastor Li Wei says that home is within. He says you have to be right with God and striving to live like Him to be content wherever you go. Do you agree?

7.  Do you think Tyler should have told his dad
    the information he knew right when he
    found out?  Do you think Tyler's dad was
    accurate in thinking some of the fault in the
    marriage's discord was because of him?

8.  Pastor Li Wei says home is found when you
    are at peace with God and content with
    yourself.  Do you agree or disagree?

9.  When Ethan starts to draw out Jezmeen, do
    you begin to feel sorry for her?  Why or why
    not?

10. When God spares Ethan's business and he
    finds Claire's Bible, Ethan is moved to
    surrender His life to Christ.  If you've done
    the same, share with your group the
    testimony of your surrender.

# Preview of Book Three

When Jezmeen Williams reveals to Ethan Adams that she's pregnant, he believes he's the father of the baby. With Ethan's newly found faith guiding his decisions, he desires to make his live-in girlfriend, Jezmeen, his wife. Jezmeen always wanted the lifestyle Ethan could offer her, but something is holding her back from saying 'yes' to his proposal.

Ethan encourages Jez to leave bartending and find a job with daytime hours, so she pursues her passion of interior decorating by enrolling in an online program to earn a certification.

Shortly after she begins school, Jezmeen gets hired as an assistant decorator at Monica Taylor's interior design franchise *Style Street*. One of her first client's is fifty-one-year-old Christian counselor, Charles Noble. He recently moved to Springfield and is opening up a private practice.

With the passing of his wife, two years prior, Charles has relocated to be near his aging parents. Charles recognizes that Jezmeen carries many emotional wounds, and he skillfully draws out her pain and insecurities. In the process, Jezmeen becomes strongly attached to the kind man. Even though Charles is more than twenty years older than her, he finds himself drawn to Jezmeen as well.

All the while, Ethan is regularly attending church and Sunday School, where he meets worship leader Ariana Thompson. Ariana seems practically perfect, and the two become friends.

While Ethan is developing his spiritual life, Jezmeen is being tutored in marketing, design, and a manipulative set of values, by her narcissistic boss, Monica Taylor. When Monica presents Jezmeen with a career offer that appears amazing, Jezmeen has much to contemplate, including her relationships with Charles and Ethan.

Ethan, too, has decisions to make. Choices involving his newly discovered biological dad, Wayne, and half-sister, Isabella, believing in God's goodness when people let him down, and knowing God's will for matters of his heart, weigh on Ethan. Book three of the Capitol Heart series concludes with *Freeing Grace* which portrays a picture of God's merciful love for His children.

# About the Author

One of the discussion questions, at the end of this book, prompts readers to share their testimony of surrender to Jesus Christ, and I feel led to do the same. My eighth-grade year was filled with acne struggles, trying to fit in, balancing sports and music commitments, and attending a year-long confirmation class at my local church in Yorkville, Illinois.

I recall our class being unruly and wild, and sometimes our sweet interim pastor retreated to his office in frustration. Somehow, we got through those weeks, and a final class assignment prompted us to explain why we wanted to give our lives to Jesus. I remember really taking time to contemplate this exchange. Did I sincerely want to go through with it?

In the end, I realized if Jesus gave His life for me, I wanted to give my life back to Him. From that day on, I started writing in my journal "Dear God," instead of "Dear Diary," I read through every copy of *Guideposts* magazine, a Christian publication, that my Grandparents would share with me, and even began putting post-it-notes of scripture verses in my parent's bathroom to encourage them.

Through the years, I have found *true* life only in my wonderful Savior. That sounds like "Christianese," you know the stuff that Christians say to one another that maybe seems...fluffy? But it is the truth.  As I write to you, I think about *all* the times the Holy Spirit has taken me through deep waters and brought me out.

After I became a Christ-follower, I still had questions…lots of them.  I struggled to accept that the Bible was the inspired word of God which caused me to doubt many basic Christian doctrines.  In college, I sifted through these beliefs.  But it wasn't until I began attending Calvary Church in Springfield, Illinois, when I was in my twenties, where the Bible was the prominent starting point, that it became the foundation for my faith.

If you have questions, I'd love to dialogue with you.  We can connect on Facebook at my page Author Laura Powell, or you can find me at www.authorlaurapowell.com.  I'd also love to hear your testimony!  Someday, believers will be together in our eternal dwelling…heaven, and I pray everyone reading will want to go home!

9 781735 359731